Michel ?-?
2021

Matanza!

Michael Horrex

AuthorHouse™ UK Ltd.
500 Avebury Boulevard
Central Milton Keynes, MK9 2BE
www.authorhouse.co.uk
Phone: 08001974150

© 2009 Michael Horrex. All rights reserved.

No part of this book may be reproduced, stored in a retrieval system, or transmitted by any means without the written permission of the author.

First published by AuthorHouse 4/8/2009

ISBN: 978-1-4389-4978-9 (sc)

Printed in the United States of America
Bloomington, Indiana

This book is printed on acid-free paper.

ACKNOWLEDGEMENTS

To all of those people who have helped with research and advice, my sincere gratitude. A special thank you to: Michelle Lovric and Valerie Powell - for their patient editing and invaluable advice - Madame Nawal Mahmoud Hassan, Virginia Poveda, Eugenio Sanchez Poveda, Maria de Los Angeles Ita and Dr. Arabi for their encouragement and information. Gracias to The Director and staff of The Bahia Serena Hotel, Almeria, Spain. Shukran Gazilan to Natasha Baron and the Sheikh Ali team for feeding me and keeping a roof over my head while in Luxor. I am indebted to Ben Hayley and Chris Griffiths for their computer wizardry and Abdu Rahim Mohammed Hassan Jaber for his tireless driving skills.

A special mention to Ammar for his superb cover illustration and to IBS Youssef for test driving the book and declaring it street-worthy.

I shall sit in ambush for them.

I shall come upon them from before them,

And from behind them, from their right hand

And from their left hand.

Thou wilt not find them thankful.

IBLIS

1

The first of the troopers died quickly, the skinner's knife releasing him smoothly into death. His companion was less fortunate. Hacked achilles tendons cripple but do not kill, neither did the sword slash that blinded him. The blade began its skilful work on chest and belly, ensuring that for him, the end would not be hurried.

Both soldiers had taken as heaven-sent, the shepherd with his fire and stone-walled hut. They'd promised protection from the wind and threatening rain, but just as they'd mistaken their sanctuary, so they'd misjudged this scruffy, simple-looking man. The sergeant, well armed and loud mouthed, had been the first to dismount. Swaggering a little – generally the best way to impress an ignorant countryman – he'd demanded food, drink and a place to escape the cold. The second trooper watched as the shepherd bowed his head respectfully and beckoned the sergeant into the security of his shelter. The dog had worried him at first. It was one of those hunters the mountain people liked to have around. Wiry and quick to react, they were bred to be vicious but this one looked docile enough.

Sitting for a while, too tired to dismount, the trooper heard his friend give what sounded like a deep sigh of contentment. Eager to escape the bitter wind, he forgot his exhaustion and eased himself to the ground. He tied his horse to a tree and walked between the pair of fire-blackened stone uprights that framed the doorway.

Without waiting for his eyes to accustom themselves to the gloom, he took a step forward, slipped and nearly lost balance. He'd trodden in something wet and sticky. At the same time, he was sickened by the smell of fresh blood. The shepherd must have been slaughtering animals inside the shelter. It was a filthy thing to do but not surprising, considering the man's ignorance. Peering into the blackness, the trooper strained to find his comrade, not realising the sergeant was already dead, his torn throat leaking blood into the dry earth floor.

Before they grew used to the dark, the soldier's eyes were blinded by the single slash of a sharpened sword. Rough hands took hold of him and threw him to the ground where his heel tendons were swiftly severed. He screamed and writhed in helpless misery as the skinner's knife flayed strips of skin from his chest and belly. The questioning had begun.

No longer fearing death, but craving an end to the agony of the blade, the soldier answered as best he could. The gold would be transported in two days' time. He swore he had no idea how many soldiers would be guarding it. The blade renewed its work.

'Three, no more than four,' he rasped, searching for an answer that would put an end to his torment. Realising the man had no more to tell, the skinner showed mercy and opened his victim's throat.

The troopers would be missed but no trace of them or their horses would be found and their names would be added to the growing list of army deserters. Neither of them had carried much in the way of money, just a few coins. For now, these would suffice.

The skinner had two days before the consignment of gold passed this way. It was time enough to wash the gore from the soldiers' clothing and alert his comrades. Tired, cold and hungry, the guards would be relieved to see a couple of men, in uniforms identical to their own, beckon from the light of a welcoming fire. The skinner and his friends would be ready for them.

He tugged open the flap of his saddle bag and dropped in the coins. As he did so, a lingering trace of sandalwood escaped from deep inside. It caught him unawares and with its tang came memories. More often than not, recollections were to be resisted.

They disturbed his dreams and tortured his waking hours. These were of a happier sort and he opened his mind to them.

He remembered the market; its shoppers flocking like sheep on a mountainside. He heard the clonk of donkeys, patiently labouring, and the yells of their furious drivers. He saw bright coloured spices jumbled in baskets and smelling of strange lands. The banner-decked souq had been their wonderland in those last days of Ramadan when, anonymous in the grind of traffic, Khaled and Ethan had jostled with good-natured crowds in their eagerness to buy. So many things were needed to celebrate an end to the month of fasting – food, new clothes, shoes and presents for friends or family.

Darkness came down and they'd pushed around shops and through passageways made homely with lanterns. Light glowed through pierced brass or ceramic shades, causing warm and starry shapes to dance across walls and floors. The friends had heard the ringing blows of metal smiths and, just a little louder, the cries of mueddins from neighbouring mosques. Some of them proclaimed their beliefs quite beautifully; their voices changing words into music. Others bellowed like bulls at a slaughter, striving to outdo the rest with the piety of their cries.

Khaled and Ethan had watched the leather workers stamp segment by segment, allowing intricate patterns to emerge. They'd marvelled at the finished goods, their fingers tracing the golden stars, the geometrical patterns and crescents that led at last to Ethan's name in Arabic script.

It was finely made, that saddle-bag. Khaled had ordered it the week before and was thrilled by the pleasure his present gave. *'For learning to read my language'* had been the excuse but Ethan knew what lay behind the gift and for the rest of his life, would use it to carry anything of value he possessed.

In his shelter, and slithering on bloody ground, Ethan opened a side pocket of the bag. He ransacked its contents until he found the small wooden box that Khaled had given him. On its top, again in Arabic, he could make out the words, *'For My Brother'*. Inside was the razor, and once more there had been an excuse. He put that fragment from another lifetime back into its box and closed the lid.

He would use it, but not yet. His beard had served him well and would do so for a little longer.

There were perfumes too in those, their glory days. Floria had blended them with oils, spices, herbs and the essence of flowers. He closed his eyes, recalling the tingling skin, soon to grow warm as she caressed their eager young bodies. Sensing how little or how much of her potions to apply, Floria had aroused in them yearnings that neither boy had previously known.

There were other, less comforting thoughts that pressed their way to the front of his mind and since a man who can no longer like himself might love his friends, Ethan first visited that day when Khaled came looking for him.

✳✳✳

2

What normal boy wouldn't swap school room for stable yard? Today was a case in point. By mid-morning, what with the sun's heat and Khaled's bone-headedness, his tutor had had enough. There's a limit to the amount of work that can be swished out of an unwilling pupil, so when his charge yawned for a second time and asked to be let out early, instead of reaching for his cane, the teacher nodded in tired agreement and the boy was off.

The yard stank of labourers' sweat, horse shit and piss. A definite step up from musty books. Feeding the horses, grooming them, cleaning out the stables and helping stack the manure were also a change for the better as far as Khaled was concerned. Of course, his view didn't satisfy everyone. According to Ali, his elder brother, he ought to spend less of the day hanging around with slaves and more of it learning about the responsibilities that lay ahead. As Sheikh Omar's younger son, he should get his nose back into his books and take more pride in his appearance. Khaled had other ideas. The yard was a happy-go-lucky place. He loved the jokes and the quick results he could see from manual labour. Most of all, he enjoyed being with young men of his own age.

One day, without warning, he'd been moved out of the intimate atmosphere of the haramlek where he'd always lived with his mother and other female members of his household. It was time, they told him, to share life with his father and brother in the salamlek. Here, the men passed much of their lives and entertained male guests in the sitting area known as the majlis. From now on, contact with his mother and other women of the household would be less frequent and always chaperoned. It was about that time, Khaled had noticed a change in his voice. He remembered trying it out with other young men, all of them speaking as deeply as they could.

A few years on, and he was still playing that same silly game with the girls on his father's estate. They liked the low down sound; he knew that for sure because it made them giggle. Afterwards, he'd catch them with their heads together and hope they were talking about him.

Girls looked him up and down a lot these days and whenever they got the chance, they'd stop for a chat. He especially enjoyed it when the pretty ones hung on to him. They'd push their bodies against his and he'd feel himself getting hard. The girls knew well enough what was happening - he'd caught them eyeing his bulge - but none of them complained. From time to time, he'd get lucky and they'd go with him to the stables. There were dark corners there.

Jews and Christians enjoyed more freedom than he did. He'd seen the way the boys and girls mixed easily together. Being friends with them had opened paths he'd never have found for himself. At first, his games with the girls had been fumbled, all-fingers-and-thumb affairs but he was getting better at them - especially when Ethan was around. Sometimes, his friend had a girl of his own. More often, they shared. It didn't matter either way.

They were fun, those times, but there were other things that made life worth living and he could do them whenever he liked. Girls were sweet fruit but you were always looking for places to take them and that wasted a lot of time. All in all, swimming, wrestling and fishing were a better bet.

Since getting away from his tutor, Khaled had worked hard. He'd fed and watered the falcons and helped carry out a lot of other jobs around the yard. He didn't mind what he did and Ethan liked him more when he caught him hardworking and filthy. Khaled swiped his arm across his face and pushed back the tangle of curls that plastered his forehead. There'd be time to sluice himself clean while his friend picked them out a couple of horses.

A collection of farm buildings surrounded the yard, blocking off any currents of air that might cool the place. That was well and good in cold weather but on days like this, it made work feel endless. The old hands had got through most of their jobs early and could now take things easy. Khaled, still the novice, had carried on working through the heat and his tunic hung heavy with sweat. He dragged himself free of its tackiness and slung it over a bush. It would be dry in no time – the sun would see to that. Meanwhile, he'd liven himself up at the water trough.

Getting permission to go hunting hadn't been easy. He'd made his father a lot of promises about studying and treating his tutor with respect. After all that, his friend hadn't shown up. More than likely, Sulieman was to blame. The stable-yard overseer had probably got wind of their plans and given Ethan some job or other to keep him busy.

Khaled's tunic already looked as good as dry. He untangled it from the bush, pulled it back on and went looking for his friend. None of the stable boys seemed to know where Ethan was, so Khaled headed for the barns. As he passed the horse trough, it reminded him he was sweating again. He plunged his head deep down, enjoying the boom of water in his ears while waiting for its chill to reach him. Still half deaf, he stood up allowing the freshness to flood his body.

None of the barn workers had any idea where his friend was. That's what they said but their voices told him they were keeping something back. Reuben's scowl confirmed his suspicions. He was a workmate of Ethan's and over the last couple of years, the three of them had grown close. 'Don't let everyone know he isn't here,' he hissed urgently while dragging Khaled to one side. 'It'll give Sulieman another excuse to swing the stick.'

Reuben was as wild as the rest of them. Given half a chance, he'd be after the girls or drinking himself stupid but he had common sense as well, so he was worth listening to. 'I've told you before; there are some of them we can't trust.' He was nodding in the direction of a twig-thin youth who was half-heartedly brushing the ground. Reuben had positioned himself so the young labourer couldn't make out what was being said. 'Saleem's idle but he never gets hammered. Not while he's useful for passing on information about the rest of us. He sucks up to Sulieman all the time.'

Khaled was ashamed of his own stupidity. A fool would know better than to go around loud-mouthing about Ethan not turning up for work, especially when he'd been warned not to trust Saleem. Khaled had never thought of the boy as more than obsequious and effeminate but Reuben knew better. He saw Saleem as a reptile and they could be dangerous.

Khaled's glee was a threat to his face; any more smiling would slash it in half, but he'd seen his friend sprint into the yard. Ethan's fair hair was dark-streaked with sweat, he was looking worried and Khaled knew why. His friend had been punished for lateness twice in the past month and the overseer would enjoy making another example of him. Ethan might be Khaled's friend but Ali had the authority and Sulieman swung a mean cane.

'Do they know I wasn't here?'

Khaled shook his head. 'We'd better get going before they find out.'

Whistling with relief, Ethan went to fetch the horses. His first choice would've been the stallion while his friend made do with the gelding, but he was feeling generous. He'd escaped his enemies so he agreed to a swap.

'The mountains?'

'In this heat?' Ethan scowled.

'We're supposed to be going hunting.'

Ethan ignored him and led them across the dry flat countryside, his horse churning dust and flinging up sand. Fear wasn't for him, not so long as he could outride it. Khaled wasn't so sure. One day he'd master a horse as well as his friend could. But not yet. Dread tore his guts too often.

Ethan looked over his shoulder and started to yell. He was pointing at an opening, half hidden by some rocks. It was a shorter route and led to a clearing shaded by trees. *Aguadulce*, the local people called it because of the small, sweet-water springs that bubbled and fed into a stream. Ethan and Khaled picked out a deeply shadowed area and tied up their horses. They'd heard the raucous jabber of boys in the sea and ran to join them.

The sand was sun scorched but their feet, toughened by walking barefoot, could take its heat. The sea was another matter. The shallows splashed viciously, scalding their ankles and forcing them further out. By the time it was slapping their thighs, the water was better natured.

'What if, one day, it didn't get any cooler?' Khaled laughed.

'We'd be boiled. It beats me how anything lives in it.'

Swimming and spearing fish were good ways to spend an afternoon. So was flogging an octopus. 'What's he doing that for?' Khaled asked his friend, the first time he saw a man smashing his catch against a rock. 'It's dead, isn't it?'

'Try eating one without beating it first,' Ethan told him. 'They're as tough as a saddle.'

One of the boys was jumping around and yelling. His name was Sergio and he was pointing to a boat half way between the shore and the horizon. 'I reckon it's a slaver. I've seen a lot of them over the past few weeks.'

The boys looked nervously at each other. Their parents never stopped warning them about ships landing and the crews carrying off young men and women. But weren't these tales to frighten children, to make them behave or go to bed early? This was Almeria. Things like that happened in other lands and to other people.

'Muslim or Christian?' several of the boys wanted to know.

'Christian,' one of their friends said, glancing anxiously at the others.

'That didn't take much working out!' Sergio told him, 'Most of them are Christian, these days.'

Khaled's eyes shifted uneasily towards Ethan but his friend's only reaction was to give him a slow conspiratorial wink. Nobody seemed to have guessed he was a Muslim. He had dark skin but so did several of the others and he wasn't circumcised. There was no reason to suspect. Anyway, he was a friend of Ethan's and that was good enough for them.

'How can you tell it's Christian when it's that far off?' Ethan asked.

'See the prow? The Arab ones are like a long beak. They're different from ours.' Sergio sounded as though he knew what he was talking about and the other boys strained their eyes to make out the distant vessel. 'Christian or not, we'd better keep an eye on it. If it comes any closer, we'll make ourselves scarce.'

The ship disappeared over the horizon and, breathing more easily, they turned their attention to gutting the catch and cooking it over a driftwood fire. Khaled walked casually over to Ethan and as soon as he was sure he couldn't be overheard, said quietly, 'They won't be back. They know what we'll do to them if they come inshore. Father says we've got plenty of defence boats.'

Worries about slavers were pushed away but it would be a while before the fire burned down to the glowing embers needed for cooking fish. A few of the boys had darted back into the sea while others started to wrestle on the beach. They were from the surrounding villages and Khaled remembered his friend telling him they learned to fight from an early age. Anyone showing weakness had his life made miserable, so they hardened themselves.

He eyed his companions' bodies and compared them with his own. A couple of years ago, he'd have seemed puny. Now, he was as well built as any of them. Working alongside Ethan in the stable yard had seen to that.

'He's good!'

'Who is?'

'Reuben's brother.' Khaled was nodding in the direction of a young man who was standing over a winded opponent. 'It looked easy, the way he did it.'

Ethan grunted enthusiastically. 'Danny's a better wrestler than

I'll ever be.' Cupping his hands to his mouth, he yelled, 'Get yourself over here, Big Man, and teach us a few of your tricks.'

Menacing and deliberately ape-like, Danny loped across the sand towards them. 'You're after a lesson?' Khaled and Ethan jumped to their feet. Of all their friends, Danny was the toughest. But it wasn't his muscles Khaled envied. Danny and his brother were cut.

Ethan had nearly choked with laughter the first time Khaled told him he wanted to be circumcised. 'A lot of misery for nothing', was the way he saw it. You wouldn't catch him putting his cock to the blade, and for the life of him he couldn't see why his friend should want to go messing about with knives either. 'We're alright the way we are, aren't we?' It was traditional for Muslim men to be circumcised. Ethan knew that, but it was usually done when they were children. For some reason he couldn't fathom, a few families linked the practice to a young man's coming of age. He supposed it was that underlining of manhood Khaled was looking for.

Danny was a good teacher. He worked with them for a long time, showing ways of tripping an opponent and how to apply pressure to joints and other sensitive areas. He had nothing but praise for Khaled. The boy knew nothing but was quick to learn. Ethan, on the other hand, irritated him. He didn't lack guts but his over-confidence was a weakness. He was a born fighter but he thought he knew it all.

'You're good in attack,' Danny told him, 'But you haven't learned a thing about defence. As long as you're taking the fight to your opponent, you think that's good enough. Maybe it is, sometimes. But you leave yourself wide open. In a real fight, I'd have blinded you or ripped your balls off by now.'

'We're supposed to be mates!' Ethan scoffed.

'That's why it's no good practising with me. You need someone who hates your guts. But I'm warning you. Pay more attention to defence, or one of these days you're going to lose and lose badly!' He'd had enough of Ethan's cockiness and headed for the shade, leaving the friends to practise together.

Ethan soon staggered back, sweating and gasping for breath. 'It'll be years before we're anywhere near as good as he is.'

'How come you win so many fights, then?' Khaled asked.

'Me? I'm just brutal! There's more than one way to fight. Danny's the best at what he does but you need to know more than that.'

'Such as?'

'Like I said, it'll take years. Anyway, I've shown you enough already. Learn too much and you might hammer me.'

'You admit I'm learning then?'

Khaled was looking for praise but that was no reason to give it to him. 'Slowly,' Ethan told him. 'Very slowly.'

'It might come in handy, sometime. When you need me to get you out of trouble.'

'That'll be the day frogs grow hair!' Ethan jabbed his friend lightly in the groin and reached for a water-skin. He gulped down part of the contents before handing it to his friend.

Khaled drank thirstily from a spout still moist from Ethan's lips. 'Is it right what Danny says? About defending yourself?'

'He's always going on about it. I don't take much notice. Anyway, let's get something to eat.' The smell of food had tormented them long enough. There'd be a period of quiet while they wolfed down the fish and moved out of the sun to sleep.

The flies were a plague. Khaled flicked his hand at them repeatedly but it didn't work. Sterner measures were required. He grabbed a length of rope that had been washed up nearby and started to thrash around, trying to slaughter the pestering swarms. Instead, he caught Ethan across the chest.

'Do that again and I'll thump you! You're more of a curse than the flies.'

Khaled looked at his young fair-haired companion as he lay back, half asleep on the sand and knew that nobody in the world had a better mate than Ethan. It felt like they'd been friends for most of their lives. In fact, they'd met seven years before - soon after the young slave started working for Sheikh Omar. Before that, Khaled had grown used to spending long hours alone. He'd study with his tutor during the mornings but once classes ended, he'd wander about looking for things to do. One day, he'd been ambling around the stable yard, talking to the horses and watching the men at work when a voice made him jump, 'You can give me a hand if you're up to it!' Khaled turned around and found himself looking at a boy of about his own age. Things were in for a change.

Colt-like and with hair the colour of straw, the boy smiled cockily. 'Don't stand there gawping! Come and help muck out the stables!' It was one part invitation and two parts order but before Khaled had a chance to argue, the young labourer had handed him a rake.

They'd worked together for most of the afternoon, cleaning out the fouled bedding and replacing it with fresh straw. Mostly, they talked about girls and beer. At least Ethan did. Khaled went along with just about everything he said. He didn't know much about such matters and to cover his ignorance, he'd mumbled enthusiastically. He didn't care. He was learning and if Ethan wanted to play the older, wiser man, that was alright as well. Khaled had found a friend and that's what mattered.

Later in the day, he'd heard one of the stable-yard workers telling Ethan off. 'That's your master's son you've been bossing.'

'His work's alright,' Ethan shrugged, 'And he does what I tell him. I'll probably keep him on.'

The man wasn't one for humour and continued trying to make the youngster see sense. He might as well have been talking to the horses. 'You'll get yourself whipped if you carry on like that,' were his parting words.

'I don't think so!' Ethan yelled after him. 'He's happy enough with me.'

He was right. Every day from then on, as soon as his lessons ended, Khaled made straight for the yard.

Strawhead, a lot of the men called him, but to Khaled's mind, Ethan's hair looked more like the sun. His new friend laughed a lot and talked to him as if he were a man. An ignorant, know-nothing sort of man. The type that needed a friendly clout from time to time.

But a man. Not the all-spots-and-no-balls kind of boy Khaled had felt like before.

He'd started going along with Ethan whenever he visited his family. They lived in a small farmhouse in the Alpujarras Mountains, close to the village of Felix. His friend's mother and sisters always made a fuss of him and he soon felt more at home with them, than he did in his own house in the Alcazaba.

Then there was Inga. She was the oldest of the sisters and as fair-haired as her brother. Khaled liked looking at her. It made him get hard and he sometimes worried in case his friend noticed. He had a feeling it might not go down too well with Ethan.

To repay the family's kindness, Khaled convinced his father to let Ethan join in some of his lessons. They were in the mornings and during the afternoons, Khaled could help out in the yard. The work would still get done.

At first, Ethan had only played a small part in the classes but as his confidence grew, he became more active in the discussions they held with their tutor. The boys had been eager to learn about the history of their country and the teacher had been just as keen to show off his knowledge.

It had been more than seven centuries, he told them, since the Berbers and various Arab tribes had flooded into Spain from North Africa. They'd brought with them the message of Islam and were seen by most of the local people as a welcome change from the Germanic nations that had tried to rule Iberia after the collapse of the Roman Empire.

'All you were any good for was knocking the cocks off the statues!' Khaled said, elbowing his friend.

'That wasn't us. It was the Vandals! We just killed the men and raped the women!'

Their tutor had threatened to crack a smile but he'd covered up with a well timed cough and a change of subject. Later, Khaled told his friend that some of his ancestors had come from Yemen in the Arabian Peninsular. They'd been close allies of the victorious Berber leaders and had been rewarded with vast tracts of land around the city of Almeria. Today, their estates reached from the gates of the Alcazaba to the fertile valleys of the Alpujarras Mountains where Ethan and other members of his Visigoth tribe lived.

Ethan's position was similar to that of a bonded servant. When he'd been about ten years old, his father had decided to buy their farm from Sheikh Omar. The family had very little money so it was agreed the boy would work without pay for a period of ten years. During that time he would be more or less the property of Khaled's father, living and working in the stable yard.

Less than a year after the agreement had been reached, Ethan's father had died, and the family found themselves facing financial hardship. Sheikh Omar had been their saviour. At first, he'd thought about releasing Ethan from the bond but came to the conclusion that it might not be the best idea. As an Arab, he understood the importance of saving face and knew that even the poorest of people could be humiliated by careless generosity. It would be better if Ethan carried on working. In that way, he could pay for the farm, safeguard the family's self respect and at the same time guarantee their future.

The boy was allowed home at weekends to help out on the land and as soon as he returned to work, he'd be asked about his family. The questioning was in the form of casual conversation but the answers gave Sheik Omar an insight into the family's affairs. He was able to make sure they never went short of food or anything they needed for the smooth running of the farm.

Khaled hadn't known much about his friend's history but it seemed wrong to him that Ethan, who was at least his equal when it came to intelligence, should be thought of as a slave. As time went by, he managed to piece together parts of the story and one day their tutor had filled in the missing details. The young men listened in silence as he told how the Visigoth kings had been weakened by feuding among themselves and were quickly defeated by the well organised Muslim armies.

For Ethan, this was interesting news. 'If my ancestors hadn't been such idiots,' he taunted, 'You'd be calling me, *Master!*'

'And how would you treat me?'

'Hard! The same as you are with me.'

Khaled's face began to burn and he looked at the ground. He hoped he did right by his friend, but he knew there'd been times when he'd used his position to get his own way. He squirmed inwardly for a while, until Ethan released him. 'You're fair. Most of the time, anyway! You are to the others as well. That's why they like you. Mind you, your brother's another matter. So is Sulieman. Give us half a chance and we'd soon show that pair of bastards what we thought of them.'

Khaled's eyebrows shot up. He wasn't sure he should let Ethan speak like that about his brother. On the other hand, his friend's comments were justified. When he'd been a boy, Ali had enjoyed making small animals suffer and for a while, he'd made his brother's life miserable as well. That was until Khaled grew bigger and learned to fight back.

Sheikh Omar was wise in most things but he'd made a serious error of judgement when he gave his elder son a powerful role in the running of the estate. Worse, from the workers' point of view, was the day Ali brought in Sulieman to be the stable-yard overseer. Between them, they managed to make the labourers' lives uncomfortable.

Khaled remembered a time when his brother had appeared tall, strongly built and imposing. In recent years, however, a lack of exercise had ruined his body. Like all idle men, he'd grown feeble and lardy. Sulieman, on the other hand, was thin and wiry. He moved in a slouch with those lizard eyes of his, flicking from side to side as they sought out trouble. The moment he found an excuse for brutality, he'd jerk into action and make life hell for anyone who refused to grovel. Ethan and Reuben were among those marked down for punishment, but they weren't alone. Khaled had noticed that Sulieman's victims were always good-looking, powerfully-built young men. The overseer found fault with their work and caned them in front of their mates.

Lazy ripples lapped the rocks and several of their friends were snoring on the sand. The sounds were lulling and Ethan was drowsing. Khaled, on the other hand, was wide awake and wondering. Why were these northern people so beautiful? Their fair hair and light skin gave them the look of angels, like the ones he'd seen painted on the walls of Christian churches. Inga had eyes like her brother's and her hair was as golden, but her mouth was soft and her chin delicate. Ethan's jaw jutted aggressively at times and he could say harsh things. Inga's lips spoke gently.

Khaled found himself thinking more and more about her. And that was the one thing he didn't dare tell Ethan. He'd get the beating of a life time if his friend so much as suspected there was something going on between him and Inga. Well, there wasn't anything going on, but there would be if he got half a chance and Ethan was no fool. Sooner or later he'd guess at the thoughts that passed through Khaled's mind.

He'd better say something first. The problem was, he'd no idea where to begin. All he knew was that most of the time he was thinking about Inga and a lot of those thoughts weren't the sort of things her brother would want to know about.

Khaled crawled next to his friend, intending to make a pillow out of his belly. A hand flicked his hair and that meant he was welcome. He wriggled about, trying to make himself comfortable. Instead, he got a clout. 'You're on my balls!' Ethan jerked and Khaled's head thumped onto the sand. Scooping up fistfuls of gravel, he started to sling them over Ethan's chest and belly. His friend didn't move or make a sound but Khaled was looking for a reaction. He scraped up another handful of wet sand and rammed it into the hairy curls at the base of his friend's belly.

'Are you after another thump?'

Khaled watched Ethan lapse back into a drowse and started to flick pebbles. There was no warning this time. His friend lunged, grabbing him around the neck and kneeing him in the ribs. 'I warned you!'

It was the sort of reaction Khaled had been hoping for. 'You haven't told me about last night.'

'What's it to you?' Ethan was trying to sound curt but it was confession time and sooner or later, he was going to talk. He let go of Khaled's neck and sat up warily. It was just possible his friend had decided to play the good Muslim and object to alcohol. If Ali had been working on his mind, the truth could be dangerous. One glance at Khaled's eager face told him he'd nothing to worry about. 'I went with to the tavern with a few friends.'

'Any women there?' Khaled's casual tone was a mask for his envy.

'One or two.'

'Did you have one?'

'All night.'

'And the other times? That's why you were late?' Khaled had screwed his face into the scowl of the interrogator. His friend had told him something but it wasn't enough. He'd have to rack him some more.

Meanwhile, Ethan's remorse wasn't burning too deeply. He should have taken Khaled to *The Barrels*. He'd betrayed his best friend. But that wasn't the problem. He'd admit to it and say he was sorry. Khaled would hate him for a while, probably give him a cursing and maybe a thump - the puppy was growing teeth!

It was the massive shadow of shame running alongside his guilt that made Ethan cringe from the truth. He shrugged his shoulders and worked at looking surly. He'd brazen things out, Khaled would forgive him and the guilt would go away. The same trick wouldn't work with the shame, though. That would stay with him. 'You know as much as you need to know,' he snarled. 'Now, shut up!'

Over the past weeks, Ethan had got a name for idleness and brawling. More often than not, he'd come back to the cabin he shared with Reuben and Danny, reeking of beer. But to risk those canings? Khaled knew his friend had been up to something compelling and it was probably to do with a woman. 'Why didn't you tell me what was going on?' he sniggered. 'Don't try saying there weren't enough girls. We've shared plenty of times before.'

Ethan knew it was true. When they were boys, they'd played around with each other. Still did for that matter. But more often these days, it was with girls. They fucked them together. And there was the smart that made Ethan flinch.

'It wasn't the girls …' He was going to lie. He didn't like doing it, not to Khaled. His friend deserved better. But it was easier this way. 'There was beer, lots of it. You Muslims aren't supposed to drink and I didn't want you in trouble. You'd have come if I'd told you. Then, when we got back, Sulieman or Ali would have smelled the drink. Even if they didn't, Saleem or one of the other creeps would have told them and it would have been you, as well as me, for the stick.'

'That's my problem, not yours. I don't need you protecting me all the time.'

'I wasn't protecting you'

'That's what it feels like!'

'It's not how it was meant! Now give it a rest!' Ethan sensed he was back in the saddle. He kept up the act until his friend thought the subject was closed. Then, very casually, and as though it couldn't be of interest to anyone, he dropped in the words, 'I'm going again tomorrow night.' He paused, enjoying the hope he could read on Khaled's face. 'Interested?'

Interested? Khaled was up and jumping!

It was what Ethan had been hoping for, but it was more than he was ready to admit. The last few times with the girls hadn't been all he'd made them out to be. Sometimes he couldn't get it up. And when he did, he'd come too soon. They'd told him he was the best, but he knew they were lying. He'd seen the looks on their faces. Floria was a good girl. She'd never complained and he didn't want her disappointed. But he knew what was missing and that was a confession hot irons wouldn't sear out of him.

'When you get your arse whipped, don't blame me!' Ethan gave another shrug. It felt like the right thing to do, and it helped the story along. His lie was smoothing the edges and he didn't feel guilty any more. In fact, he was happier than he'd been for days. He needed Khaled with him and that was the truth. Things went better that way. He never had any trouble getting it up when his friend was there. That's what worried him. Maybe it would always be like that and it wasn't right. Someday, he'd have to like Khaled a little less.

Michael Horrex

For the time being he wouldn't think about it. There was something he wanted his friend to see. He'd found a way of putting his muscle to use and that should be good for a few beers.

***

3

It was night by the time they arrived at a wedge of buildings that hugged the wharf. The street lamps had been lit but several were running out of oil and smoked filthily. The gloom was broken here and there by lanterns flickering from the windows of shops or glowing warmly in the doorways of taverns. Khaled's eyes latched onto the girls. Groups of them, with painted-up faces and dressed-down bodies, worked hard to coax the boys inside. Any of them would have done as far as he was concerned but Ethan shook his head and hurried him past. He knew where he was going and Khaled followed like a tamed dog, through the maze of alleyways.

They came to a stop outside a muck-encrusted doorway. It had been red at one time, but there wasn't much left of the original paintwork, just a few faded patches grinning through the grime. Along the bottom of the wall, there was the stain and stink of human piss while, higher up, a crudely painted sign showed three barrels. It was a rough dive in the worst part of town and Ethan was standing like he owned the place.

The shouts of drunken men, a rattle of dice and the stench of sweat reeled through the open doorway. They promised a different world and Khaled couldn't get inside quickly enough. He pushed around, mouth open and eyes straining, until he got some idea of his surroundings. It was a drinking den, dingy and heaving with loudmouths, all of them happy to curse and jostle, while swigging from earthenware pots. There was nothing much by way of furniture; a dozen rough wooden tables and the same number of half-broken stools had been slung to the sides of the room. The light, what there was of it, came from a few old oil lamps that glimmered from hooks in the wall.

A couple of young men were busy selling a dark frothy liquid. It reeked of yeast and Khaled guessed it was *beer*, that famous brew Ethan was always talking about. He watched the men refill the pots then hand them back to their customers. Their in-the-know smiles suggested the liquid held some arcane, almost mystical significance.

'The beer's the best thing about this place.' Ethan was holding up his pot and yelling to make himself heard above the din. 'It's better than wine when you've got a thirst on.' To Khaled, it tasted bitter, vinegary even. But he'd get to like it. Ethan told him the beer was good, so that had to be the case. All he needed was time.

It was the rawness of *The Barrels* that Khaled loved. There was more life among those curses, the yells and that smell of sweat than he could have hoped to find in one small room. Nevertheless, he'd stick with his friend. Ethan was on good terms with the crowd.

Khaled recognised some of the young men from the beach but most of the customers were strangers. He was certainly the only one of his kind in the room which shouldn't have surprised him; not many Muslims would go into a place where alcohol was drunk. Several of the customers were eyeing him and, feeling a brief ripple of insecurity, he edged closer to Ethan.

Moments later, and he was in trouble. Reuben was pushing his way towards them. He was sure to call him *Khaled* and that would give the game away. Instead, his friend gripped him by the arm and winked his hello. It was safer than using his Muslim name.

Most of the crowd had reached that happy stage of drunkenness when life is to be enjoyed and all men are brothers. One of them lumbered unsteadily towards him. 'Your mate's going to win us a lot of money tonight,' he slurred, ramming a pot of beer into the newcomer's hand. It fitted comfortably. Khaled liked its size, its reassuring weight and the roughness of its baked clay surface. He was happier than at any time in his life. He loved *The Barrels*. He could

Matanza!

spend the rest of his life here with Ethan beside him and maybe a few of their friends. They'd make it their home, just like the pot was making its home in his warm fist.

The man who'd brought him the beer was bellowing at him but most of his words were lost in the racket. Khaled understood him to say something like, '*How much are you putting on?*' He'd no idea what that meant and looked around urgently. Reuben came to his aid. 'Too much!' he yelled into the man's ear.

The noise was deafening but it served a purpose. The friends could speak to each other without being overheard and Reuben snatched the chance to clear up a few points. '*Put something on Ethan*, that means *make a bet*. There's a couple of Jews over there.' He was nodding in the direction of two dark skinned, eager-looking men crouched over a table in the corner of the room. 'They'll take your money, if you think *Strawhead's* got a chance.'

So that was why his friend had dragged him to this particular den. He'd arranged to fight and wanted his mates with him for support. Khaled downed beer after beer and knew he could fly. Everything was possible. Ethan would win. He didn't doubt that for a moment - just as he knew everyone in the room was his friend. He had no difficulty keeping up with the other men when they talked about beer, the fights they'd won and the women they'd fucked. A few of the stories were true. Most of them were lies. It didn't matter either way. They were all part of the game and he could play it as well as anyone.

He needed a piss in a hurry and Reuben went with him. They had the wall to themselves and that was a definite advantage. Nobody likes pissing with strangers. Khaled sneaked a look at Reuben's well-cut cock and felt more uneasy with his own. Something had to be done about that piece of skin. It told him he was a boy.

While they were watering the wall, somebody shoved past, making Reuben piss on his own feet. He looked over his shoulder, ready to curse. Then, recognizing the thug who'd pushed him, he changed his scowl to a smile. His feet weren't that wet.

By the time they got inside, the man had elbowed his way through the crowd. His size and loose-limbed walk told the world he was strong, so nobody stood in his way. 'That's Bruno,' Reuben hissed. 'Fighting's the way he makes his living.'

The man stood at least a head taller than anyone around him. He was ugly from scarring and at one time or an other, his nose had been smashed flat to his face. Khaled jerked with revulsion when he saw the man had no ears. In their place were two ragged holes surrounded by scar-silvered skin. 'It's never him, Ethan's planning to fight?'

'Don't worry about it.' Reuben did his best to sound convincing. 'He's big and he's ugly but that's all he is. *Strawhead*'s in with a chance.'

Khaled watched Bruno gulp down a couple of beers while swapping jokes with the crowd around him. They'd pushed forward, wanting to borrow some of his glory, while keeping a respectful distance between themselves and their man.

At last, and it was at a time of his choosing, Bruno handed his pot to one of his friends. He began to strip, showing off his powerful legs and thighs followed by a muscle-bunched torso and shoulders. His supporters yelped with excitement while he worked steadily through a well-practised display of flexing. Every move was designed to work up the crowd and intimidate his opponent.

Khaled couldn't take his eyes off the man. His back and shoulders were ridged with badly healed lash marks while other parts of his body showed signs of having being burned.

'They did that to him in the north,' Reuben said. 'He's one of theirs but Christian or not, that didn't stop them sending him to the mines. The story goes he was caught stealing food for his family. It's not like it is down here. Not where he comes from. Here, everybody gets enough to eat. Up there, it's church and army first. By the time they've had their fill, there's never much left for the poor bastards who grew it. Anyway, Bruno got ten years. He escaped twice. The first time, they brought him back and gave him the lash. They cut off his ears and branded him with red hot rods. That was to make sure none of the others got any ideas about trying to escape. It didn't stop him, though. Next time, he made it to Granada. Some Muslims took him in and he's been living there ever since with his family. He moves around the area, fighting so his family can eat.'

Khaled took a good look at this monstrous being. Bruno couldn't afford to lose and desperate men made dangerous opponents. He knew he should try and stop this madness before his friend got hurt. On the other hand, something told him he wanted to see the men fight. Back at the stables, whenever there was a brawl, he found himself hollering along with the other workmen. He was always sorry when Sulieman or some of the labourers broke it up.

He pushed his way through the crowd until he was standing next to Ethan. 'You didn't tell me you were fighting!'

His friend shrugged. 'I don't tell you about a lot of things I do. How do you think I get the money I need for beer and girls?'

That was good enough. Ethan wanted to fight so it was out of Khaled's hands. Besides, being told his friend had a life apart from the one they shared was galling. It would serve the bastard right if he got hammered.

Khaled switched his attention to a few of the supporters who were working their way around the room and collecting wagers. Apart from their share of the takings, Reuben told him, the fighters were hoping to make money from side bets.

'Can you beat him?' Khaled asked his friend.

'I wouldn't be here if I couldn't.'

'Wait till I get back!' He grabbed Reuben by the arm and the pair of them shouldered their way through the mob until they reached one of the tables where the Jews were taking bets.

'Let me do it,' Reuben yelled. 'Danny and I have known him all our lives. He won't try any funny business, not with us. How much do you want to put on?'

'All of it.' Khaled handed his friend a leather bag, lumpy with coins.'

Hefting it in his hand, Reuben stared at his friend in amazement. 'Are you mad? There's a fortune in here.'

'It's for all of us.'

'If you're sure.' Reuben shrugged with resignation. Khaled was probably making the mistake of a lifetime but there was nothing he could do about it. 'If Ethan loses, you'll be on water for a year.'

'Good for my soul! Anyway, he'll win. He said he would, didn't he?'

There was no answer to that. Reuben emptied the coins onto the table. The man counted them and they agreed the amount. Once the bet was recorded, they pushed their way back to their friends. Khaled was looking confident while Reuben muttered a prayer of thanks that it wasn't his money!

Ethan unbuckled the leather belt of his tunic, yanked the single item of clothing over his head and threw it to Khaled. He was nothing like as tall as his opponent but in many ways he was the more impressive man. Bruno's bulk bordered on the grotesque. Ethan had the finely honed physique of an athlete. Every muscle was sharply defined while his bronzed skin and golden hair gave him the heroic look of an invincible warrior.

Like the proud tunic bearer to a demi-god, Khaled held his friend's clothing where everyone could see it as the crowd moved towards the inner yard. At the entrance, they were forced to wait. The landlord's son was still busy sprinkling the sand-covered ground with water while his brother raked it smooth. Once the young men had finished their work, the mob roared into the yard. They formed themselves into a quick rough circle, leaving the centre clear for the fighters.

Bruno swaggered, biceps flexed, into the ring of spectators. He acknowledged his supporters' yells, while ignoring the catcalls from his rival's friends. A few moments later it was their turn to roar. Ethan, arms raised and grinning, strutted confidently towards his opponent.

The fighters circled each other - watching for an opening and waiting for a chance to attack. Ethan dropped his guard contemptuously and walked into a right fist. Bruno followed up with a series of hammer blows to the head and body. Ethan stumbled, hurt and with unfocussed sight, into a callous wall of spectators. They heaved him back towards the centre of the ring where Bruno stood ready. He landed a left to the jaw and lightning flashed behind his victim's eyes. Pain swamped thought and a shocked numbness took hold of him.

Ethan's supporters groaned in disbelief. Their man had left himself open and he'd paid the price. He was fighting to drag air into desperate lungs. The sweat sprayed from his hair as he shook his head. The crowd sensed his grogginess and they watched Bruno move forward.

The giant unleashed a merciless barrage of blows to the ribs and stomach, finishing with a wicked left, driven deep into the youngster's groin. Ethan groaned and crashed to the ground, where he lay writhing in agony. Reuben's reaction was instinctive. He leapt forward, forcing his body between the two men in an attempt to shield Ethan from further punishment. The crowd roared its fury. Four of Bruno's supporters fought to wrench Reuben away, impatient for their man to press home his attack.

It was Khaled's turn. He had no plan, but his friend was hurt. Without thinking, he elbowed one of the supporters in the face and tripped another. The pair of them crashed heavily into Bruno, dragging him to the ground. The crowd erupted into a brawling rabble, shouting and lashing out as tables and stools were hurled around the room.

The landlord and his sons could see the night's profit disappearing in the rampage. They waded, strap-wielding and cursing, into a mob driven by fury and deaf to threats of violence. Their attempts to regain control had no effect until, bellowing to make himself heard, the landlord jumped onto one of the tables and threatened to cancel all bets.

The fear of losing money was a powerful one. Growling their resentment, the brawlers backed down. Some sort of order was restored but the landlord and his sons were taking no chances. They singled out Khaled, Reuben and a couple of Bruno's supporters to make their point. 'No getting in the way of the fighters. Try it again and you'll get this!' The landlord rammed his strap into Khaled's face before turning on the mob. They were included in the threat, his bulging eyes and twisted mouth told them as much. Reuben nodded, obedient as a whipped schoolboy. The rest of them did the same.

Khaled shifted uneasily on his feet. It was the first time anyone had brought him to heel so publicly. He noticed some of Bruno's men wearing equally cowed expressions and felt a little less humbled. Reuben elbowed him in the ribs. It was a welcome nudge that meant, 'Behave! The landlord's a man of his word and that's a hefty looking strap.' But it also said, 'You're one of us. We're in this together'.

Ethan's friends had gained him time. And that was as much as they could do. Their man was on his feet but his legs were jelly. Bruno looked fresh. Any moment now, he'd move in and finish the job.

The pain in Ethan's balls had eased and he was starting to think. If he was going to turn things around, he needed to hang on to his concentration. He forced his mind to slow down. For the moment, he was in no state to fight. If he tried, Bruno would hammer him into the ground. Ethan circled his opponent. He moved cannily and kept his distance.

Gradually, the young fighter felt his strength returning. There was no more time to waste feeling sorry for himself. He feinted with his right. Bruno fell for it. Exploding into attack, Ethan ripped shot after shot to the head and belly. Bruno staggered. But it wasn't enough.

Ducking low, the young giant grabbed Ethan's legs. He slung him to the ground and followed up with a series of savage blows to his unprotected body. Ignoring the pain, Ethan wrapped his legs around his opponent. Thigh and calf muscles straining, he gripped Bruno in a crushing lock. Slowly, he turned him until he lay on his back with Ethan astride. His friends went wild as he hammered Bruno's head, slamming it mercilessly from side to side.

The man wasn't fighting back. Instead, he lay motionless and bloody under Ethan's attack. Reuben and Khaled glanced quickly at each other. They moved forward and seized hold of their friend's arms, fighting to rip him away from his helpless opponent. Khaled's voice at last cut through Ethan's madness. 'It's over. Are you trying to kill him? You've won, you bloody fool!'

Reuben and Khaled pulled Ethan to his feet while some of

Bruno's supporters crowded forward to help their man. They dragged his unconscious body to the side of the yard and drenched his head and limbs with cold water. It was crude but it was the only treatment they knew.

Ethan's supporters roared and bullied their way to the betting tables to pick up their winnings. It took Reuben longer than most. He had a lot to scoop up and it needed some counting. That done, he swaggered back, humping four bags heavy with coins and slammed them at Khaled's feet.

'Divide it up!' Khaled yelled, trying to make himself heard above the din. 'Ethan gets half. There's plenty to keep the rest of us going.'

Sweating like a horse, Ethan gloried in triumph. His supporters shouted and chanted his name while he jumped and punched the air. Khaled was whooping his own happiness. The sweetness of victory was heady stuff.

Keen to be seen with the winner, a lot of men had changed sides, hoping to filch some of his triumph for themselves. But one of Ethan's friends wasn't cheering. Danny's face displayed a mixture of impatience and anger as he heaved his way through the mob. Some of Ethan's supporters had dragged over vats of water and were using beer jugs to drench their hero's body. He washed off the sweat, the sand and the clotting blood, then reached for the strips of cloth his friends held ready. Before rubbing himself down, he fingered his balls.

'Still there?' Danny asked abruptly.

'A bit bruised. No harm done.'

'You're lucky. I've warned you enough times. You've got the balls for attack but you haven't got the brains for defence. One of these days, someone's going to do you real harm.'

Reuben couldn't believe what he was hearing. 'Shut your mouth,' he yelled at his brother. 'He won, didn't he?'

'He was lucky. Next time, he might not have us behind him.'

The look of triumph was wiped from Ethan's face and he gave a slight nod. That was as far as he'd go in front of the others, but he knew Danny was right. He'd dropped his guard and his opponent had punished him for it.

Reuben punched him on the shoulder, 'He's an evil bastard, that Bruno!'

'He's got a family to feed,' Ethan said shaking his head. 'He did what any other fighter would do in his place.'

'He'll be alright. His mates always make sure he gets his share.'

Strangers were crowding around, slapping Ethan on the back and behaving like they'd known him all their lives. Khaled elbowed them aside and put his arm around his friend. Ethan was his father's property and he didn't mean to share him. It was a squalid thought and before it could form into an ugly idea, he was ashamed of it. Khaled briefly gripped his friend's shoulder then let his own arm fall to his side.

Ethan grabbed his tunic, dragged it over his head and fumbled to buckle the belt. Even with both hands ramming down, there was no controlling his erection. Apart from a couple of sniggerers, nobody was bothered. He was a winner and that's what mattered. Crowding Khaled and Ethan with them, they moved back inside. Strangers who would later boast about drinking with the winner, thrust jugs of beer towards him. Ethan gulped down a couple of mouthfuls before catching hold of Khaled's arm and the pair of them headed upstairs. He didn't know why fighting made him hard, but it always did and right now, it wasn't beer he needed.

News of his win had spread. Before they were anywhere near the top of the stairs, Ethan and Khaled were surrounded by girls, giggling and anxious for a cut of the money. Ethan shook off their clawing hands and pulled Khaled towards one of the rooms. He tapped lightly before opening the door. Inside the room, a young girl with an anxious face was sitting on the edge of a bed. She looked up nervously then threw herself towards Ethan. He wrapped his arms around her slim waist but when he went to kiss her, she pulled back. 'Your mouth tastes of blood.' Her scowl became a wince as she fingered his cuts and grazes. 'Don't do this again,' she begged.

'What's the matter with you, Floria? I won, didn't I?'

Khaled could hear annoyance simmering in his friend's voice.

'What about next time?' The girl asked. 'I don't want to see your face cut and bruised like this.'

'It's nothing,' Ethan snarled impatiently, shaking the girl off.

'No, you've got to promise me you'll stop fighting.' She turned to Khaled, her eyes appealing for support. But he owed his friend the greater loyalty.

'It's no good looking at me,' he shrugged, 'He's his own man.'

Desperately, Floria turned back to Ethan and his smile gave her the hope she was looking for. He moved to kiss her again and this time, she didn't pull away.

The girl shared Khaled's brown-eyed, black-haired, Mediterranean colouring. Her features were delicately formed and lovely. But he wanted to do more than gaze at the girl's beauty. His eyes flickered repeatedly towards her firm breasts and the nipples that pressed tightly against the fabric of her dress. He needed to touch, to caress the curves of her thighs and the swell of her hips. He looked around guiltily, not sure he should be there. Ethan's hand on his shoulder told him that he should.

'This is the one I've been telling you about,' he said, pushing Khaled forward. 'We work together in the stable yard.'

The girl's smile lit up the room. 'You never stop telling me about him and now I can see why. He's even more beautiful than I imagined.'

It was no more than a touch, a greeting and not meant to provoke, but her hand on his arm was enough. Khaled tried forcing his fists against his cock, and like Ethan downstairs, he found it just as useless. So what, he shrugged, it's what we're here for.

Ethan and Floria were squabbling again and this time it was about him.

'Only if you like him,' his friend was saying.

'Instead of you, you mean?' Floria sounded hurt.

'No, together! It's his first time here.'

Floria was giggling and Khaled's face started to burn. Fuck Ethan! Now she'd think he was a boy with no idea about anything. But she smiled into his eyes and ran her fingers through his black curls. He wasn't up to much conversation after that, but he saw Ethan getting his clothes off so he did the same.

Floria liked what she saw. Mumbling something about the gods being kind to her, she grabbed the two men, pulled them onto the bed and wriggled between them. Her hands explored their muscular chests and played games with their balls. She ran her fingers up and down their cocks before starting to work them.

Ethan slapped her hand away. She'd make him come too soon and he'd had enough of that. Using his knee, he forced her legs apart and started to thrust into her. Khaled watched them move together until, groaning a curse, Ethan sank down. 'I'm sorry …,' he began.

'What for? Playing rough or loving me?'

'Not loving you enough.'

'There's more to come. Get some rest and next time, you'll smash the bed.'

She lay for a while, whispering into Ethan's ear. Khaled couldn't make out the words but his friend's face showed they'd done him good. He was smiling and gave a slight nod. Floria pulled her body free, and reached for Khaled. She went down on him; slowly at first, then rougher. Careful not to let him come, she took his cock out of her mouth and moved up the bed. He started to roar his protest then realised she was getting ready to take him. Nervous at first, then feeling her rise to meet him, he started to thrust urgently. He didn't last much longer than Ethan.

Later, half asleep and totally happy, the three of them lay together. Floria wriggled to the edge of the bed, scrambled across their clothes to a small table and flicked back the red and white checked cloth. As soon as Ethan saw the loaf of bread, the jug of beer and the bowl of olives, he swung his legs over the edge of the mattress and followed her to the table. He tore off three chunks of bread, handed one to Floria and tossed a second piece to Khaled before starting to wolf down his own share. They carried the food and drink back to the bed and spent time eating and swigging from the jug.

Ethan had gnawed the salty flesh from an olive until all that was left was the sticky stone. He squeezed it hard, hoping to see it fly. Instead, it slithered out and glued itself briefly to Khaled's chin before flopping onto his chest. 'You learned quicker than I expected, Little Brother.'

'*Little?* Khaled's as big as you are. And I'll tell you something else. He's quite an expert, that boy.' Floria was busy nibbling Ethan's ear. It made her words sound strange so he didn't take them to heart.

'It won't work, Floria.'

'What won't work?'

'Trying to make me jealous.'

'Are you sure?'

'I'm sure. Khaled and me, we're best mates.'

Ethan was ready for another fuck, only this time he'd try taking things slower.

***

4

Ethan was still half asleep when he remembered the yard. He shook Khaled awake and the pair of them dragged on their clothes. Promising Floria they'd see her soon, the friends headed for the stairs. They hammered the road until they were in sight of Khaled's home, then jumped down and led the horses. It should have made things quieter but they'd forgotten the cobbles. The horse-shoe clatter rang around the yard but at that hour, it wasn't likely there'd be anyone to hear it.

Inside the stables, they felt on safe ground. Khaled was whistling with relief when Ali and Sulieman edged out from behind one of the stalls. The pair of them were looking for trouble and the state of Ethan's tunic told them they'd found it.

Khaled was still full of himself after their night with Floria and it got in the way of his common-sense. Missing the danger in Ali's expression, he started to smirk. 'Ethan's not late for work, if that's what you're hoping!' The words were intended to grate and they did. His friend was blood and beer-stain scruffy and in addition to that, Sulieman was happy to point out the boy's grazed knuckles and the bruises to his face. Ali and he had seen marks like these before. They meant Ethan had been in a brawl.

The pained face his master was wearing encouraged Sulieman to lay on more poison. 'He's started taking your brother with him.'

Ali's eyes brightened and there was still more to come. 'They've been to the harbour,' Sulieman complained, 'Drinking with the sluts that infest those taverns down there.'

'In that case, Ethan needs a good thrashing. Father might have stopped you using the whip, but you've still got your cane. Lessons given with stripes are learned quicker.'

Khaled moved forward, until he was standing between his friend and his accusers. 'How come you know so much about the harbour?' he asked cockily. 'A favourite place of yours, is it? Funny, we didn't see any boys there. But I expect you know where to look. Anyway, Father knows all about Ethan and me. We've got his permission.'

There was a smug smile on Ali's lips that told Khaled his bluff wouldn't work. 'Father gave you time off to go hunting,' his brother replied, 'Not to spend the night drinking and brawling.' Turning in Sulieman's direction, he snapped, 'Take Ethan into the barn!'

'Thrash him now, or make an example of him when the others get here?'

Ali nodded to himself. He could see the sense in Sulieman's suggestion. 'Let him get the trestle set up,' he said. 'Then he can wait. The twenty strokes he's going to get should give him plenty to think about.'

If he'd had any sense, Ethan would have looked worried. Instead, he grew surly. 'Twenty. Is that all? I was expecting thirty!'

'In that case, we mustn't disappoint you. Sulieman, give him forty!'

The overseer started in Ethan's direction but found himself checked by a grip on his shoulder. 'It'll be the mistake of your life!' Khaled's tone was calm but carried a menace. For a moment, Sulieman hesitated. Then, confident he had Ali's backing, he shrugged off the youngster's hand.

It wasn't much of a punch. Later, Ethan would tell him it was pathetic. But it was enough to make Sulieman lose balance. He staggered briefly before ending up in a pile of freshly raked manure. Red faced, he lay there for some time, his clothes heavy and reeking of horse shit.

'When Father's finished with the pair of you …' They'd lost face and Ali was turning to bluster.

But he'd misjudged his brother. He was no longer the boy that Ali had once pushed around. 'If you're running to Father, we're coming with you.' Khaled's voice sounded confident, scornful even. 'He's going to hear our side of the story, not just the lies you cook up.'

They headed for the house and Ethan hissed urgently at his friend, 'I got you into this. If your father won't listen …'

'Don't start playing the hero. I was with you from the start.' There was no way Khaled was going to let his friend shoulder the blame. Apart from that, his friend's temper would wreck any chance they had of avoiding punishment. 'Keep your mouth shut when we get there and let me do the talking. The mood you're in, we'll be sleeping on our bellies for a month.'

'The mood *I'm* in? You're the one who's just belted Sulieman!'

Khaled's scowl quietened him. He'd said enough but he remembered what their tutor had told them about Pyrrhic victories. This might well be another one. Having his friend speak up for him was better than gold. On the other hand, if things didn't go their way …. He felt the muscles in his arse clench.

***

Sheikh Omar was pacing anxiously around the majlis. Ali had woken him earlier to tell him Khaled and Ethan were missing. Since then, he'd been waiting for the workers to arrive. One of them would surely know what had happened to the boys. Now that he saw they were safe, he thanked God and struck Khaled across the face. 'Your mother has been worried to death. She heard there were slavers in the area.'

'I was with Ethan. You said we could …'

'Don't try telling me you were out hunting all night,' his father interrupted angrily. 'Hunting whores, maybe.'

This was Ali's chance and he blasted his brother with a catalogue of complaints. There was the drinking and Khaled's lack of respect for his elder brother. Added to which, he'd just humiliated Sulieman, a trusted overseer. Ali watched his father's expression harden. Things were going very nicely.

Sheikh Omar's face showed anger but there was also a hint of disappointment in his expression that Ali had failed to notice. Turning to his younger son, he said, 'This *friend* of yours. He's dragged you down to his own level. That's the truth of it, isn't it?'

'No Father. Ethan hasn't dragged me anywhere!' Struggling to keep his tone respectful, Khaled continued, 'I went to the port. That much is true. And, yes, I drank some beer. But that wasn't Ethan's fault. He knows Muslims aren't allowed to drink and he warned me I'd be offered alcohol if I went with him. But I pestered him to take me.'

'And the fighting. What do you know about that?'

This question was trickier and Khaled wasn't sure how to answer. In spite of the slap he'd just given him, his father hated violence. Khaled wouldn't lie but he could try watering down Ethan's role. 'There was a fight, Father. That much is true.' He'd spoken the words casually, hoping they'd make fighting sound like an everyday sort of matter. They didn't.

'That's why we shouldn't drink alcohol,' his father told him angrily. 'It brings out the worst in us.'

'Ethan had to defend himself, didn't he? A man has a right to do that. You're always telling me I should learn to stand up for myself.'

Ali was getting worried. There was a faint chance his father might be persuaded by Khaled's answers. It was time for more poison. 'The drinking and brawling are only a part of it.' His tone was reasonable but his intention deadly. 'They've been going with whores. We mustn't forget that, Father. Ethan's corrupted him, like I've always said he would. He needs the cane. So does Khaled, before he gets completely out of control.'

Sheikh Omar didn't reply. Instead, he walked over to the window and stood tugging his beard while looking at the harbour. It was already busy with seamen and merchants, yelling or growing violent with over-worked mules. This was his favourite view but today, it would take more than the beauty of the bay to brighten his spirits.

He was weighing Ali's accusations against Khaled's answers as he searched for the truth that must surely lie in the middle. There was something in what his elder son said. Khaled was headstrong but wasn't that to be expected from a young man of seventeen? Ali's increasing viciousness towards the workers sickened him. Discipline was necessary but there had been far too many punishments meted out recently. He had come to realise that Ali and Sulieman were the wrong men to wield so much authority.

In part, Sheikh Omar blamed himself. He'd been hard on Khaled these last few months. Anxious for his favourite son to do well, he'd pressured him into studying harder than was necessary. The boy was intelligent. His tutor said he absorbed facts without difficulty. More importantly, he was able to use and interpret information. It had been a mistake not to give the boy more responsibility.

Khaled put an anxious hand to his unshaven face. He usually took care with his appearance, especially whenever he went to see his father. After their all-night outing, he and Ethan hadn't had a chance to wash, let alone use the razor. He didn't know it but his stubble was working for him.

Sheikh Omar had noticed with quiet satisfaction the dark shadow strengthening his son's features. It wasn't surprising Khaled was going with whores. He should have been married a year or more ago. As for his friendship with Ethan, it was intense but mainly positive as far as he could see. His son needed to mix with people from different backgrounds. That was the best way to learn respect for them and their religions. On the other hand, delinquent behaviour, if that's what it amounted to, couldn't be tolerated.

Ali had no time for thoughts like these. He didn't believe in trying to understand people. It made a man indecisive. The case against Khaled and Ethan spoke for itself. Taking his father's silence for agreement, he went to fetch one of Sulieman's canes.

'Ethan's been improving your riding as well as showing you how to fish,' Sheikh Omar said to his son. 'And he's been teaching you, I don't know how many other useful things, as well. That's all to the good. And it's important for a young man to know how to defend himself. I agree with that. But by letting yourself be taken to places where alcohol is drunk …' He paused, before turning his attention to Ethan. 'Who do you blame for this?'

Khaled had told him to stay silent and so far, he'd managed to keep his mouth shut. Now, however, his master was asking him a direct question. He had no choice other than to reply. Ethan looked briefly in Khaled's direction and saw his friend give a slight nod. 'I blame myself, Master.'

'No!' Khaled protested angrily.

His father glowered him into silence before turning again to Ethan. 'Did Khaled force you to take him?'

'I'd like to see him try.'

Omar ignored the rebelliousness in Ethan's voice. 'In other words, it was your idea?'

'Yes, Master.'

'So, it's you who deserves to be punished?'

'Yes, Master.'

'But Khaled admits pestering you to take him!'

'He's just saying that to get me out of trouble. He could have pestered me as much as he liked. I wouldn't have taken him if I hadn't wanted to.'

'And why were you so keen to have him with you?'

'He's my friend, Master.'

'You enjoy his company?'

'I love it when he's with me.'

Khaled's heart was thumping. His bloody fool of a friend was determined to take the blame and Ali would win. 'Don't listen to him, Father. Ethan didn't do anything, apart from what I told him to do.'

'In that case, it's time you started to behave more responsibly. Actions have consequences. Not just for you but for others as well.'

Sheikh Omar looked out of the window again as he continued to weigh both sides of the story. 'Your friend's loyal, Khaled,' he said at last. 'You are too, for that matter. If he gets a caning, I've a good mind to make you watch every stroke that's laid on him.'

'That's not fair, Father. Why him and not me? Because he's a slave?'

'You're right. It isn't fair. If anyone deserves to feel the rod it's you and not him. But it will hurt you more to see your friend punished, knowing it was your selfishness that caused it.'

Looking even more serious, Sheikh Omar came to what he considered the most important matter. 'You and Ethan have been going with whores!' He let his words hang for a while before continuing. 'That doesn't worry me as much as Ali seems to think it should. It's better you satisfy yourselves with women than spend the rest of your lives playing around with each other.'

Again, his words hung in the silence.

'In two weeks, it will be Ramadan. Immediately before that, you will be circumcised. After the Holy Month of Fasting, I'll arrange for you to be married.'

This was something new. Khaled had known that sooner or later, his parents would raise the subject of marriage. His father had always said he wouldn't be pushed into marrying someone he didn't want but that wasn't the same as saying he could marry whoever he liked. And there was Inga.

'May I tell Ethan to wait outside, Father?' Sheikh Omar nodded and Ethan glared suspiciously at his friend.

'I need to speak to Father,' Khaled told him. 'Trust me, Brother. It'll be alright.'

Ethan walked sullenly to the door. At the last moment, he looked back at his friend. Khaled's smile was more reassuring than his words.

As soon as Ethan had left the room, Khaled started to jabber nervously, 'Most of what happened was my fault.'

'We've been through this before,' his father said impatiently.

'Forgive me, Father, but there's more to be said.'

'Then you'd better explain yourself clearly and at a normal speed. I've only got one pair of ears.'

'I'll try, Father. But you see, Ali and Sulieman are always punishing Ethan for no good reason. They enjoy doing it. He's not the only one. They pick out the good-looking boys and get them to do things. Things I can't describe to you, Father. If they agree, they get presents. Time off. Easy work. That sort of thing. If they won't go along with it, their lives are made hell. Ethan, Danny and Reuben are honest and hard working but because they won't let Ali and Sulieman do what they like with them, they get thrashed.'

Sheikh Omar took a long look at his son. The boy was taking a deep breath and that had to be a good sign. With any luck, it meant he'd finished blethering. Khaled had expressed himself badly. Nevertheless, his words had the sound of truth about them. At some stage the boy would have to learn to speak like an educated man instead of gabbling like an inarticulate labourer. But his son didn't lie and that was unusual in a young man. Normally they'd say anything to get out of trouble.

Placing a hand on Khaled's shoulder he said, 'You are right about Ethan. I'd free him if he was an ordinary slave but he's bonded to me for another three years. I can't break the agreement I have with his family. Ethan understands that. He knows how important the farm is to them. I can't free him but I can give him to you.'

Khaled's mouth opened in amazement.

'From now on, he'll be your responsibility. If he suffers injustice again, you'll have no-one to blame but yourself. You'll want to free him, I know you will. But you can't. Not for another three years. After that, the farm will belong to his family. Then you can do what you like. In the meanwhile, you'd better see to it that he's fairly treated.'

Khaled was finding it difficult to take in exactly what his father had said.

'Are you man enough to be entrusted with another person's life?' Sheikh Omar asked. 'Because, believe me, that's what owning a slave amounts to.'

This was deep water and Khaled was floundering. 'I'll try,' he said at last.

'I know you will.'

Khaled hesitated, not sure how to continue. There were other people involved, besides Ethan. In the end, he surprised himself by asking his father outright. 'Can I have Reuben and Danny as well?' He could tell from his own voice that he expected a refusal, so he'd better explain his reasons. 'They're good friends, Father. Not just to me but to our family.' His confidence was growing, 'Will you give me the chance to prove I deserve their loyalty?'

Sheikh Omar's expression didn't change. He was thinking things through. 'Yes, you can have them,' he replied at last. 'But make sure you never give me any reason to regret my decision. Now, you'd better leave me alone for a while. I've got their transfers of ownership and the small matter of your circumcision to arrange.'

'And you said something about me getting married, Father?'

'That as well.'

Khaled's chest tightened. He was on a mountain edge. He needed to walk warily but wasn't sure he could move. The lump in his belly felt real enough. Everything else was moving too fast to get a hand-hold. 'There *is* a girl,' he started nervously. 'Inga. She's Ethan's sister.'

His father's expression was impossible to read, 'A Christian? The sister of a slave? There are other women, you know.'

'Not like her, Father.'

'Does Ethan know about this?'

'Not yet, Father. I haven't said anything.'

'You can't marry him, so his sister will do. Is that what this amounts to?'

'No, Father. That's not it at all!'

Sheikh Omar smiled, 'If you're too young for a sense of humour, my boy, you're too young to get married. We'll talk about it later. But Khaled, please remember I'm not blind. I see very clearly the way things are between you and Ethan.'

'We're like brothers, Father.'

'Brothers or Lovers?'

When he thought about it later, Khaled realised the question had been long overdue. At the time, it had taken him by surprise. He looked at his father, briefly anxious, 'Ethan and I are more than friends. And I thank Allah for it. He doesn't give many people what he's given to us. If you're asking whether we love each other, the answer must be *yes*. But believe me, Father, there is nothing in our relationship of which I could ever feel ashamed.'

'I do believe you, my son. Love between men is no bad thing, provided there is still room in your hearts for the love of a woman. But make no mistake; this emotion we are talking about can be a dangerous thing. It's often described as a form of insanity and in all too many cases, the irrational behaviour it provokes has led to the death of one or both partners.'

'But, Father ...'

Khaled's attempt to speak was brushed aside. Sheikh Omar was determined his son would listen. 'This is particularly true in the case of one man's love for another. The Greeks regarded it as the most dangerous form of love. They saw how often it caused outbursts of violent jealousy.' His expression hardened and his voice took on a deeply serious tone. 'That sort of love won't do you much harm as long as you know where it can lead. But be honest with yourself and, above all, be careful.' He paused, waiting for his son's reaction.

'I understand, Father.'

It was enough. Khaled's voice showed he had taken the words to heart. 'After all,' his father continued in a lighter vein, 'Achilles had his Patroclus and Alexander the Great had his Hephaestion. They would probably agree that Ethan deserves his Khaled.'

'And do I deserve my Ethan?' Khaled asked, matching his father's tone.

'Only you know the answer to that. Do you?'

'I try to.'

'As far as marriage is concerned,' Sheikh Omar said, returning abruptly to the original subject, 'We'll give ourselves until the end of Ramadan to think about that. You'd better find out how Inga feels. If she's mad enough to agree, you'll need Ethan's permission. That is, unless you're planning to treat your best friend as a slave. If you are, he'll have nothing to say on the matter.'

'Ethan is my brother.'

'So you keep saying. In that case, what I've said stands. He's the head of the family so we'll get him in and the three of us can discuss the bride price.'

'Should I tell him about it now, Father, or wait?'

'First, get things clear in your own mind. If you're certain you're making the right decision, talk to him and Inga. I'm not sure which of them you should speak to first. That's a decision you'll have to make. When you've done that, we'll talk again.'

***

When Ali returned, cane in hand, he was surprised to find his father alone. He could see from the expression on his face that the old man's attitude had changed. Sheikh Omar did not favour the mealy-mouthed style of many men he knew and believed in approaching matters directly. 'You will have no more to do with the people who work for me,' he said to Ali's astonishment. 'Instead of helping with the running of the estate, you and Sulieman have abused your authority. You show no respect for the people who work for us and for that reason they show you none in return. You have become a cruel man, Ali. I only hope that Allah will forgive me for the mistake I made in giving you the opportunity to indulge your viciousness.'

'I don't know what Khaled has been saying,' Ali stammered, 'But I have done no more than was necessary to maintain discipline among the slaves and ensure that we get a good day's work out of them.

Sulieman agrees they need a firm hand and if trying to maintain order among a group of idle, semi-rebellious scum is wrong …'

'Your choice of words proves my point. There are no *'idle, semi-rebellious scum'*, as you call them, on my estate. They are people who have always worked hard and without complaint. That was before I was foolish enough to give you authority over them. Several of them have taken the trouble to teach your brother skills that will be of enormous use to him and that's in addition to their normal duties'.

'They've taught him to drink alcohol and behave like a member of the vulgar brawling rabble. And now you take his word against mine.'

'Don't think your brother has poisoned my mind against you. His words have simply confirmed my suspicions. Ethan has been a loyal worker and a good friend to your brother. Nevertheless, you and Sulieman were keen to see him punished. No doubt you would have enjoyed the spectacle.'

'Father, I assure you…'

'I want no assurances from you. They would be as valueless as words written on water. There is, however, one last duty you will perform and that is to throw Sulieman off the estate. You brought him here. Now you can get rid of him. Make sure he understands that if he comes near my property again, he will be punished for trespass. Now get out. I'll send for you again when I can bear to look at your face.'

***

5

Khaled's euphoria was beginning to fade. He'd set off confidently enough, striding, whistling, and slapping the pillars. But the whistling had stopped and, now, he walked more like a man on the road to execution. The responsibilities his father had outlined were daunting.

He didn't know Danny as well as he knew Ethan. When they were younger, the difference in their ages had created a distance. That had more or less disappeared but how would he react to the idea of belonging to a younger man? A lot depended on the way the news was broken. Khaled knew he'd better thrash things out with Ethan before he spoke to the others.

His friend was lounging, long-legged and scruffy, on the steps to the inner courtyard. He'd been watching a cat carry out a raid on a band of sparrows. Belly brushing the ground, it had fixed on its victim and edged forward. But it pounced too soon and the entire flock struck back with a salvo of squawks. Chastened, the cat withdrew. Ethan guessed it would be some time before it tried again. Meanwhile, the birds chirped and glanced nervously around before continuing their grub hunt among the brick and cobble paving.

The fountains that splashed and trickled water into their shaded basins should have calmed him but Ethan hadn't forgotten Sheikh Omar's face. He'd been courteous, dignified, and patient. But under that civility, Ethan had sensed a man angry enough to flog an army. Khaled dumping Sulieman in the shit had been one of their better times but it was going to cost.

He recognised Khaled's footsteps and jumped up. 'Who's getting it? You, me or the both of us?'

'Neither of us. Father accepts what I told him.'

'So why the hangdog look?'

'I'm frightened of what you'll say. Let's get to my room. There's something I need to tell you'.

'It must be important. You're twitching.'

'I'm not twitching. I'm pissing myself.'

They walked along the corridor with Ethan asking and Khaled not telling. 'Just say it,' Ethan snapped at last. '*I've got a secret*'. That's for girls!'

Khaled needed to talk as much as Ethan wanted to hear. It was babble at first. Words filling in silence. When they ran out, he got to the truth. 'Father has given you to me. You, Danny and Reuben.'

There was nothing he could read into Ethan's nod. He wasn't even sure his friend had heard him. 'I can't free you for another three years,' he started to explain. 'It's because of the bond. Father says it's alright for Reuben and Danny. I can free them now but I can't do the same for you.'

Ethan had heard but that wasn't the same as understanding. Being bonded to Sheikh Omar was a fact of life. It was uncomfortable at times but he'd grown up with it. Khaled was his friend. True, they weren't equals but it had always felt that way. 'He's given me to you. Like a present, you mean?'

Khaled had guessed it wouldn't be easy. He'd expected anger or resentment. Things he and his friend could laugh about later. What he hadn't bargained for, was the humiliation in Ethan's voice. 'It's only for three years,' he tried to explain. 'Less, if we work together. Until we can get the bond paid off.'

'You'll own me, like a dog or a horse?'

'Of course not.'

'That's what it'll be like.'

'Father thought it was a good idea.'

'And you? What about you?'

'I thought so, too. At first.'

'Now you don't?'

'I've seen your face.'

'It's the only one I've got. You can get used to it while you're being kind to me. Like you're kind to the horses. You'll enjoy that, won't you? Being kind! Maybe give me extra food, when I'm good. And I'll be good, Master. No shitting in the wrong place. Just on the straw in the corner of the stable, so it's easy to clean up.'

Khaled had asked for the truth and that's what he was getting. Ethan had turned away from him, his fists covering the tears while his body jerked with sobs.

'I was afraid of what you'd be like.' He tried putting his hand on Ethan's shoulder but rocks were softer. 'It's not like you think, Brother. I'll help you get the bond paid off. Nothing will change except you'll have Sulieman and Ali off your back. If you don't like the idea, say so. I'll tell Father I'm not ready for the responsibility. He's half expecting that anyway.'

'Danny and Reuben won't be going anywhere,' Ethan said after a while. 'They're happy enough here. They're safe with your family. Not everybody treats Jews like you do.'

'And you? How do you feel?'

'About Jews?'

'Stop playing the fool, Ethan! You know what I mean.'

'Will it make any difference to us?'

'Yes, massive. We'll be working together, to get the bond paid off. Maybe we can do it in a year.'

'You'll treat me fair?'

'You told me I did.'

Matanza!

'If you don't …!' The threat became a truce.

Khaled's guts had started to settle but there was something else he needed to say and Ethan wouldn't want to hear that either. 'There's one more thing.'

'What's that?'

'No more fighting at *The Barrels.*' His tone was matter of fact. He hoped it would cut and dry things. It didn't.

'Who says?'

'I do.'

'Fighting pays. I need the money.'

'There'll be no more fighting and there's an end to it.' It was matter of fact again and it didn't work any better the second time.

'What's the problem, Khaled? I like fighting and you like watching.'

'That's because you haven't lost yet.'

'I won't lose!'

'You will. You'll end up with your tail between your legs. They all do in the end.'

Ethan flinched. Nobody ever had or ever would win for ever. He knew that well enough. A time came when even the toughest man had had his day. He just hoped *his* day was a long way off. 'What if I don't agree?'

'You'll agree!'

'And if I don't?'

'I'll have you whipped.'

'*Ha! Ha!* That'll be the same day shit smells sweet.'

'I mean it Ethan. Not about having you whipped. About the fighting. I don't want that look on Floria's face again, when she sees what it does to you. But I'll give you a better reason. You're my property and I want to keep you in good condition.'

'It didn't take you long to start throwing that up. Like I said before, Master, *Ha! Ha!*'

'I'm not joking, Ethan!'

'I'll think about it.'

'You'll do more than that. Anyway, do you want the good news?'

'I can't wait.'

'You'll be earning in future.'

'I already earn. That's what the fighting's about.'

'It's time you were paid something. For teaching me to stand up for myself and ride properly. You'll get more than you do at *The Barrels*.'

'I don't need your handouts.'

'They're not handouts, you bloody fool. They're wages.'

'Slaves don't get wages.'

'My brother does.'

At *The Barrels*, his friend was king, not a stable boy stinking of horses. Khaled realised it was going to take more than money to make up for that. Ethan had turned his back. He was giving the matter some thought. At least that's what he hoped it would look like. Khaled knew better 'You're not bloody crying again!'

It was a while before Ethan trusted himself to speak and when he did, the words were choked, 'You're a good man.'

'It's easy with you.'

'It's better when you're there!' Ethan blurted.

'What are you talking about?'

'With the girls. It's better when you're there.'

He was a fool to speak like this. Khaled wouldn't want to hear it, but he'd said too much to walk away from the idea. 'It shouldn't be like that. It should be just me and the girls. But I'm better at it when you're there.' He stopped. Not because of his throat. It was dry but that wasn't the reason. His eyes were searching the floor, looking for an excuse he was never going to find.

Khaled saved him with a headlock and a punch on the shoulder. 'You must know it's the same way I feel.' And that was as much as they were going to say. There was a silence before Khaled started to laugh. 'Being good or bad with the girls. You needn't worry about that. Not for a few weeks, anyway. You heard what Father said, he's having me circumcised.'

And that was too funny for them to keep quiet any longer. 'You brought it on yourself,' Ethan shouted. 'You're always going on about how it makes a man of you!'

Khaled wasn't so certain. Now his time had come, he could see drawbacks to being circumcised. 'It'll be the end of everything with our friends. Like the beach and the drinking. As soon as they see what I've had done, they're going to start asking questions. They'll soon find out I'm a Muslim.'

'They already know that! They're not stupid, you know, just because they work with their hands and don't read Aristotle. I was as bad as you at first, thinking we could keep it quiet. Khaled, they've only got to look at your face to see you're not one of them. And as far as the blade is concerned, I'm getting it done as well.'

'The other day, you said it was madness!'

'I've changed my mind. Slaves can do that, can't they? It was Reuben and Danny. They're always saying girls can't get enough of them. They reckon it's because they've been cut. Well, the girls won't be able to keep their hands off us, either!'

'You don't know what you're talking about.'

'Yes, I do. Reuben told me about it. He says you go in harder and last longer. That's got to be good.'

'You've just decided you want it because I'm getting it done.'

'Something wrong with that?'

'No.'

'Well then.'

'Alright, I'll speak to Father and get him to arrange it for you as well. It'll be too late then to change your mind.'

'I'm not going to change my mind.'

'A few days from now, and you'll wish you had!'

***

6

'Father wants us to eat with him.'

'What about Floria. It'll be our last chance before Ramadan.'

'Father eats early.'

It was a large gathering and later, there'd be dancing girls. Khaled and Ethan walked into the high-arched majlis and Sheikh Omar immediately beckoned them to join him. Two young slaves arranged their cushions, while a variety of meats, fish and pastries were laid out in front of them. They mightn't have felt hungry when they walked into the room, but the spicy smells and flavours had sparked their appetites. The food became irresistible.

Ethan couldn't believe his luck. Several of the dancers were as good as naked and the few clothes they wore revealed more than they hid. The girls picked him out for special attention, returning again and again to run their fingers through his blond hair or sneak inquisitive hands inside his tunic. He was wrestling with an erection when Khaled kicked his foot. The girls had been his father's idea so there was no need to feel guilty.

Once the dancing was over, jaded old men turned to their water-pipes. A few years ago, Khaled and Ethan would have been happy with the jugglers and acrobats. They'd have found the snake charmers and fire eaters exciting. Now, they had Floria. They wouldn't be seeing her until later, though. In the meanwhile, the souq and its racket would take their minds off the girls.

Ramadan was coming so lines of extra stalls had been set up by brash-voiced foreigners. In a couple of packed alleyways, Khaled and Ethan found rock salt from the Sahara, gold from Egypt, silks from Damascus and rhino horn from Africa.

Smoke wafted from clay pots or water-pipes and the air grew heady with hashish. The clatter of the metal smiths, the croaking of horns and the thump of tabors merged to produce sounds that pulsed zestily through the shoppers' bellies. The friends eased past the rich, the silk-dressed and the snooty, before laughing with a smoke-faced gang of charcoal burners. They pushed indulgently through bands of ready-arsed boys until one of them went too far. Blocking his path, he reached out to ruffle Ethan's hair. Khaled winced as his friend slammed aside the offending hand and saw the boy cringe back into the crowd.

'That was harsh.'

'I can't stand those bastards pawing me.'

Turning corners, they entered worlds where a smack of spices mingled with the sweetness of honeyed cakes and freshly picked fruits. Stalls displayed oils of musk rose, lemon, lime and orange blossom. The perfumes had been blended for seduction, and were an essential feature of the bedroom or hammam. Following the advice of a slippery-tongued salesman, Khaled and Ethan chose a couple of varieties made from sandal wood and cedar. They were specially imported from Alexandria and were guaranteed to enhance a man's performance. The vendor, a hook-nosed Yemeni, knew for a fact that King Solomon had used identical oils when striving to bed Balquis, Queen of Sheba.

Perfumes, created to an ancient and secret formula, were designed to inflame the female passions. He told them this in confidence, as one man speaks to another, and could thoroughly recommend the type given by Paris to Helen of Troy. By a lucky chance, he had a small supply of the self-same oils to hand. He owed it to the ladies, indeed he was honour bound, to sell them only to the most handsome and virile of men. He was pleased to say that both Ethan and Khaled measured up.

The old rogue made a careful show of wrapping their purchases in squares of dyed cloth while telling the boys how wisely they'd chosen. 'There isn't a woman born who can resist such perfumes,' he assured them.

'You'd better let me do the rest of the buying,' Ethan murmured, pushing his friend away from the stall.

'I buy things all the time. There's never been a problem.'

'And there never will be, as long as you're paying double. It's the way you talk. You sound like you've got money, so they skin you alive.'

'I speak the same as you do.'

'And a horse brays like a donkey.'

'Who's the donkey?'

'Work it out for yourself, Master!'

Without warning, Khaled started to retch and Ethan nodded him in another direction. They'd come across the tanners' yard before and decided then, it was a place best avoided. For as long as they could stand the vile smell, they'd watched half naked men and boys treading putrefying hides in massive vats of stale urine.

Khaled tried smothering his nose and mouth with his hand. 'I'd do anything before I worked there,' he said, gagging at the still strong stench.

'Some men don't have the choice. Anyway, you're happy enough with what they turn out. Leather's just bits of dead animals.'

When she saw what the boys had brought, Floria closed her eyes and gently inhaled the enticing aromas. She knew all there was to know about oils. Some of them tingled, while others grew warm. They could turn boys into men and men into lovers. Khaled and Ethan stripped before leaping onto the bed. Floria wasn't far behind them.

Matanza!

Later, Ethan said they wouldn't be seeing her for a month, but that wasn't what she wanted to hear. She clung on tight until they honeyed things with a promise. They'd be back as soon as Ramadan was over. It was all they were willing to say, so it had to satisfy her.

'We'll have a couple of surprises for you,' Ethan said, nudging his friend.

'No! Tell me now!'

She begged and she flirted but her lovers gave nothing away. 'Keep yourself for us,' was as far as they'd go.

Khaled watched Floria hand back most of the money Ethan offered her. She took enough to last until their next visit and no more. He saw her hands on his friend's body and his fists clenched. He knew that feeling for what it was now, but it didn't help. Jealousy isn't to be softened.

'Why did you give her all that?' he asked, angry as they walked down the steps.

Ethan shrugged, 'I don't want her going with anybody else.'

'What makes you think she won't?'

'Floria's not a whore like the others. Inga told me about her. She needs the money for her mother and little sisters. Her father's dead, the same as mine. You don't know what it's like, Khaled, not having anything. I had to fight to get the money I needed. It's the same for Floria.'

'She doesn't act like a girl who's forced to do what she does. She enjoys every bit of it.'

'That's because it's with us, you fool.'

'With *you*, you mean! Ethan, tell me the truth. Do you want me to get out of the way, next time?'

'No!' Ethan bellowed. 'That's not what I want at all. I like her. She's better than any girl I've ever been with. But apart from that, what can you do with a woman?'

It was what Khaled had hoped his friend would say and hearing it, freed him to be kind. 'Why didn't you tell me before, about the money? I could have helped.'

'You do already. That money you give me. It changes everything.'

'You earn it. Anyway, I'm talking about Floria. I could ask Father.'

'What for? Money to pay a whore?'

'No! I'd tell him it's for something else.'

'Lie, you mean?' Ethan shook his head violently. 'Don't start that, Khaled! You never lie to your father. That's why he believed you and not Ali. You don't lie to me, either. Not about important things. That's why I trust you. Start lying now and we'll never feel the same about you.'

'But money is something I could help with. Something worthwhile.'

Ethan stopped and grabbed his friend by the shoulders, 'You're a stupid bastard, you are! Being a man we trust. You don't think that's worthwhile?'

*

Next day, Ethan rode up to the farm. He wouldn't be around for a few weeks and wanted to make sure his family wasn't short of anything. It was Khaled's coming of age and he had to help out. That's what he told them, and it was all he was going to say. Circumcision wasn't the sort of thing you talked to women about. Besides, he needed to be back in time to join Khaled and his father for the evening meal.

Reuben and Danny ate with them, but they were sitting a short distance away with another group. Ethan found himself next to a young man called Hamdi. He was wearing a simple cotton tunic, like the ones Ethan and Khaled found comfortable. For some reason, that made him easy to talk to. His father, on the other hand, was a serious-looking man called Abdul-Aziz. He was dressed formally in tailored robes and a turban, similar to those worn by Sheikh Omar. Ethan would have to think long and hard before trying a conversation with him.

From the way Ethan was lounging and laughing, it was clear he had no idea why Hamdi and his father were there. Khaled enjoyed watching his friend's expression change when he told him it was to put them to the blade.

After they'd eaten, the young men headed for the inner courtyard so they could talk without being overheard. They wandered for a while, past the flower beds and night-scented bushes, before stopping at one of the fountains. The water splashed vigorously into its marble basin and a couple of shadowy fish, their bodies just visible in the fading light, chased streams of fast-moving bubbles.

'They think it's food,' Ethan said.

Hamdi wasn't listening. Instead, he started to tell them about his father's job. It was a hereditary one and someday, he hoped he'd be entrusted with the task of circumcision. It was tricky work, needing skill and experience, so for the time being, he was happy enough to watch and assist.

'What do you mean by *assist*?' Ethan wanted to know.

'With the ointment and bandages.'

'*Bandages!*' The word conjured a hundred images and none of them comforting. 'That's what you've got in the bag?'

'Amongst other things. There'll be some bleeding and it's my job to stop that. The ointment's to help with the pain. It speeds up the healing as well.'

Ethan grunted and flicked his fingers along the surface of the pond. 'How long before we're back to normal?'

'A month. Maybe less.'

Khaled copied his friend and played casually with the water. 'Painful, is it?'

'Not bad. I've brought some poppy juice.'

'Poppy juice! What good is that going to do?' Khaled's nervousness was making him snappy.

'I know all about that!' Ethan boasted. 'Poppy juice gives you funny dreams.'

'We're not here for funny dreams!' Khaled was growing impatient. It was time to come to the point. 'We've heard about men being butchered,' he told Hamdi. 'They were no good with women, afterwards.'

No wonder they were jittery. With people feeding them stories like that, it was surprising they wanted to go through with it at all. 'You'll have to trust us,' Hamdi said defensively. 'I know what I'm doing and my father's the best there is. Ask anyone. They'll tell you.'

Ethan decided it was time he took over. The way Khaled was talking, anyone would think they were afraid of a little nick! 'We've got a couple of friends,' he said. 'They're Jews. You saw them while you were eating. They'll be out soon. Then you can talk to them properly. They've both been well cut. That's the way we want you and your father to do us.'

'Anything Jews can do, we can do better!'

'That's as maybe, but we don't aim to be back for a second dose.'

'No, but your sons will be. Sooner or later, they'll all fall into our hands.'

'That's if you do a good job! Do us permanent harm and you'll be short of customers in the future.'

'Hamdi!' It was Danny's voice. He and his brother were walking through the arched entrance to the courtyard. 'Your father told us to come and find you. It's time to get your victims ready.'

'We're on our way to the hammam,' Hamdi said, opening the top of his bag and fishing out a pot of ointment. 'This is what you need. It'll cut the pain to nothing and help stop the bleeding as well.' He didn't plan to discuss the matter further. His father had told him that too much information made the patients nervous. 'One of you had better show us the way to the hammam,' he said. 'A man could get lost in this house of yours.'

Khaled led the way, pulling Reuben and Danny with them. 'You've never seen the baths and there's plenty of time for a swim.'

Danny's eyes were wide open, 'They're big enough for that?'

'One of them is. Wait until you see it.'

He took them along a corridor and down a flight of steps that led to the green and blue tiled hammam. Torches in gilded sconces flamed upwards. They provided the main illumination while a more fascinating light flickered through star-shaped piercings in the domed ceiling. Additional torches blazed on the roof, giving the impression the stars twinkled as they helped light the interior of the building.

Ethan and Khaled loved the hammam and headed there whenever they got the chance. The scented steam rising from the baths reminded them of summer mornings by the sea. During the winter months, there was no better way to spend an evening than having the day massaged out of them before going to bed.

Reuben and Danny's eyes were caught by the smaller baths. They ranged from numbingly cold to steaming hot but Ethan had a better plan. He challenged them to a race in the massive pool that dominated the hammam.

While he was clambering out, Hamdi missed his footing and thumped, arse first, down a couple of steps.

'Hard stuff, marble!' Ethan taunted.

Hamdi nodded slowly, like a man storing a grievance. Then, remembering his new friends were only a short walk from the blade, he gave them a broad smile. 'Father's waiting,' he said and tossed them some towels.

The steamy air made drying difficult. Reuben, Danny and Hamdi pulled their tunics over still damp bodies while Ethan and Khaled were handed a couple of white cotton loin cloths. Grabbing his bag, Hamdi led the way back. Bruised arse or not, he was the man in charge.

Most of the guests were taking the opportunity to nose around the palace. Their eyes inventoried the contents and the quality of the furnishings. There was money there, they could see that. Sheikh Omar, Abdul-Aziz and the fathers of six possible brides were the only men left in the majlis. Hamdi strode self-importantly to join them.

'Reuben and Danny are here, Father. We'd like them to stand with us, if that's allowed.'

Sheikh Omar nodded his agreement. In the villages, groups of young men underwent the ceremony together and he saw no reason why Khaled and Ethan shouldn't have the support of their friends. It was going to be a strange circumcision, he thought. The only Muslim was his son. His best friend was a Christian and they'd brought a couple of Jews along, to give them courage.

Khaled and Ethan stood side by side, their arms resting lightly on each other's shoulders. Reuben and Danny moved to either side of them and Hamdi told his patients to uncover themselves. He dolloped ointment over their foreskins and then stood back so his father could get to work. Sheikh Omar noticed with quiet satisfaction that both his son and Ethan could put a donkey to shame. Abdul-Aziz would have earned his money by the time he was finished with that pair.

The ointment struck cold, just as Hamdi had told them it would. Maybe he knew what he was talking about after all. Murmuring a brief prayer, beseeching the blessings of Allah, Abdul-Aziz stepped forward. The blade glinted in his hand as he made ready to cut. Ethan felt his friend's grip tighten on his shoulder and turned to look at him. Khaled was breathing through tightly clenched teeth and his gaze was fixed on the inscribed calligraphy decorating the opposite wall. 'There is no victor but Allah', he read repeatedly in an attempt to take his mind off what was being done to him. 'There is only one God and Mohammed is his prophet.'

Ethan didn't have long to wonder what his friend was going through. Abdul-Aziz was already moving in his direction. It was the young Christian's turn to grip his friend's shoulder.

As soon as his father had finished, Hamdi plastered more ointment onto his patients' cuts, then bandaged them tightly. His father's work had taken moments. Hamdi would need more time to control the bleeding.

'Your blood was mixed on the blade,' he told them. 'People say that makes you brothers.'

Khaled and Ethan managed to smile. Their stoicism under the knife had impressed Sheikh Omar and the men who'd watched with him. They saw that Khaled would make a fine, manly husband and immediately attempted to open negotiations with his father. Each of them emphasised the advantages his daughter could bring to the marriage but Sheikh Omar was not impressed. Although the men spoke respectfully about his noble family, it was Khaled's future wealth that played the most significant part in their calculations.

He listened politely but explained that his son's wishes would have to be taken into account. A few days earlier, he'd promised Khaled there would be no forced marriage and Sheikh Omar was a man of his word.

'I suggest we let the young men go to their quarters,' he said at last. 'Then Hamdi can give them whatever attention he thinks necessary.' The men nodded in agreement and the friends started the long walk to Khaled's room.

As soon as they arrived, Hamdi reached for his poppy juice and poured out a couple of measures. Khaled spluttered most of his dose onto the floor. 'It's as bitter as an old man's curse! Are you trying to poison us?'

'It's what you need!' Hamdi's tone was authoritative. 'But, if you'd prefer …'

'Don't take any notice of him,' Ethan roared, 'Give us the juice!'

'You've made the right decision.' Hamdi was enjoying the role of the medical man who demands his patients' unquestioning compliance. 'It'll reduce the pain and then you'll be able to get some sleep. As for those *funny dreams*. Don't worry about them. Some people pay good money for this stuff. Isn't that right, Ethan?'

Ethan didn't answer.

'Believe me,' Hamdi continued, 'It's far better than the alternative.'

Obedient as a chastened school boy, Khaled held out his cup for a replacement dose and Hamdi gave what sounded like a stifled snort.

'What's so funny?' Ethan snarled.

'The other reason for the juice. It stops you getting hard.'

'No chance.'

'You won't say that in the morning. Keep taking the juice or you'll know all about it.'

Danny was enjoying himself. It was the best spectacle he'd seen for a long time and there was always pleasure to be derived from the discomfort of close friends. 'You Muslims must be mad, going through this at your age. Jews have got more sense. They do it to us when we're about a week old. We don't know anything about it.'

'It's not all Muslims,' Khaled told him. 'Most of us have it done when we're young. Some tribes, and mine's one of them, think it's a significant experience for a man, so it's worth remembering.'

Ethan and Khaled had been shuffling around on the cushions, trying to get comfortable. Then, without warning, the pair of them were snoring. 'The magic of the poppy juice,' Hamdi smiled. 'Give them the same again if they start feeling sorry for themselves. You can mix it with honey if they start complaining about it being bitter. That's what we do with the children. I'll be back in the morning to see how things are.'

***

When he returned, Hamdi found the four friends washing down a meal of dates and figs with mugs of fruit-flavoured buttermilk. 'It's Ramadan?' he said severely. 'What are you doing breaking the fast?'

'Father says it's alright for a few days because this is the same as being ill. It doesn't matter about Danny and Reuben. They're Jews and Ethan's a Christian.'

'Very convenient!'

For the next couple of weeks, Khaled and Ethan didn't move

far from their room. Their friends came to see them every day and helped pass the time with games of backgammon and chess. Hamdi dosed them less and less with the poppy juice and his patients started looking for things to do. Danny humped in a couple of logs. 'Try exercising with these,' he told them. 'Reuben will bring you some heavier ones in a couple of days' time. Make sure you use them.'

Khaled's father visited at least twice a day to check on their progress. He brought them books, most of which remained unread, and fruit from his wife. She always sent her best wishes but never commented about their circumcisions.

Even with their friends' company, the room became a prison and they bristled for a change of surroundings. Apart from that, Ethan was feeling guilty. He'd left the running of the farm to his mother and sisters for the best part of a month. He needed to make sure there were no problems.

The emptiness of his absence penetrated like a cruel winter; nipping away the buds of thought and feeling. Worse, Khaled couldn't get Inga out of his mind. He'd put off saying anything to his friend because he wasn't sure how he'd react and, of course, he'd had no chance to speak to Inga. In fact, when he thought about it, he and Inga had never talked about anything of importance. You didn't with girls.

He'd better ride over to the farm and have a word with Ethan.

***

7

When God created the world, he took Ethan's farm as his model. That was Khaled's view and had been since his first visit. Set high in the Alpujarras, it enjoyed a cooler climate than he was used to on the coast. The air was crisp and at sunrise or sunset, the mountains glowed like copper.

The surrounding hills had been terraced, to make the most of their rich red soil and the dry-stone retaining walls provided a bonus crop since thyme, rosemary, sage and oregano sprang from their cracks. In spring and early summer, Inga and her mother collected the tasty caper buds and pickled them in soured wine. They went well with their home-cured hams, while any buds they missed rewarded them with a starburst of flowers.

In sheltered areas, protected from the frost and winter winds, sweet-scented orange and lemon trees jostled for space with the chumberas. These strange, cactus-like plants produced a show of yellow flowers and pear-shaped fruits. They were good to taste but treacherously spined. Apart from a few leather-fingered old men, only the goats and Ethan had mastered the art of eating them. Khaled watched his friend make a wad from a piece of sack-cloth. He used it to rub off the fruit's fine needle-like protection and then held the *chumbos* with it, while cutting into their juicy flesh. The seed-filled fruit had a delicate flavour. It reminded Khaled of the pomegranates his mother had peeled for him when he'd lived with her in the haramlek.

The cottage was roofed with launa, a thick waterproof clay that insulated it from both heat and cold. Along its low, south-facing wall, pergolas provided shade and leafy corners where hens cackled and laid their eggs. Khaled had caught the last of many a summer's evening with Ethan and his family under that lattice-work of vine shoots.

To the accompanying throb of cicadas, they'd gorge on grapes and figs while watching the colours of the mountains change from yellow to orange and finally to purple. On cooler nights, a tripod brazier, smouldering with vine twigs, kept them warm. The heat and smoke dissuaded the biting insects from closing in, while skewers of spiced meat fizzed and spluttered over the fire. No food had smelled or tasted better.

The valley, generously planted with almond, olive and fig trees, plunged fertile and green towards the bay of Almeria. Here, spice-laden dhows and white-sailed feluccas skimmed like gulls over the blue sea. On sharp-frost winter days, the air was clear as running water and old men from the village spoke of seeing the mountains of Africa. The Alpujarras was an undiscovered land where Khaled and Ethan walked between rocks and through mountain passes, amusing themselves with the echoes of their voices.

The first time they'd climbed the cerro, they'd felt like the only men in paradise. It wasn't much more than a ridge that bordered the farm but they'd conquered it together and that made it *their* mountain. The air shocked, like a splash of iced water. 'And there's only you and me to breathe it,' Khaled gasped to his friend. 'Lucky we came or there'd be nobody to see how beautiful the place is.'

'It does alright by itself,' Ethan told him. 'The last thing it needs is us.'

***

Some distance from the cottage, two brown and white long-haired goats were tethered to limit their marauding. They chomped greedily on anything within reach, but it was from their milk that Inga's mother made her fierce-flavoured cheeses. She served some of them while they were crumbly and only a few days old. Others were steeped for months in olive oil. She waited for their rinds to turn pink, before dusting them with crushed herbs. Either way, the boys couldn't get enough of them.

Khaled's mother loved them as well. Whenever Ethan returned to work, he took with him some fresh fruit, eggs and a basket of cheeses, sprinkled with rosemary. 'For the Sheikha Souad,' his mother would tell him.

Khaled was always surprised to hear people use her name and title. It made her sound like a strange and distant figure when he'd only ever thought of her as *Mother*. Beautifully dressed, with her black hair perfectly groomed, she walked like a queen. Khaled supposed it was why some people were a little afraid of her. That and her tongue. She could speak sharply at times but he heard more than her words. He sensed the concern that lay beneath them, just as he saw more than her outward expression. When he was a boy, she'd never been too busy to put her arms around him when he was unhappy or smile encouragement when he was anxious. But he no longer lived in the Haramlek. He belonged to the world of men and could no longer look for his mother whenever he needed a kind word.

Inga's hens were flapping, scratching and cackling so she didn't hear him arrive. Khaled stood gazing at her. Loving the way her long blond hair flooded her face as she ducked to collect eggs and place them in her basket.

'There's one under that bush!' He sprinted to pick it up and handed it to her, together with the small bunch of cornflowers he'd picked along the way.

'I didn't know you were coming,' she said, flirting through long eye lashes.

Khaled saw the mischief in her smile. Maybe she could read his thoughts. He started to explain why he was there, but the words came out lame and he changed direction. 'I've got to speak to Ethan.'

Inga didn't let him off so easily. 'He's been with you for a month.'

'I didn't know I needed to talk to him. Not until he'd gone.'

'Children! You can't be apart for more than a few hours.'

He'd heard comments like that too often to be offended. She was always teasing Ethan and him about their closeness, describing them as each other's shadow. He took the basket from her hand while putting on his hurt look. That usually had the right effect on women.

It didn't work with Inga. She nodded him bossily towards the farmhouse. 'He's a boy with a man's body,' she thought. 'Let me get you something to eat,' was what she said.

'I mustn't, Inga. It's Ramadan.'

'I'm sorry, Khaled. I forgot.' Now she was angry with herself. She should have remembered he'd be fasting. 'As soon as the sun goes down, then. We can have cheese and some of mother's bread. She baked it before she went to the market with my sisters.'

Inga held up her basket proudly. 'The hens have done well, haven't they? I've found a dozen eggs already and there'll be more to come. I'll boil us a couple later. They'll go well with fresh bread and butter.'

Khaled was standing, all hands and feet, like a boy who didn't know where to put himself. Inga hadn't seen him this edgy for a long time. When he was with Ethan, they were either clumping around or sprawled untidily, taking up most of the space. On his own, he seemed smaller.

Fumbling with the latch, she realised she'd caught some of his nervousness. 'You'd better come in, out of the sun, and tell me what you and my brother have been up to.'

Khaled was about to follow her into the house when something made him hesitate. 'Do you think Ethan will be long?'

'I don't know. He's taken some rabbits over to the neighbours. If they get talking about horses, you never can tell.' Turning to look at him she asked, 'What's the matter with you today? It's because

Ethan isn't here. That's why you're so jumpy.'

'No, it isn't that,' he stammered defensively. 'I'm not used to being with girls. Not when they're alone.'

'Don't be ridiculous! We've known each other since we were children.'

'We're not children any more, Inga.'

She shrugged. If that was the way he wanted things.

'You're really pretty!' he blurted, immediately wishing he'd kept his mouth shut.

Inga had known for a long time that Khaled liked her. She'd loved him for longer than she could remember but they'd never spoken about their feelings. Thoughts put into words became reality and then they were dangerous. You couldn't step away from them. Better leave things as they were. Dreams never hurt anybody.

Khaled's father was unlikely to accept a non-Muslim wife for his favourite son. Inga knew that, but she was more worried about her family's reaction. They'd never believe the son of one of the richest men in Almeria wanted her for more than a plaything. It was safer all round if everyone carried on thinking of Khaled as Ethan's friend - a young man whose good looks would always guarantee a warm welcome from her mother and little sisters.

'Why did you pick the flowers?' she asked him.

'They're like your eyes.'

'Red from the pollen?'

'Blue. Like pieces of heaven.'

She took his hand and pulled him into the kitchen. It was cool inside. The thick stone walls and shuttered windows kept out the heat of the day but it was the intimacy of the cottage that Khaled liked best. He stood the basket of eggs on the table, noticing how years of daily scrubbing had worn away the soft wood, leaving the hard grain to stand proud.

'It's making me hungry,' Khaled said, 'The smell of your mother's bread.' He walked to one of the windows and opened the shutters, just enough to see into the small inner courtyard. It wasn't formally laid out like those in his own home. Instead, it was planted haphazardly with orange, lemon, fig and pomegranate trees. They provided a mottling of shade and when he and Ethan had been younger, they'd spent warm afternoons watching the grey flickering shadows. They were swift moving and impossible to catch but sometimes the shapes paused. Then they became birds, animals, clouds or imaginary monsters.

One day, they'd given him an idea. He'd scratched a shape into the dusty earth and asked his friend what he thought it was.

'Looks like a dog to me,' Ethan told him.

They made themselves comfortable, bellies on the ground, while Khaled traced the word *KELB* into the dust. It was Arabic for *DOG* and as he formed each of the letters, he sounded them out. Ethan got the idea and was soon able to repeat the trick for himself. Khaled tried other words and Ethan quickly learned the sounds the shapes represented. He could already speak Arabic and often did when he was alone with Khaled. With their other friends, they spoke that strange mixture of languages which over the centuries, Andalucians of all races had made into a dialect of their own.

'Try writing it.' Khaled held out the stick and Ethan took it clumsily. Reading was one thing. Writing was another. He had no difficulty in his own language but Arabic went from right to left and most of the shapes were still strange to him. He hesitated, not sure he could do it.

'Go on, write!' Khaled urged, watching as his friend concentrated on scratching a few letters. 'That's *KELB*,' Ethan told him. And it was.

'Try my name.'

'That's easy.'

Again Khaled watched, whooping his encouragement as Ethan slowly scratched the Arabic words for, *KHALED DOG TURD*. It was a good start.

A year or so later, he handed his friend some sheets covered with verses, then winced as Ethan burst out laughing, 'What's this?'

'It's poetry. I wrote it.'

'Why?'

'I get ideas and try writing them down.'

'Why don't you just speak them like the rest of us?'

Khaled tried to explain that sometimes his ideas needed sorting out so he could express them better. Besides, Ethan wouldn't listen.

'That's not true. I always listen. When you've got something to say, that is. All these words you've written. You've got your ideas wrapped up inside them. You're just hiding behind a lot of fart-arsed words. What's the matter, ashamed of your thoughts or something?'

'No.'

'You must be or you'd speak them out, the same as I do. You don't need all this shit!'

'Sometimes I wish I'd never taught you to read Arabic!'

'No you don't. You enjoyed doing it. The same as I liked learning. Just cut out the shit, that's all I'm saying.'

'Why do you keep calling it *shit*?'

'To stir you up!'

Khaled smiled at his memory, and then turned back to Inga. 'I love being here. I don't know how Ethan puts up with my home. It's the size of the place. It won't let me think properly. Ethan feels the same, I know he does. It's so big it crushes the ideas out of us. Does he say anything about it to you?'

'Not about your home. He's too busy talking about the things you do together. At least some of them. I know he doesn't tell me everything you get up to.'

Khaled wondered how much she knew. She'd caught him and Ethan playing around with each other more than once. But that was boys' stuff. Floria was her friend and girls gossiped.

Inga noticed his cheeks beginning to darken. She'd learned over the years that he didn't go red like she and her brother did but embarrassment still showed on his face. She'd teased him long enough.

Khaled pushed his guilt to one side and watched her hunt out a small terracotta jug. He loved the way she took such care arranging his little bunch of blue flowers. 'They're nothing special, Inga. Just cornflowers. They're not worth the trouble you're taking.'

'They're special enough.'

'Did Ethan tell you why he's been staying with me for the past few weeks?'

'Not really. He didn't say much about it at all. He was helping with your coming of age ceremony or something. He wouldn't say any more. Why, what was it all about?'

His face burned again, 'I can't tell you that, Inga. It's not something women should know about. But it means I'm ready to get married. Father says it's time for that. I suppose he wants grandsons.' They laughed and Khaled put his hand on her arm. He expected her to pull away. Instead, he felt her tremble.'

'Do you like me?' he whispered.

'You know I do. You don't need to ask.'

'Enough to …' he hesitated. 'I have to … speak to Ethan!'

'No, carry on. This is an important conversation we're having.'

'Enough to marry me?'

Khaled's words had shot out like stones from a shepherd's sling. Unexpected, but hitting their mark. They were what she'd hoped he'd say but now that he'd spoken, she was struck silent, like a stunned rabbit.

'How can I marry you Khaled?' she said at last. 'There are too many differences. Not between us. Between your family and mine.'

It was his turn to look anxious. He knew what the biggest difference was and it wasn't something he could brush aside. 'It's because I'm a Muslim, isn't it?'

Inga nodded.

'Father says …'

'What does he say?'

'He says the differences between Christians and Muslims are invisible to a wise man.'

'It's not just religion,' Inga said. 'The way you and Ethan speak about it, I could become a Muslim tomorrow. It's the way I'd be expected to live. My life isn't very exciting but it's the one I know. I don't think I could live the way your mother and sisters live. In every other way my life is poor compared with the way I'd live with you. But I can do as I please and go where I like.' She smiled her mischievous smile again, 'I'm even free to talk to a beautiful young man without being afraid of what my brother might say.'

'And being with me would ruin your life?'

'I'm not saying that.'

'Life for our women is not like you think.'

If Inga had thought she could lighten the mood, it hadn't worked. The obstacles were too serious to be joked away but she needed to make her position clear. She decided to risk everything and speak in words that couldn't be misunderstood. If she'd miscalculated, Khaled might think her too forward. It was a risk she'd take. If he rejected her, she'd know where she stood. That was better than wishing for the rest of her life she'd told him the truth.

'I love you Khaled but I can't live away from the world.' Her words sounded petty, as though something less noble than religion was preventing their happiness. But as far as she was concerned, independence and freedom were not small things. 'If there is some way we can be together, I'll do it. Even if we're not married, I'll have your children, if that's what you want.'

'I want more than that and so do you. Let me take you to my mother, Inga. She'll show you how we live.' He put his arms around her and rocked her gently. She remembered her father doing that when she was a little girl. It made her feel safe and at home.

'If you don't want to speak to my mother, we'll find another way,' Khaled told her, 'Ethan will help us.'

'I didn't say I wouldn't talk to her. It needs some thought, that's all. And as far as Ethan is concerned, do you think he can change the world? Life isn't like that!'

'Sometimes, when we're together, we get the feeling we can change the world.'

'Silly boys playing games,' she whispered and pulled him close.

They heard the door open but didn't feel the need to move apart. It would only be Ethan coming home. They heard him take a sharp breath but before either of them had a chance to react, Ethan lunged at his friend and wrenched him away from Inga.

'Bastard!'

Khaled didn't fight back. His limbs felt useless and his mouth incapable of speaking. Ethan flung him against the wall, then hammered his face and body. Khaled slumped to the floor.

Inga fought to pull her brother away but her kicks and blows had as much effect as if she'd been slapping a wall. 'Get off him!' she screamed. 'He wants to marry me.'

'Marry you, you little fool!' Ethan spat out the words. 'People like him don't marry your sort!'

'My sort? What do you mean my sort? I'm no different from you. I'm your sister!'

'I work in a stable yard. I'm his slave. The sons of Sheikhs don't marry the sisters of slaves. They use them as whores.'

'And what about you, Ethan? Does Khaled use you as a whore?'

Her brother turned to face her, his fists raised. She didn't care. Let him hit her if that's what he wanted. 'You think I can't see why you're so angry? You're afraid I'll take him away from you. Do you think you can marry him yourself?'

Ethan's face had drained of its colour. His teeth clenched as he took a step towards her. Inga saw the look of hatred on his face and realised she was afraid. But she had gone too far to take back her words. 'You love him!' she screamed, 'You've always loved him. Do you think you're the only one who has that right? Can't I love him as well? Can't he love me? Maybe not the way he loves you. But enough.'

Ethan looked at his knuckles. They were raw and bloody. They'd seemed like a badge of bravery when he'd fought Bruno. His friend had been with him then, cheering him on, ready to defend him when he'd been helpless. Now, Khaled lay unconscious, his face a swollen mass. For the first time in his life, Ethan recognised the nature of his anger.

His sister had dropped to her knees. She was cradling Khaled's bloody head in her arms. For a long while, Ethan could only stare at his still, bleeding friend. Terrified of the answer, he finally found the courage to ask, 'Have I killed him, Inga?'

'No, but you wanted to.' Her tone was harsh and unforgiving. But her brother wasn't looking for pity. It was the last thing he expected or deserved. 'If I've hurt him, I'll kill myself.'

'You won't need to,' Khaled muttered through cracked and swollen lips, 'I'll do it for you.'

Ethan crouched beside his friend. 'Do what you like. Just be alright!'

'I'll be alright!' Khaled grimaced, mocking the concerned tone in his friend's voice. 'But if you've ruined my face, I'll rip your balls.' Remembering that Inga was listening, he turned to her and asked, 'Can you get me some water from the spring?'

She snatched up a jug from the table and was about to run into the yard when he called after her, 'Take some time bringing it. Ethan and I have things to say.'

She closed the door behind her and Khaled tried to stand. He needed his friend's help. Together, they got him to a stool and he sat for a while, fingering his face and jaw. 'It hurts,' he said, touching his nose. 'Does it look broken, to you?'

'If it is, I'll...'

'Yes, you said. You'll kill yourself.'

'Why didn't you fight back? I've taught you better than that.

Just standing there and taking what I threw at you. You should have come back at me or at least moved out of the way.'

'I know. Somehow, I didn't want to. I couldn't believe it was happening. Then it was too late.'

'I could have killed you ...'

'You didn't.' Khaled fell silent for a while before starting to explain. 'Inga won't be long, so try and understand what I'm saying.' He moved his lips as little as possible, his tongue felt too big for his mouth and he knew his voice sounded muffled. 'I've never touched your sister before today and if you're honest you'll admit nothing much was going on when you came in. I give you my word, nothing more than that has ever happened between us. I didn't come here sneaking around, trying to catch her on her own. I came here to talk to you. I was going to ask if you'd let me marry her.'

Ethan shook his head slowly, 'Inga likes you a lot. But ...'

'She's already told me about the problems,' Khaled interrupted. 'That's why we need you on our side.'

'And if I don't want to be on your side?'

'We'll manage. But Ethan, don't do that to us. You remember once, when we were talking about Floria, you said there were things we did together that we couldn't do with women. Remember that?'

'Of course I do.' Ethan sounded confused. He couldn't understand where the conversation was leading them. 'What's that got to do with Inga?'

'Think about it,' Khaled continued. 'We spend most of our lives hunting, swimming, fishing and sometimes even fighting. How much of that could we share with a woman? And you know what Berbers and Arabs are like. We're always fighting among ourselves. Father's heard Ali might be joining forces with a cousin of ours. We could be in for trouble. Then there are the Christians. They get more threatening by the day. But what matters now, is we sort ourselves out.'

The door opened and Inga came in carrying the water. The men were deep in conversation and much as she wanted to listen, she knew she had no part in what was taking place. She put the jug on the table and left them to it.

Ethan poured some of the water onto a piece of cloth and started to wash the blood away from Khaled's face. 'Have you spoken to your father about this?'

'He said it was time I got married. That's when I told him about Inga. But I didn't know if she'd have me. I wanted to be sure. I didn't think there'd be a problem with you. We've always known where we stood with each other. Look, I'll never do anything like this again. I'll tell you what's on my mind. But you've got to listen to what I'm saying because it's important. Father is happy for me to marry Inga. He's offered me land next to yours as a wedding present. We can make it into one big farm. We'll be partners.' Khaled clenched his teeth. The pain in his jaw was flaring again. 'You'll burn in hell for this,' he spat at his friend. 'I'll see to it that you do!'

'It's not only the Alpujarras you've got tied up, then? You've got influence down there as well.'

Khaled almost managed a grin and Ethan reached over to feel the bridge of his friend's nose. 'There's nothing wrong with it,' he said impatiently, 'It's a bit swollen, that's all. Have me whipped or something, if it'll stop your whining.'

'It's crossed my mind.'

'I'll bet it has. You won't do it though. You haven't got the balls. You think too much and that makes you weak. Me in your place and you in mine, I'd have had your back in ribbons by now. But you! You'll probably write a poem about it!'

Khaled felt another grin starting until the pain put an end to it. 'Inga, she's what's stopping me. She wouldn't like it if I had her baby brother whipped.'

'Don't you believe it. She'd probably give you a hand! And what about those rich men? The ones who were trying to snare you for their daughters. What's your father going to do about them?'

'It isn't me they're interested in. Father knows that. It's what I'd bring to the marriage.'

'And what would Inga bring to your marriage?'

'She loves me. It's not as unusual as you think. Father's mother was a slave before grandfather married her. That's why we've got lighter skin than most of our people. Grandmother was a Berber, her skin was very pale and her eyes were as blue as yours. Berbers are a lot taller than Yemenis, the other side of my father's family. That's why I'm as tall as you are. I get it from her.'

'And your father's agreed to this, the marriage and the farm?'

'All of it. You'll be able to kick me around as much as you like then.'

***

8

Inga had never forgotten that hot, dry-grassed summer's day. Time for the afternoon sleep was approaching and she'd followed her brother and his friend in the direction of the cave. From a distance, she'd watched them push their way through the bushes screening the entrance, and then drag closed the wooden door behind them. Her curiosity had told her to move closer but she knew she had no right to enter. Hiding behind a rock, she'd sat in its shadow until her inquisitiveness drove her to creep forward. Inga had eased aside the wooden barrier, wincing at the scrape of hard wood on packed earth.

Draughts had played games with her hair while her eyes took nervous moments to get used to the darkness. At last, in the faint light that reached them from the open doorway, she'd made out the shape of Khaled's head and shoulders. His brown muscular arm was thrown protectively around the golden body of her brother as they lay sleeping under the same blanket. Inga had always thought it strange, this love between Ethan and his friend and felt excluded by it. She'd stood watching for as long as she dared before pulling the cave door closed behind her.

It was a useful place to store milk and cheese but it came into its own during the autumn when salted hams were preserved in its crisp dryness. From the day when Ethan first brought Khaled home, it had been their private space. Somewhere dark, safe and hidden in which they could escape the world. Ethan had worried at first about the hams and how his Muslim friend would react to them. 'They're to get us through the winter,' he explained. 'So we've got enough meat.'

'It's safe from me,' Khaled laughed. 'Bad things happen when you eat forbidden fruit.'

'That's only if you get caught.'

'You always do.'

'Not always. You don't know half the things I get up to.'

'So you're always telling me.'

They ate their main meal with the family, Khaled chewing warily and Ethan looking sheepish. As soon as it was over, they threw the remainder of the cheese and some grapes into the saddle bag. They'd decided to sleep in the cave and the food would do for later. They carried it in silence, with some wine and a couple of blankets. Their mood lightened as soon as they'd pushed the wooden door closed. Ethan lit the oil lamp and Khaled set about building a fire. They piled the sticks onto the heat-cracked stone that served for a fireplace and found themselves chatting easily to one another.

Leaving the fire to manage itself, Khaled thumped the dust out of a large straw-filled sack and dragged it over to where Ethan was sitting. They might as well be comfortable while the warmth built up. Ethan had remembered something from their past and it was making him shake with laughter. He could see Khaled's expectant face in the firelight. His friend was hoping to be let into the memory so Ethan decided he'd tantalise him for a while.

For Khaled, there were a thousand possibilities, most of them embarrassing and all ready to be dredged up. 'What's so funny, *Strawhead?* You might as well tell me before you piss yourself.'

'Remember when you used to creep out of your house at night?'

Khaled was confident enough to laugh at himself, these days. He could see how ridiculous his antics must have appeared. 'I couldn't sleep properly in that great place.'

'Things must have been bad if you preferred our rough old straw mattresses and Danny snoring like a pig!' Ethan felt a need to goad building inside him. He could resist it if he tried but where was the fun in that? He picked a handful of grapes from the bunch and, taking careful aim, hurled them one by one at his friend's head and body.

There's only so much damage a ripe grape can do and Khaled was happy enough to go along with the game. He rolled around, half-heartedly avoiding them until the assault petered out. Then, growling with mock anger, he grabbed up as much of the ruined fruit as he could find and crushed it into a threatening pulp. It was Ethan's turn to play along. He made no attempt to move when his friend lunged forward and plastered the wet sticky mass across his face and then down over his chest and belly. He remained motionless, waiting and watching until there was no more pulp to spread. Then, he pounced, grabbing Khaled's head and pulling it close to his own.

'Lick it up, dirty boy!'

'And if I don't?'

'You will!' Ethan's tone was menacing. 'You've had your fun, now you're going to pay for it!' He tightened his grip and Khaled felt his face rammed hard against his friend's chest. He knew he would surrender, but not yet. The sweet-juice smell of grapes and the musky warmth of Ethan's body excited him. He held out for a few, face-saving moments and then started to lick the juice from his friend's face and body.

The fire had come to life and they watched a tendril of smoke find its way towards the roof, before disappearing into the darkness of a small fissure. Ethan turned to his friend, 'The grape juice. Didn't it sting those cracked lips of yours?'

'I suppose it must have.'

'Why did you do it, then?'

'You told me to.'

'Do you always do what other people tell you?'

'When it's what I want as well.'

The fire was crackling and starting to throw out heat, but they were surprised by a chill in the air. 'It must be freezing outside,' Khaled said. 'I've never known it like this inside the cave.' He squatted next to the fire stone and poked a couple of small logs into the centre of the flames. A mass of sparks exploded in his direction. Just in time, he scrambled out of harm's way. There was a tang of singed hair but no damage.

Ethan reached out for an extra blanket and shrugged it around his shoulders, 'Coming under?'

'I'm not sure.' Khaled sounded as if there were options to be weighed.

'Can't trust yourself?'

'Can you?'

'Probably not.' Ethan pulled back part of the blanket and his friend crawled in beside him.

They lay for a while, watching the fire. The flames leapt around the logs as the smoke trailed upwards. It was a comfortable silence, broken because there was something Ethan needed to say. 'Those memories we talked about. I keep them in the good part of my head but there's a place for bad thoughts as well.'

'Is that where I'll go?'

'No, you don't belong there. I keep people like your brother and Sulieman in the bad part.' Ethan's voice had taken on a bitter edge that Khaled hadn't heard before. 'They made a fool of me in front of the others.'

Khaled threw back his half of the blanket and sat up. He guessed Ethan was talking about the canings. But why? At the time, everyone had been impressed by his stoicism. Reuben had described how his friend was made to strip and bend over the trestle. His workmates had watched in surly silence while stroke after stroke hammered down. Once the thrashings were over, they'd seen him shrug, then stroll over to the water trough and start washing. Even when his friends angrily pointed out the finger-thick welts and bruises that darkened their hero's buttocks, Ethan never said a word.

'They told me you walked away from them as if they were nothing,' Khaled said. 'They thought you were so leather-arsed, Sulieman couldn't make much of an impression.'

'I wasn't going to let that bastard know he'd got to me. It hurt like hell. You know it did. You got a good look at the marks so you know the impression he made. They weren't going to tame me, that's all. Not like some animal that's had its balls off. I used to tell myself it was making me stronger, like those Spartans your tutor told us about. He said they were flogged during training to see whether they'd flinch. It was supposed to toughen them up. I thought, if they could take it, so could I.'

'Ethan the Spartan!' Khaled smiled. He wasn't sure whether he should show sympathy or help his friend deal with the memory by laughing at it. 'I used to think you enjoyed it. You were always showing off your marks.'

'Only to you.'

'Maybe I was the one you were trying to impress.'

'Mmm.'

'What's that mean?'

'What do you want it to mean?'

There was a part of Khaled, dark and hidden, that had enjoyed Ethan's canings. They'd given him a chance to be useful by spreading ointment across the bruises but he knew that wasn't the reason. It was Ethan getting thrashed that had excited him. 'What would you say if I told you I wanted to give it to you?'

'The cane? I wouldn't mind if it was you. Not hard though. Just for a laugh. Then I give you a dose. Is that the idea?'

It wasn't, so Khaled changed tack. 'You were paying for your forbidden fruit!' He dodged a non-too-friendly clout and wriggled back under the blankets. 'Being made to strip, that must have been the worst part.'

Ethan shook his head, 'Nah. We always work stripped when the weather's hot. It's easier to get the filth off your body than out of your clothes. You know that yourself. You've washed with us at the trough enough times. Getting your clothes off in front of your mates is nothing to worry about.'

'Even with slimy creatures like Saleem gawping at you?'

'Reptiles don't count. No, it was being bent over and beaten like a boy,' Ethan said sullenly. 'That's not something they should do to a man. Not in front of his mates. The bit I hated most was not being able to fight back. I've been hurt worse in fights, but I was never humiliated by it.'

'That's because you won!'

'It might have made a difference.' Ethan gave a brief smile, and then continued bitterly, 'Ali and Sulieman liked whipping us like dogs. I'll never forget the shame and I won't forgive it either.'

Khaled hadn't realised his friend had suffered such a loss of face. 'You didn't say anything about it at the time. You should have told me.'

'Sulieman made sure you weren't around. He did it while you were in the house, studying with your tutor. Even if you had been there, you couldn't have stopped it. Ali was older than you so he had the authority. And what would Danny and Reuben have thought if I'd come running to you every time Sulieman got his cane out?'

'I'm not talking about stopping it,' Khaled said. 'But the three of us could have told you there was nothing to be ashamed of. None of us could have taken it the way you did.'

Khaled's words helped and common sense told Ethan his friend was right. He didn't believe it, that was the problem. He lay for a while, studying the roof of the cave as it wavered in the light of the fire. 'I never understood why Ali hated me so much.'

'He was jealous. Of our friendship. On top of that, he knew he'd never be the man you were, so he and Sulieman took it out on your arse.'

'You think too much,' Ethan laughed! 'You say you don't like studying but you'll end up as wise as your father. Do you remember what Ali called me, the first time you took me home?'

Khaled did remember but he'd hoped his friend had forgotten.

'He said I was a yellow-haired, speckle-faced kaffir and I stank like the horses. He told you to get me out of the house and back with the animals where I belonged. You got him pinned him up against the wall. He was ready to shit himself when your father came along and spoiled the fun.'

'He'd heard us yelling. He told Ali you were no kaffir because Christians and Muslims believed in the same God. Then he said it wasn't surprising if we smelled of horses because we'd been doing men's work in the stable yard. We could soon wash ourselves clean but the stench of dissipation wasn't as easy to get rid of as the smell of honest sweat.'

'I didn't know what *dissipation* meant but Ali did. He thought your father was talking about him.'

'He was.'

'That was the first time you let me wash in your room. Then, when we didn't stink any more, we went to the hammam and soaked in the baths. I was in paradise. You even had our food brought there so we could spend more time playing around in the water. We slept in that great bed of yours, with the cotton sheets and the mattress filled with feathers. You were always saying you couldn't sleep there but we managed it alright. Like a couple of dead men.'

'You were still speckle faced in the morning, though!' Khaled enjoyed tormenting his friend about the small brown marks on his face. It could make Ethan furious and that was worth seeing.

'They'll never come off,' he said moodily. 'The sun makes them worse. My sister's got them as well.'

Her freckles were one of the things Khaled found irresistible about Inga but he knew Ethan felt differently about his. 'I don't know what you're worried about. They look alright.'

'You haven't got to take the stick I get.'

'What, from Reuben and Danny? They only do it because it makes you wild.' There was something Khaled had wanted to ask for a while but he'd been afraid he might get an answer he didn't want. 'Do Reuben and Danny say anything about us being together so much?'

'They did at first. I think they were jealous. Especially Reuben. Before you came, we were good friends. We still are. Not in the same way we're friends, you and me, but near enough. When we got close, they thought neither of us would want them around any more.'

'Do they still think that?'

'Nah, that was at the beginning. They soon realised they'd got an extra mate in you. You're always asking them things. You ask Danny to teach you how to fight and Reuben about the horses and the falcons. It makes them feel important.'

Khaled smiled with relief. The reply was better than he'd expected. 'I don't know much that's of any use compared with the rest of you. That's why I'm always asking questions.'

'You do right to ask. It makes them feel part of everything.'

'They *are* part of everything. The four of us make a good team.'

Ethan nodded. He liked the idea of a team so long as he and Khaled were special. They moved closer together, partly for warmth and partly because they wanted it that way.

Half way through the night, Khaled was jolted awake. He'd been dreaming. It was nothing he could understand, just a jumble of fears. For a while he didn't know where he was. Then, he recognised the security of Ethan's nearness. He lay, breathing the warm reassuring body smell of his friend, and wished the night would last for ever.

'Do I stink or something?' Ethan sounded mildly defensive.

'No, you smell alright. Anyway, I thought you were asleep.'

'I was until you woke me up. I could feel your breath on my body. I must stink or you wouldn't keep sniffing me.'

'I like the way you smell.'

'Get back to sleep!'

9

They were playing for time in their makeshift bed. Under the covers, things were snug. Out of them, they'd be bitter. The trouble was, Ethan needed a piss. He cursed the donkey whose wheeze-rasp braying had jarred them awake and flung back the blankets. It laid Khaled bare to the chill. He curled up and away from it, like a dark, furry animal eager to hang on to its sleep. Ethan stirred him with a foot and wrenched open the door.

From the farmhouse, he could hear the morning babble of women's voices as they rattled pots and made up the fire. Out here, the world was quiet and unhurried. The sun hadn't heated the land and the brisk air nipped at his sluggishness. Cold or not, this was Ethan's favourite time, when the day was yet to come.

Checking to make sure no-one was around, he walked into the crisp light and pissed vigorously against the trunk of an olive tree. The yellow stream tracked frothily through the dust, leaving a miniature wadi in its wake before disappearing without warning into the ground.

Years before, his northern tribe had believed in spirits that lived in sinewy old trees like this, and were prepared to die fighting anyone who disagreed with them. The Christians had dismissed them as primitives with painted skins, who muttered and mumbled their false beliefs. Today, there were new generations of men, all claiming to believe in the one true God while teaching Christians, Jews and Muslims they could never be friends.

This tree had been old when his grandfather was a boy and had looked then much as it did now. It would continue to grow bigger, harder and stronger until they were long years dead, those men, who were so certain of the truth. But these were gloomy thoughts for a bright morning and Ethan shook himself free of them. That was the trouble with thinking; it made you miserable.

He heard a thump from inside the cave and pictured Khaled, still half asleep, badgering himself from a now empty bed. Ethan looked over his shoulder and saw his friend shambling towards the tree. They grinned lazily at each other's nakedness. 'Some beast you've got there,' Ethan said, nodding at his friend's erection. 'If that's what you meant by bringing something to the marriage, my sister's in for a surprise.'

Khaled smiled, still half asleep but smugly satisfied with his friend's compliment. He mumbled that it was always the same, first thing in the morning and that Inga must have caught sight of Ethan's at one time or another.

They washed at the spring, the water's iciness shocking the last traces of tiredness out of them, then towelled their bodies dry. Using their fingers, they hooked mint flavoured paste from a pot and rubbed it around their teeth. Ethan was watching his friend with interest. A lot of Muslims wouldn't use tooth cleaner during Ramadan because it amounted to breaking the fast. Khaled obviously thought differently. They pulled on their clothes, refilled their water-skins and walked to the farmhouse.

A bundle of food for the journey was waiting on the kitchen table. Inga knew their habits and guessed they'd rather eat once they'd built up an appetite. For now, she offered them buttermilk and a handful of dates. 'Is it alright Khaled, to eat? I know it's Ramadan but you're going on a journey. That makes a difference doesn't it?'

'It can do. Besides, I've got Ethan with me and he's no good on an empty belly. I'll make up by fasting for an extra day when Ramadan's finished.'

'You'll really do that?'

I'd feel guilty if I didn't.'

When the time came to leave, Inga clung to them while her little sisters begged them not to go. Ethan's mother was sitting quietly at the table with tears in her eyes. She hated it when they went away. It would only be for a few days but she had the fear she might never see them again. She shouldn't do it. It would only irritate her son, but she couldn't stop herself from telling them to come back soon. Instead of looking angry, as he usually did when she said something like that, Ethan kissed her on the forehead. She looked up at Khaled, hoping he'd kiss her too, and wasn't disappointed.

She'd said nothing about his bruised face. It wasn't her place to comment on the young men's business, but it reminded her that Ethan had a temper and it had often got him into trouble. Her husband had told her it was normal for boys to fight but she knew her son took things to heart. He felt pain more intensely than most people, just as at other times he was capable of being happier and more loving as well.

Over the last few years, his outbursts had become fewer and she'd noticed a growing gentleness about him. Khaled had given him that. When Ethan's puppy died, Khaled had calmed him before his grief could turn to anger. Her son had been too ashamed to let himself cry in front of her or the girls. With his friend, he'd allowed the tears to wash the misery out of him. Later, she'd heard him ask Khaled not to tell anyone.

'About the puppy?'

'No, that I cried. You won't tell Danny and Reuben!'

'It wouldn't matter if I did. You're man enough to cry.'

Next morning, Khaled had disappeared and with him, Ethan's saddle bag. The family couldn't understand why he'd gone without a word but later in the day, they'd seen him come riding back. Instead of jumping down to the ground as he usually did, they'd watched him climb slowly from his horse, holding the saddlebag carefully in one hand. He'd given it to Ethan and inside, curled up and fast asleep, was a new puppy. And what an affectionate, bounding little creature it had turned out to be. Its enthusiasm for life suited the boys. 'If it doesn't stop wagging its tail,' Inga said, 'It'll wear out and drop off.' She'd used the local word *'rabo'*, when talking about the animal's tail and it appealed to the boys.

'*Rabo*, that's a good name,' Ethan decided, 'We'll call him that.'

The farm was a second home to Khaled and leaving was as hard for him as it was for his friend. They'd said nothing to Ethan's mother about the wedding. Inga would pick the right time to break that piece of news. Promising they'd be away for the shortest time possible, they headed back to Khaled's house.

In the mid-day heat, they stopped beneath some trees to rest their horses and let them drink from a stream. Ethan clambered around until he found a few wild figs the sticky-beaked birds had over-looked. They were ripe to bursting and the boys sucked out the sweet juicy seeds before wolfing down the bread, cheese and olives that Inga had packed.

'Everything alright?' Ethan asked.

'Why shouldn't it be?'

'Not angry about the fight?'

A cacophony of sound filtered through the leaves above them. 'I'm as happy as those birds up there,' Khaled told his friend.

'They're not happy,' Ethan said. 'You've only got to look at them to see they're fighting mad and squawking menaces, *'Get away! This is my branch! Keep your distance!'*

'What happens if they don't do as they're told?'

'The others squawk louder.'

'And if that doesn't work?'

'They get really angry and ruffle their feathers.'

'Birds do war better than we do.'

The sun hung low in the sky. It had lost most of its intensity by the time they reached Khaled's home. A breeze had freshened the first part of their journey but by mid-afternoon, it had become a driving Levante wind. Hot, sweat-soaked and coughing dust, they rode into the yard and made straight for Khaled's quarters.

Their rowdy feet in the corridor alerted a house slave. He stared in disbelief at his sand dusted master and his equally ghost-like friend. Khaled and Ethan could manage without his help and he was told to leave.

They dragged off their sodden clothing, dumped it in a pile on the floor and darted to a wooden vat that stood ready-filled with water. Plunging in a couple of jugs, the friends took it in turns to drench each other. They roared with shock as the cold water sluiced the plastered mess from their hair and bodies, briefly reviving the dusty smell of their journey, before flushing it away.

Ethan loved soap. In his opinion, it was the best thing Arab civilisation had produced. He held the slippery block in his lather-coated hands, took aim and squeezed. His friend knew what was coming and dodged sideways as the soap shot out, missing its target and thumping into the tiled wall. Khaled grabbed it and shot it back, catching his friend hard in the middle of the chest.

They rinsed off the foam, rubbed themselves down with rough cotton towels and cleaned their teeth with a spicy, clove-flavoured paste that stung their mouths with its freshness. 'It's better than the mint,' Khaled said. 'Father gets it from Damascus. We'll take a pot to the farm, next time we go.'

He ransacked his cedar wood chest, looking for a couple of tunics. It was well stocked with clothes - his mother saw to that. Once he was married, it would be his wife's job to make sure he was well turned out. He was excited by the idea of having Inga look after him. They'd spend their time talking and making love. Except when he was off hunting with Ethan and that would be most days.

He wondered how his mother would take to the idea of him and Inga getting married. He'd better go and have a word with her before they ate dinner.

'Do we stink less?' he asked his friend.

'We're as fresh as we'll ever be.'

'This'll help.' Khaled picked up a bottle of distilled herb oils and splashed some under his arms before handing the rest to his friend. 'You need this more than I do.'

'Don't be too sure about that. We can usually smell you coming.' Ethan liked the fresh, tingling sensation the liquid left on his body. He slapped a palmful over his balls and the next moment he was jumping. His face screwed into a mask of misery as the herb oils nettled the sensitive skin.

'Don't worry. It goes off after a couple of days.'

Ethan's mouth opened, ready to curse. But it was alright; the smarting was already beginning to fade. 'Have you ever done that?'

'Most people try it once. Not many do it again.'

'Let's have a look at your cuts.' Ethan rinsed the remainder of the herb oil from his hands before running a finger carefully over his friend's still swollen nose and lips. 'They're healing but you've got a couple of black eyes, as well. Did you know?'

'Bad enough for Father to notice?'

'He'd be blind if he didn't. Listen Brother, if he asks what happened, tell him the truth. I lost my temper.' He was finding it hard to look his friend in the face. 'It's not the first time I've done it, either. It frightens me sometimes.'

'No, you had good reason in my case. Or thought you had. But you're right about your temper. You might go too far one day. We all thought you were going to kill Bruno. We never said anything at the time because we were carried along with your win. But you'd never have stopped hammering him if we hadn't pulled you off.'

Ethan nodded guiltily. 'I get like that sometimes. I think it's because of the canings.'

'Not that again!' Khaled scoffed. 'You can't blame everything you do on a few strokes of the cane. Anyway, it was Sulieman who gave you the stick, not Bruno!'

'Sulieman wasn't there. Bruno was.'

'So what about me? What was I paying for?'

'Loving Inga.'

'Who told you that?'

'She did. She said I was afraid of losing you.'

The cry of the muezzin told them it was sunset and the hours of fasting were at an end. 'Here!' Khaled threw his friend a tunic and pulled another over his own head. 'I'm going to pray and then see mother. I won't be long but I've got to tell her about Inga. As soon as I get back, we'll go and break the fast with Father. He'll be expecting us.'

'Are you going to say anything about eating on the way?'

'He probably won't ask. If he does, I'll tell him. He'll understand.'

10

Souad turned her head and smiled at the young girl who was brushing her hair. She hadn't seen her son for nearly a month and was feeling nervous. As soon as she'd heard that Khaled and Ethan were back, she'd decided her make-up needed attention. Her son would be coming to see her, impatient to talk about his choice of a bride. Omar had already told her the girl was a Christian and of excellent character. He'd approved the match, so that was the way things would be!

She checked her reflection in the mirror and nodded to herself. Things weren't too bad at all; scarcely a line on her face and not a trace of grey in her long, dark hair. It would be a pity to cover it but Khaled was coming and the only man with a right to see her hair was Omar.

One of the girls handed her a finely woven scarf and Souad nodded her approval. The colour set off perfectly the green of her silk dress and yet, she hesitated. There'd be time to put it on when she knew Khaled was definitely on his way. Perhaps a little more kohl around the eyes and a touch more colour to her lips …

There were excited whisperings and a young girl ran to warn her that her son was already at the door of the haramlek and asking to see his mother. Souad grabbed the headscarf and arranged it over her hair. She watched as Khaled crossed the room towards her. The grin on his face told her he was full of news and burning to share it. He'd never been able to keep secrets from her. One glance at him, when he was a boy and she'd know if he'd been up to mischief.

Souad caught herself wondering what he'd look like with a beard. His father would be pleased to see him with one but she wasn't so sure. She hadn't caught so much as a glimpse of her husband's face since he'd given up shaving and that had been soon after they'd married. While Khaled was young and beautiful, the world had a right to his face. But enough was enough. She'd been looking at him, not as a mother looks at her son, but as a woman looks at a man.

She greeted him with a warm embrace and a mild rebuke. 'I take it you're not here to ask after my health.' It was the tone she'd used when Khaled was a boy. Deep and gentle, her voice could at times sound disapproving, but it never failed to reassure him of her love.

There were the politenesses to be observed. His mother offered him fruit juice. The selection was wide but he settled for pomegranate without honey. She passed him the cakes. Sticky-sweet, one of them filled Khaled's mouth and stuck to his teeth. Souad hoped he wouldn't try to speak for a while; it would disgust both of them.

It was the first time they'd seen each other since his circumcision. She'd guessed what was going on from the women's blether but she'd known better than to ask her husband outright. Whenever she'd manoeuvred the conversation around to their son's health, Omar had assured her that Khaled was well. She'd made sure plenty of fresh food was taken to his quarters every day and when the servants returned, they brought with them all of the tittle-tattle it was fit to repeat. They told her Ethan was with him. It hadn't surprised her. A month apart would feel like a lifetime to that pair.

Civilities were exchanged and then Khaled let loose the idea of his marriage. It was his father's suggestion, he told her, but didn't she agree he was of an age when he should choose a wife? Casually, as if it were of no significance, he asked how she would feel about a Christian bride.

Souad's eyes and mouth opened wide and she shook her head in disbelief. Anyone but Khaled would have been convinced the news had come as a surprise. But he'd seen her astonished look too often.

It had worked well when he was a boy. Then it was enough to make him ashamed of whatever he'd done. These days, he was less easy to tame.

'You know about it!' She heard the challenge in his voice. 'Father's already told you.'

'Well, perhaps he mentioned something. It's hard to remember. So many things happened during Ramadan.'

'And what do you think of Inga?' he asked directly.

'Khaled, you know I've never met the girl. Your father tells me her brother Ethan is very nice. He seems to think that's some sort of a recommendation. I'm not so sure, myself. He's that boy who's always getting into fights, isn't he?'

'Mother! It's no good pretending you don't know who Ethan is. I'm sure Father has told you more than enough about him over the years.'

'He's mentioned him once or twice. The girls tell me more.'

'More? About what?'

'Oh you know the sort of rubbish girls talk. He's handsome, strong, and the two of you are more interested in each other than you are in them.'

'That's not difficult. Some of them are as fascinating as dead fish.'

'And from the state of your face, life with Ethan is anything but boring.'

'It was a misunderstanding.'

'And, as I'm sure your father has told you, something to be avoided in the future.'

'He warned me of the dangers of jealousy, if that's what you're talking about. He also said that love never hurt anyone.'

She took an impatient breath. 'In that case, I must have imagined all of those people in the cemeteries who died because they loved the wrong people. Those Greeks, for a start. Your father never stops talking about them.

Khaled, you can lie to me and you can lie to your father. You can lie to whoever you like, but never lie to yourself. Ask Ethan straight out whether he can tolerate the idea of your marriage. If the answer is *'No'*, you're playing with fire.'

'I don't need to ask him. We've discussed it already.'

'And to judge from your face, nearly killed each other. Not much of a start to married life with his sister!'

It was time to leave. Khaled embraced his mother and kissed her warmly on the mouth. She felt his strength, the hardness of his muscles and her own tinge of envy. It would be a lucky woman who found herself in those arms. 'Is she beautiful, Khaled?'

'Yes, Mother, she is.'

'As beautiful as Ethan?'

'Nearly.'

He managed to duck in time. The hairbrush clattered harmlessly to the floor. 'Don't throw things, Mother! You always told me it wasn't the sort of thing a well brought up person did. Besides, you know I was only joking. Inga's very beautiful. You'll love her.'

'Will she convert to Islam?'

'If I ask her.'

'And will you ask her?'

'No. That's for her to decide.'

'But you love her?'

'Very much.'

'And she loves you?'

'Yes. Surprising, isn't it?'

'Not really. If she didn't, she'd be the only woman in Almeria who wasn't in love with my son. Stop looking so worried Khaled, you have my blessing.'

***

11

Ethan had walked over these rugs before, but this was the first time he'd noticed the intricacy of the patterns and the subtle blending of colours. From lower down, the incised wall decoration and horse-shoe arches also struck him as more magnificent than he'd remembered them. Khaled's father had invited them to sit with him on the carpeted floor of his reading room and Ethan was working hard to look confident. Inside, he wasn't convinced and his heart throbbed like a warning drum.

He knew he'd never be able to sit like an Arab. Lounging was alright when he was with Khaled but in his master's presence, things were different. He'd tried every way he knew to sit with his feet decently hidden; so as not to give the impression he wanted to walk over his host. That was the explanation his friend had given for not showing the soles. Whether it was the real reason or not, he had no idea. It seemed more likely it was something to do with the bottoms of the feet being dirty but he wasn't taking any chances.

He needed a piss. It was the same when he was waiting for a fight to start at *The Barrels*. Once things got moving, he'd be alright. His hands wouldn't, though. He'd been clenching his fists so tightly, the finger nails were cutting into his palms. He wished to God he was back in the stable yard or, better still, in the mountains. There, he was a man in control of his life. In this massive room, he was a boy on the fringe of a rich man's world.

It was ridiculous thinking he could hold his own in conversation with his master. He'd make a fool of himself. Khaled would be ashamed of his crudeness and blame him for destroying his chance of happiness with Inga. Ethan was sweating like a pig. No, pigs were dirty animals he mustn't think about them, not here in a Muslim's house. Besides, pigs don't sweat. Horses sweat. He was sweating like a horse so he must stink. Ali had told him he stank. Ethan sniffed furtively under his arms but all he could smell was soap and that bloody herb oil. Only the night before, Khaled had told him he liked the way he smelled. He wondered what Sheikh Omar knew about him and Khaled. Could he tell what they got up to in the cave? Of course he couldn't. Nobody knew. But maybe they'd guess.

'Aristotle had some interesting ideas,' Sheikh Omar announced, putting down his book and leaning towards his guest. 'Everyday, I thank Allah for sending us Ibn Rushd. You Christians call him Averroes. Without his translations we'd know nothing of Greek learning.' He paused briefly, studying his guest's reaction.

Ethan's chest had clamped tight and he was having to force air into his lungs. His palms were damp and he only hoped no-one would notice him drying them on his thighs.

'As you no doubt remember from your studies,' Sheikh Omar continued, 'Averroes taught that philosophical truth is derived from reason, and not from faith. Since these are separate domains, they do not conflict and need not, therefore, be reconciled. Would you agree with that?'

Sweat was running down Ethan's back and there wasn't much air in the room. This meeting was turning out to be far worse than he'd expected. In need of help, he turned to his friend but the expression on Khaled's face showed he was equally mystified. The boys had made an attempt to study the works of Aristotle with their tutor. It hadn't amounted to much and the idea of discussing him or Averroes frightened them into silence.

'It's surprising he said so little about Alexander the Great,' Khaled said, trying to cling on to the conversation. 'After all, he was Aristotle's pupil.'

'Ah yes, Alexander has always been one of your great historical heroes, but you must surely agree that Aristotle would never have approved of his imperial ambitions. He and Plato regarded the city state as the logical end to social development and framed their conceptions of the ideal society upon it. The state needed to be small, of course, so that everybody knew each other and recognised their strengths and weaknesses. Would you say they were right?' Sheikh Omar's head tilted questioningly.

The young men looked at each other even more blankly. Khaled's bluff had been called and they had nothing to fall back on. His father brought their squirming to an end by giving a sudden snort, followed by a deep belly laugh. 'You're fine boys,' he told them, 'But you'll never make academics.' Obviously deciding he'd tormented them enough, he added, 'I've never understood a word those Greeks were talking about, either!'

Ethan and Khaled smiled gratefully. Sheikh Omar's diplomatic lie meant they could breathe more easily. The three men relaxed into their cushions while slaves padded inconspicuously around the room and made ready to serve the meal. Ethan was still struggling to give the impression he felt at home while watching two young men of his own age move quietly between Sheikh Omar and his guests. He saw one of them pour rose water from an intricately engraved silver jug so they could rinse their hands before eating. The second man caught the surplus water in a bowl. Ethan looked around again, nervously wondering what he was doing here, waiting to be served by people who had always been his equals.

Khaled caught his eye and gave him a slow wink. 'There's nothing to worry about,' he said quietly. 'Remember, you're the most important man in the room. You're letting me marry your sister.'

They broke the fast with milk and dates, while skewers of crispy spiced lamb were served with rice, nuts and raisins on shiny copper trays. Vegetables, in red and yellow sauces, still bubbling in earthenware pots, were placed in front of them. Later, fruit, buttermilk and juices were arranged a little to the side, on low brass-topped tables.

Ethan was dazed by choice and at first ate nothing. Then, remembering that to refuse food could be taken as an insult, he started to pick at the olives. His appetite surged back, spiked by their saltiness. The worry now was that he might overdo the gluttony. Glancing at his friend, he saw Khaled devouring everything in front of him. It was probably safe to follow his example.

While the three of them ate hungrily, polite but insignificant topics were lightly discussed. 'Nothing offends an Arab more, than to come straight to the point,' Khaled had once told him. 'That's why it takes us so long to get anything done.' Omar ordered coffee and nodded approvingly as the hot, cardamom and cinnamon flavoured liquid was poured from a height into small conical cups.

Satisfied his guest had been well provided for, Sheikh Omar asked the servants to wait outside and turned towards Ethan with a serious expression on his face, 'You and your sister are Christians. No?'

'Yes, Master, we are.'

'Do you know what the Christian King of Abyssinia did when several of our Prophet's closest supporters were being pursued by their enemies?'

'Khaled told me something about it,' Ethan replied. 'He helped Mohammed's men by giving them sanctuary.'

'That's right. Mohammed's enemies wanted them dead. They offered the Christian king a mountain of gold if he would give them up but he refused. Instead, he drew a thin line in the sand with his staff. 'The difference between Muslims and Christians is no wider than that line,' he told them. In other words, it was insignificant. If he hadn't done that, Mohammed's supporters would have been murdered and there would be no Muslim religion today.' Khaled and Ethan were craning their necks towards him. Sheikh Omar was a good story-teller.

'The King of Abyssinia was right,' he continued. 'There are no important differences between us, only those that men invent for their own ends and then attempt to dignify by describing as a *faith*. The prophet Abraham was the father of the Jewish religion. The prophet Jesus was a Jew. He preached love and brotherhood. His followers are, of course, known as Christians. The prophet Mohammed, Peace be Upon Him, was given a message from God which perfected those religions. The result is what we call Islam. It means that we submit to the will of Allah. Sincere followers of the three great religions, Judaism, Christianity and Islam are all *People of the Book* and worthy of each other's respect. The way in which you and your sister worship is no concern of mine. It is between you and God.'

Ethan was amazed by the man's words. 'Khaled and I are always saying that, Master! The important thing is the way people lead their lives and how they treat one another.'

'You and Khaled are right. There was a time when the *People of the Book* lived in a spirit of co-operation and harmony.'

'Master, can I ask you a question?' Ethan asked eagerly.

'You can ask. Only God knows whether I'll be able to answer it.'

'All this thinking, Master. Is it a good thing? I mean, can a man do too much of it?'

'In order to answer your question with the seriousness it deserves, Ethan, I must refer to Socrates. He taught us that the unexamined life is not a life worth living. What do you think he meant by that, Khaled?'

'Well, I suppose he meant we should question and examine our own beliefs and those of others.'

'Go on.'

Khaled was starting to enjoy himself. He'd never thought himself capable of conversing like this with his father. 'Most men would say that thinking is what separates us from the animals.'

'How do you know the animals don't think?'

'I don't know, Father. I just think they don't.'

'So by thinking, you have come to the conclusion that animals are inferior to us. You are capable of thought and they are not. Is that what you're saying?'

'That's right, Father.'

'But by you own admission, you don't know. You only *think* that they are incapable of thought. So by thinking, you have come up with your totally unfounded prejudice against the poor animals. Now do you see why Ethan's question was a good one?'

'It's not as easy as it seems'

'Indeed not. Perhaps Ethan is right. Men *can* think too much, if all they are doing is scratching around to discover differences, in order to make other men miserable. God wants us to be happy. He doesn't want us to ruin our lives by complicating them. In that Golden Age I referred to earlier, men believed in *God*. Today, all too many of them believe in *religion*.'

'Are you suggesting, Master, that God doesn't believe in religion?'

'If he does, it isn't a religion that teaches us to hate one another.'

'Don't they all do that?'

'Religions might. God doesn't'

Ethan still only half believed his sister and Khaled were to be married but his doubts were settled as soon as Sheikh Omar started to speak about the *bride price*. Ethan had never expected to be involved in such a conversation, but as the only male member of his family, it was inevitable negotiations would be conducted with him. He had no experience of bartering over such important matters and shuffled closer to Khaled, looking to his friend for support.

The young man was at a disadvantage. Sheikh Omar recognised the fact and took a different approach from the one he used when dealing with hardened men of business. He spoke frankly and fairly, allowing Khaled to make suggestions helpful to his friend. The situation was an unusual one because as far as material goods were concerned, Inga and her family had little to offer. There was the farm, but that was still partly owned by Khaled's family.

To Ethan's surprise, Sheikh Omar seemed mainly concerned that the bride price, which he would pay on Khaled's behalf, was sufficient for the young couple to live in a comfortable and dignified manner. His son needed the freedom which only life away from the formality of his home could provide. If things had been different, he might have chosen a similar way of living for himself. Unfortunately, his responsibilities to the many workers and tenants meant he had no choice other than to continue in the traditional way. One day, Khaled would have to shoulder those responsibilities. For the time being, if he could enjoy a normal life, then he should be allowed to do so. It certainly wasn't reasonable to make a son wait for his father's death before receiving the money which would let him live as he wished.

The sum offered to Ethan was substantially more than the outstanding loan. This meant the bond would be cancelled as soon as the marriage took place. There would be more than enough money for the construction of further farm buildings. Khaled and Inga could have their own home while Ethan would be able to build a third house for himself and his future family. Repairs to the farm buildings would be carried out and a substantial investment made in livestock. The difference these changes would make to Ethan's family was hard to imagine.

An even more significant gift was that of the rich, fertile land that lay next to the farm. This would create a massive estate, reaching from the small village of Felix to the sea. The tenants and farmers would in future work directly for Khaled and Ethan instead of for Sheikh Omar.

'Khaled, I have watched the way you treat servants and others who are less well placed than you. I am confident that neither you nor Ethan will forget those men and women have the same right to happiness and fair treatment as you have. Their well-being will be your responsibility.'

'I can answer for both of us, Father. With the help of Allah, we'll never betray your trust in us.'

'As you probably know, much of the land next to the coast is of little use for farming but it still has its value. It means you will have easy access to the sea.'

The negotiations were more or less at an end. Sheikh Omar turned to Ethan and asked, 'Do you trust my son?'

The question was surprising, but Ethan answered immediately.

'With my life, Master.'

'And your sister, would you trust Khaled with her life?'

'Yes, Master, otherwise I would never have agreed to them getting married.'

'Then there is little more to be said. What we usually do at a time like this is read together the *Fatiha*.' Ethan continued to be puzzled by those two strange questions followed by an unknown word until Khaled came to his rescue, 'We recite it together to seal a contract.'

'That's right. Khaled tells me you have taught yourself to read and write Arabic.'

'I didn't teach myself. Khaled taught me everything I know, and it still isn't perfect.'

'In that case, will you trust him to guide you through it?'

'Of course, Master.'

And so, with Khaled's help, they read together the first Sura of the Koran.

The farm and their plans for the future were the main topics of conversation, but thinking Ethan would be interested, Omar told him about the small Fortress of Zugaiba that dominated the village of Felix. It had been built a couple of centuries earlier, to protect the inhabitants of the village from slave-taking pirates or ambitious neighbours. Eventually, it would become Khaled's responsibility. At the moment, there were only a few guards stationed there but because of its strategic importance, as a watchtower close to the Alcazaba of Almeria, it could become indispensable in an emergency.

The boys had jumped to their feet and were ready to take their leave when Khaled's father held up his hand to detain them. 'Ethan, there is one more thing. Did you do that to my son's face?'

'The bruises and the cut lips, Master? Yes I did.'

'This isn't the first time you have been quick to use your fists. The swollen nose and black eyes, I take it you are also responsible

Matanza!

for those?'

'Yes, Master.'

'Did he deserve what you did to him?'

Khaled attempted to deflect the question but Ethan was too quick for him. 'No, Master, he didn't deserve it. I was wrong.'

'Khaled seems to have paid a heavy price for your mistake, or perhaps the mistake was his and concerned your sister's honour?'

'I thought that at first, Master, but it wasn't true. It was about Khaled and me; about our friendship.'

Sheikh Omar remained silent for a while, leaving Ethan to move guiltily from foot to foot. Then, as though he were thinking aloud, the older man said, 'It's a strange friendship that results in such violence.' Switching his gaze from Ethan to Khaled, he asked, 'You are still friends?'

'We are more than friends, Father. We are brothers.'

'You said that before and I warned you then of the jealousies that can arise when one man loves another. Be careful, the pair of you.'

Sheikh Omar smiled, indicating that the lecture was over. 'Ethan, what is it that you call my son?'

The young man answered hesitantly, 'I call your son by his name, Master. I call him Khaled.'

'Yes, but I have sometimes heard you call him by another name.'

'Yes, Master. Sometimes I call him *Little Brother*. He was born just one day later than me. It's a joke.'

'Yes, I can see that now. Do you think there is any other significance in your birth dates?'

It was the first time Ethan had been made to think seriously about horoscopes, but to be asked the question by Sheikh Omar gave the subject importance. 'Next to the souq, Master, there are people who tell fortunes,' he replied. 'They use star charts and birth signs. They said that our birth dates explain why Khaled and I are close.'

'And what do they predict for your futures?

'They wouldn't tell us that, Master.'

'Maybe it's just as well. Some things are better known only to God. But who are we to argue with the stars? They help us to navigate and by using our astrolabes, we calculate dates and draw up our almanacs. Since the stars decree that you and my son were born to be brothers, I would like you to call me 'Father' as he does. Will you do that, Ethan?'

'I'll try, Master.'

They returned to Khaled's room and dropped onto a pile of cushions where they lay for a while, silenced by thought. Eventually, Khaled smiled, 'It wasn't as hard as we expected, was it?'

'I can never thank you enough.'

'It's the other way around,' Khaled said, leaping to his feet. 'You're letting me marry your sister.'

Moving to sit cross-legged on the carpet, Ethan said, 'Your father is offering so much. I've never known such generosity!'

'It's not all give. He expects us to work hard in return and make the farm a success.'

'I don't see how anything can stop us,' Ethan replied. 'We know the meaning of *work*. It'll be the best farm in Al Andalous.' His face took on a serious expression as he realised there was something he needed to ask. 'Khaled, what do you think about me marrying Floria?'

'It's a good idea.' The question was unexpected but the speed of Khaled's reply showed he'd already given the matter some thought. 'The way she looks at you is quite different from the way she looks at me. She likes me but she doesn't love me. With you, it's a lot more. That's why I once asked if I should get out of your way.'

'You didn't need to.'

'Ethan, don't take this the wrong way, but this morning you couldn't afford to marry Floria. In fact, you couldn't afford to marry anybody. Soon, you'll have enough money to marry anyone you like. Do you think she'll still satisfy you?'

Ethan's expression changed to one of irritated bewilderment. 'You chose my sister when you could have picked anyone you liked. You've just said Floria and I have got something special. Now you're telling me the opposite. I don't want your questions, Brother. I want to know whether you'd accept her as a sister-in-law.'

'It's you she's marrying, not me. It doesn't matter whether I'd accept her or not,'

'It matters to me.'

'You once told me I didn't know what it was like to be poor,' Khaled began. 'You said Floria did what she did to feed her family. I've thought a lot about that. At first it felt like we'd been taking advantage of someone who'd got nothing to sell apart from her body. On the other hand, if we hadn't gone to her, you two would never have met. So a lot of good came out of it.'

'We can't carry on, though. Going with the same girl.'

'Not with Floria. She's going to be your wife!'

'She'll be expecting us as soon as Ramadan is over.'

'You'd better go on your own.'

'Come off it, Khaled. We're not married yet!'

12

Two days later, Ramadan ended. Khaled helped Ethan with the work so they could get off early. They sluiced themselves clean, shaved and scrubbed their teeth until the gums bled. Ethan remembered the price he'd paid for drenching himself with body freshener, and this time, he splashed it on sparingly. They picked out a couple of Khaled's best tunics, told each other they looked good and went to meet up with Reuben and Danny. The four of them knew what they wanted and headed straight for The Barrels.

They were too full of the evening ahead to notice they were being watched. Nor did they pay much attention to the tavern in the next alley. It was a dead looking place that never got many customers. If Khaled and his friends had bothered to look through the doorway, they'd have seen a couple of low-voiced men talking as they hunched over a table.

'His brother won't agree to that. He wants him hurt, but he'd never go that far.'

'Then you've been wasting my time, Sulieman. I'm not here to talk about what can't be done.'

'I'm not saying it can't be done. I'm telling you his brother mustn't find out, that's all.'

'He won't find out.'

'And you're sure there's no way back?'

'There's no way back.'

At *The Barrels*, the friends didn't bother with beer; they thumped straight up the uneven stone steps. Danny and Reuben grabbed the first good-looking girls to catch their eyes, while Khaled and Ethan made for Floria's room.

She'd been shopping for clothes, and she'd bought well. Her simple, close-fitting dress hinted at things to come. The rest lay in her lovers' imaginations. Floria had chosen the food and drink with equal care. Beer made men piss and flop, so there'd be none of that. Instead, she'd spiced up the wine with cinnamon, ginger and cloves. She'd buttered the asparagus and spent some of Ethan's money on oysters. Love potions and witchcraft, some might say. She preferred to think of them as tricks of the trade. This was going to be her night. It wouldn't be bad for the boys, either.

She knew they'd be coming. Even so, they took her by surprise. When Ethan and Khaled burst through the door, they found her sitting by the unshuttered window, drying her hair in the evening sunshine.

'Pigs!' she screamed, catching Ethan's head with her brush. 'You keep me waiting for a month. Then, when you finally get here, I'm a mess!'

'Come here *mess*!' Ethan grabbed her into his arms and kissed her violently. Khaled felt left out. That was until Floria winked at him, 'Come on, it's both of you I want!'

They ripped off their clothes and stood for a moment, eyeing each other's nakedness. Floria's fist was between her teeth. It was bitten knuckles or the giggles and men's cocks were no laughing matter. 'A couple of surprises!'

'Don't you like them any more?' Ethan looked like a boy who'd worked hard picking out a present for his girl, only to see her disappointed.

'Of course I like them. They'll take a bit of getting used to, that's all.'

She grabbed for him, and that meant things were fine. Then she started with her tongue and things weren't so good. Ethan watched helplessly as his semen jetted out, flooding her face and breasts. 'I'm sorry …'

'For what? Loving me?' She pulled him towards the bed.

'No, for coming too soon. I wanted it to be good for you.'

'It will be. You've been waiting too long, that's all.'

Ethan humped his way to the other side of the bed, making room for Khaled. 'Let's see if you can do any better, Little Brother.'

Khaled knew he could. He moved astride the girl, kissing her face, her throat and her breasts while she wrapped her legs around him and pulled him close.

He didn't last much longer than Ethan. They crashed among the ruined sheets which made his friend feel happier about things. Catching Floria by the shoulder, Ethan threw her onto her back. It wasn't love but it was what they'd been waiting for.

Later, the three of them lay together, half asleep, exploring each other's bodies, until they heard Danny's voice. Ethan shook himself fully awake. 'We'd better get going as well. We've got work in the morning.'

Since Sheikh Omar had thrown Sulieman off the estate, the workers had been careful not to show sloppiness. Danny had been promoted to overseer and the first thing he did was smash up the canes. Nobody wanted to let him down. He was a fair man.

This time, when Floria said goodbye to her lovers, there was no struggle, only the tears in her eyes.

'Why was she crying?' Khaled wanted to know as they walked along the small passage towards the steps.

'She won't be shagging you again.'

'You told her about Inga and me?'

'I didn't need to. Inga got there ahead of me. You know what girls are - they talk. That's not it, though. We worked something out while you were snoring. She's moving into the farm so she can cook my food and wash my clothes. It'll give Mother a break. If things go right, we'll get married.'

Khaled put his arm around his friend's shoulders and they walked down the steps together and into a nightmare.

***

13

Danny and Reuben were waiting for them, huddled in a doorway and cursing the weather. Thick clouds darkened the moon and a gale lashed the alleyway, whipping up dust and dried leaves. Earlier, the sun had blazed in the blue Almerian sky while a light breeze rustled the palms. Now, the friends used cupped hands to shield their eyes as the cold wind drove grit into their faces.

It was Danny who noticed they weren't alone. He nodded towards a group of figures holed up in the doorway of a warehouse, 'Anyone know who they are? They're not from the town.'

'I don't like the look of them,' Ethan answered uneasily. 'Let's get back to the tavern!'

As they turned, a second gang of roughnecks detached themselves from the shadows and moved quickly to block the alley.

'Trouble!' Danny shouted, 'We're going to have to fight our way out.'

Rocks and stones glanced off the wall next to their heads, forcing them to back into a doorway. It was the wrong move. The gangs moved in and the friends knew they were trapped.

Using fists and knees, they laid out several of their attackers but the result was never in doubt. The weight of numbers crushed them to the ground while cruel boots and fists slammed into their unprotected bodies. Eventually, they lay bloody, silent and unmoving.

Several of the attackers used lengths of rope to tie their wrists and ankles, while others led a horse and wagon from the next alley. Their unconscious bodies were thrown roughly into the back of the cart and it was led off towards the harbour.

As consciousness returned, Ethan lay shivering and filled with pain. The air was cold, yet the overpowering stench of damp wood and tar made it stifling. In the nearly total darkness, it was impossible to make out anything more than vague shapes. Only the pitching, rocking motion beneath them told him they were at sea.

His arms were behind his back, held by something he couldn't see. When he tried to move his legs, pain burned into his ankles. For the first time in his life, he was gripped by terror. Was this where he would die - alone and helpless in the dark? The breath rasped desperately in his throat. He needed to call out, to know if any of his friends were with him. All he could manage was a harsh croak. Then, he heard Reuben's voice. He was calling for his brother and Danny yelled back. Ethan heard an urgent shuffling and guessed they were trying to drag their way towards each other. Then there was Khaled's voice. He hollered a reply and heard his friend working through the darkness towards him.

They were tied in the same manner and Ethan struggled into a position from which he could try and loosen the cords around his friend's wrists. It would be a long job. He was working blind and his own ropes made it next to impossible to move. Danny was having more success; he'd managed to force his hands free and after briefly rubbing his numb, chafed wrists, started to tear at the cords which held his ankles.

They had no means of telling how long they'd been on board but as the sun rose and the level of light increased, they realised they were down in the boat's hold. The only way out was through a metal gate. It was old and rusty but they could see it was well chained and locked. A large grill had been let into the deck above their heads and through it, the sun started to warm their bodies. By dragging themselves closer to the source of ventilation, it became easier to breathe. They listened to the coarse shouts of the crew and learned they had already rounded Cabo de Gata and were heading north.

'Quick, lend a hand here. One of the dogs has got loose!' A seaman, brute-faced and with a leather quirt dangling from his hand, peered between the bars of the gate. He could see Danny was no longer tied. Half a dozen members of the crew, all carrying knives and hefty lengths of wood, ran to help.

'Get back against the bulkhead, where we can see you,' one of the men shouted gesticulating with his curved dagger. The prisoners shuffled away from the entrance as the gate was unlocked and all seven crew members poured into the hold. They kicked and clubbed their victims while menacing them with their blades. Obeying a roughly shouted order from their leader, Danny was seized by four of the seamen and flung against the gate. Using the same ropes with which he'd originally been tied, he was spread-eagled and made fast to the bars. One of the men approached with his dagger. He touched the tip menacingly against Danny's face, throat and back before hacking away his tunic and leaving him naked.

The seaman holding the quirt positioned himself behind and to the side of his prisoner. He took a swift couple of paces forward and using his full weight, brought down the whip. Ethan saw Reuben wince as the lash cut across his brother's shoulders. Moments later, a second stroke tore savagely at Danny's back. Varying his aim, the whipper struck without warning, targeting the shoulders, back, buttocks and thighs of the helpless man. Ethan saw Danny strain every muscle in a futile attempt to free himself. He could only guess at the agony searing through his friend's body. For Danny, nothing would exist beyond the burning hell of the lash and the jeers of his torturers.

The whipper swaggered in front of his unconscious victim. 'You'd like a chance to get back at me,' he sneered at the prisoners. 'I can see it on your faces. Don't even think about it. You'll get the same as he got.'

Turning to the grinning seamen he yelled, 'Get their wrists and ankles properly chained but leave them enough slack so they can get to the water. When you've done that, bring in the trough and let them drink from it like the infidel pigs they are. We don't want to arrive with a cargo of dead slaves.'

Danny was starting to regain consciousness. 'Chain him!' the seaman ordered. 'Make sure he can get to the water. We'll get a good price for a slave of his size.'

'With that back?' one of the crew members sneered, 'They'll see he's been whipped. It's the sure sign of a trouble maker.'

'Where he's going, they all end up like that,' the man told him. 'Mines are hard places and the one this bunch are going to is the worst I've come across in a long while. The rock face is like iron so the overseers have to use plenty of whip. They say Almaden's worse. I've never seen it and from what I hear tell, I'm not in any hurry to see it, either.'

He was laughing, enjoying the picture of suffering he was painting. 'They're told how much they've got to get out of the ground every day. If they go over that, they get paid extra. If they don't, they lose money. They make up the shortfall by breaking more rock the next day. It's not a bad system. Everybody wins. The mine owners are happy because there's no drop in output and the overseers don't lose out either. They see to it the slaves put in the extra work. When there's money at stake, you can be sure they'll do that alright. I'll tell you something else. These slaves are the best we've had for a year or two. Sulieman said they were a strong bunch. We'll be in the money as soon as we've sold them on.' Crashing the metal gate shut behind them, the seamen clambered back on deck, arguing excitedly about how much they were going to make and the women and drink it would buy.

Reuben, Khaled and Ethan dragged themselves over to where Danny lay on his belly. They helped him drink by soaking parts of his ripped tunic in the trough and squeezing the water into his mouth. At the same time, Reuben was using more pieces of rag to wash his brother's tortured back. Once the blood had been swabbed clear, they could see the extent of the damage. Danny's body was a mass of welts and bruises that reached from his shoulders to the thighs. Mercifully, however, the quirt had torn the skin in very few places.

The friends watched Ethan piss onto one of the rags. They knew what was coming. It was an old trick used by labourers when any of them had an open wound. Reuben folded another piece of rag and

Michael Horrex

put it between Danny's teeth. 'Bite on that,' he said quietly and held his brother while urine was swabbed across his cuts.

***

14

Reuben and Danny were the first to be missed. When they didn't turn up for work, Sheikh Omar sent for his son. As soon as he was told that Khaled and Ethan couldn't be found either, he realised something was seriously wrong.

Ethan's family, meanwhile, suspected nothing. He'd been staying with Khaled for most of Ramadan when they didn't see him for a few days, they weren't particularly worried. It wasn't until the sheikh's men arrived at the farm, asking where Khaled was, that both families knew their sons were missing. To add to her fears, Inga was afraid Floria might be blamed for the boys' disappearance. She decided that for the time being, it would be better not to say anything about her friend.

Sheikh Omar suspected that Khaled and Ethan had been visiting one of the waterfront taverns on the night they went missing. He sent several of their workmates to enquire and they soon traced the young men's movements to *The Three Barrels*.

At first, Floria was careful not to say too much in case she caused trouble for her lovers. However, as soon as Sheikh Omar's people convinced her they were only interested in finding the missing men, she gave them as much help as she could. Better still, she spoke to several customers who'd been drinking in the tavern on the night of the friends' disappearance. From what they told her, she was able to piece together a number of disturbing facts. The most worrying was that a slave ship had been seen close to shore. Floria went straight to the sheikh's home. As soon as he heard she was asking to see him, he told the servants to show her to the majlis.

Khaled's father wasn't at all as she'd expected. Instead of the cold, remote figure she'd imagined, she found a gentle, smiling man who welcomed her warmly. In spite of his beard, she could see a clear resemblance between him and his son. Omar's face was older, of course, but he had those same dark eyes and fine white teeth. His hair was no longer black but it curled like Khaled's as it framed a still-handsome face.

She told him everything she'd managed to find out and he immediately recognised the gravity of the situation. If Khaled and Ethan had been taken to the north, there was little chance of getting them back. Relations between the Muslim and Christian-held territories had worsened to such an extent over the past few years that diplomatic contacts were no longer possible.

'How well do you know my son and his friend?' he asked.

Floria had no idea how much Sheikh Omar already knew about their relationship. The man spoke kindly enough but she was still afraid he might blame her and Inga for the boys' disappearance. She explained that Ethan was the man she was going to marry and Khaled was his best friend.

'In that case you must know Inga,' Sheikh Omar said.

'We've been friends for most of our lives,' she told him. 'I was born in Felix and we played together as children. I used to see Ethan as well, but only from time to time. At that age, boys and girls don't have much to do with each other. These days, I only see Inga occasionally. My mother and sisters still live in the village, so when I visit them, I try to fit in a visit to Inga's home as well. There's the market, of course. Sometimes we meet there.' She started to wonder if being her friend might damn Inga in the old man's eyes so she quickly added, 'Inga's a good girl. She's not like me.'

Omar looked at this frank, open-faced girl and placed a fatherly hand on her shoulder. Its warmth reassured her and she smiled up at him. 'It took courage for you to come and speak to me,' he said.

'May I ask you a question?' She watched his face carefully, afraid she might be going too far. His smile remained gentle, however, and she felt safe to continue. 'How is it you could agree to a marriage between your son and a poor Christian girl?'

'I've known Inga's family for a long time,' he told her. 'The father was an honest, hardworking man. As the children were born, I naturally heard about them as well.' He looked away for a moment and Floria noticed a catch in his voice as he added, 'It was a sad business about the father. He was a young man when he died.'

Floria was still looking puzzled, 'But Ethan is your slave and Inga is his sister.'

'My son loves her and I love my son,' he smiled. 'Her brother Ethan has worked on my estate for several years. It's true he's a bonded servant but that's not the same as being a slave. It was agreed between his family and mine that he'd work for ten years, as a way of paying for their farm. Three more years and he'll be as free as you or I. He's grown into a fine young man. If Inga is anything like her brother, Khaled is a lucky fellow.'

'Sheikh Omar, do you know how I earn my living?' Floria looked straight at him, waiting for his reaction.

'Yes,' he replied, returning her look. 'I also know that your father is dead and your family is poor. It's easy to be virtuous with a full belly. Now you and Ethan have agreed to marry, I'm sure there will be room in your life for only one man. The one who will be your husband.'

'Ethan knows I'll never betray him.'

'Even with Khaled?'

'There was no betrayal,' she managed to stammer.

Sheikh Omar followed with an even more alarming question, 'Floria, would you say that my son was a good lover?' Her eyes opened wide with astonishment and he knew she deserved an explanation. 'I'm sorry if my words shock you,' he said, 'But I need to know the answer. You must believe me when I tell you that it's neither malicious nor idle curiosity that prompts my question.'

The man seemed to know more or less everything there was to know about her relationship with Ethan and his son. This further fragment of information, intimate though it was, could hurt no-one. Even so, she wasn't sure how to answer and felt her way slowly, searching for the right words. 'A lot of men have used me,' she began. 'They took what they wanted and left as quickly as they came.' There was an expression of understanding on the old man's face that encouraged her to continue. 'Khaled and Ethan are different. They treat me as every woman hopes to be treated; as a person with feelings and the right to be respected. Yes, Sheikh Omar, I would say that your son is a very good lover.'

'You say that and yet you must realise no two people could be closer than Ethan and my son. Do you believe they are men who have room in their lives for women?'

'They love women! There's no doubt in my mind about that. They live for each other, it's true, but they'll make wonderful husbands.' She'd spoken as frankly as she could but there was something she needed to ask, 'You do believe we'll see Ethan and Khaled again, don't you?'

He'd anticipated her question but that didn't make it any easier to reply. 'Only Allah knows the answer to that,' he said. 'In the past, whenever my son and Ethan were together, his mother and I were confident they'd be safe. We allowed Khaled to move around freely because we believed it was necessary for him to gain as much experience of life as possible. We were not blind to the risks but by over-protecting him, we felt we'd be denying him the right to develop as an individual. Clearly, we under-estimated the danger. There is comfort to be drawn from Ethan and Khaled's closeness, however. They would defend each other with their lives and that gives us reason to hope. At the same time, we must be realistic. These are dangerous times and relations with the Christians in the north have never been worse.'

'But Ethan ...'

'Ethan is a Christian,' Sheikh Omar finished the sentence for her. 'Unfortunately, his co-religionaries might no longer see him as such. For most of his life, he has lived and worked with *infidels*, which is how they regard Muslims and Jews. They could view him as a heretic.'

Floria's legs felt as though they would no longer support her. It was only Sheikh Omar's steadying grip on her arm that saved her from falling. 'I'm sorry to have spoken so bluntly,' he said.

'No, I must thank you for your frankness,' she replied, forcing a smile. 'And I must apologise for acting so foolishly. It won't happen again. I usually have little sympathy for people who behave feebly when faced with the truth.'

'We must let Inga and her mother know what you've found out,' he continued. 'They have the right to know. With Ethan gone, there are only women at the farm and it wouldn't be appropriate for me to visit them alone. If you're feeling strong enough, will you come with me?'

Floria nodded.

***

15

They were held for half a day in a small, dark warehouse, close to the harbour. When the seamen's leader returned, he had with him a flamboyantly dressed man whose heavily accented Spanish told them he was from the north. The crew members were treating him with great respect and addressed him as Don Garcia.

'Let's see what you've got for us this time,' he said. 'If they're as good as you say, we might be able to do a deal.'

One of the seamen wrenched back the shutters, and sunlight flooded the room. The prisoners, dazzled by its glare, were made to stand in a confused and defenceless group while their tunics were hacked off. Reuben was the first to be dragged forward for inspection. He was ordered to turn around and, as far as his wrist and ankle chains would allow, flex his muscles.

The purchaser nodded approvingly and moved on to look at Danny. He could see the man was strong and in prime condition but in several places the lash had sliced away skin, showing raw flesh beneath.

'They speak for themselves, those cuts,' Garcia said. 'This one's a troublemaker!'

'Those few marks?' the seamen's leader snorted defensively, 'They don't add up to anything. He'd got his ropes undone, so we gave him a few strokes with the quirt to teach him a lesson. He knows better now. He's not rebellious or anything like that. If he was, we'd have given him a good working over with the lash.'

'Learned your lesson, have you boy?'

'Yes, Don Garcia.' Danny looked at the floor, ashamed of his nakedness.

'I hope that's true, for your sake,' Garcia said. 'That whipping was nothing to what you'll get if you give us any trouble.' His tone was granite cold. Danny's offence might have been trivial in itself but discipline had to be maintained. 'You did the right thing,' Garcia told the seaman. 'If they think they can get away with that sort of thing so soon into their captivity, there's no knowing what they'll try later.'

He spent time looking closely at the merchandise, running his hands over the men's bodies, prodding and testing until he seemed satisfied with their physiques and general condition. It was their hair and skin colourings that puzzled him. Turning to one of the seamen, he asked, 'Are they all Muslims? They've been circumcised, but apart from that, they're nothing like the ones I've had from you in the past.'

'I don't know whether they are or not. They're infidels and that makes them slaves as far as we're concerned.'

'We're not infidels,' Danny tried to explain, 'We're Jews. The first one of us you looked at, he's my brother.'

'Jews! Muslims!' Garcia sneered, 'You're all infidels to civilised men.' He moved on to examine Ethan. 'What about you, boy? You don't look like the others.'

'I'm a Christian, Don Garcia. My family came from the north.'

'That explains the hair and the skin but, how come you've been cut? Are you sure you're not a Jew or a Muslim?'

'A lot of men are circumcised,' Ethan replied angrily. 'They're not all Muslims or Jews.'

Garcia drew back his fist, ready to strike, and then appeared to have second thoughts. He slid his hands slowly over Ethan's body, fingering his muscles and toying with his hair. 'If you're speaking the truth, we might be able to use you in a different job. But God help you if you're lying.'

Khaled recognised the danger in Garcia's face. He'd seen Sulieman eyeing his friend in a similar way and it had always led to trouble. 'He's not lying,' he told the man. 'We've known him for years. He's a Christian. We were circumcised at the same time. But that doesn't mean …'

Garcia silenced him with a glare before moving closer to the young prisoner. 'You've got the look of an infidel Moor. Am I right?'

'I'm a Muslim, Don Garcia, not an infidel. Christians, Jews and Muslims all believe in the one true God. Allah is the same God that you worship. You say Jesus was his son. We believe he was a prophet of God, second only in importance to Mohammed.'

An angry murmuring came from the fishermen and Garcia knew he couldn't afford to let the remarks pass. 'Watch your blasphemous tongue,' he spat at the boy, 'Or you'll get it ripped out.'

The seamen were growing impatient. Garcia was wasting time and looking for excuses to beat down the price. One of the crew members stepped forward and confronted him, 'They're strong healthy slaves, Señor. You can see that for yourself. Can't we talk business?'

'We can. But at half the price you're asking.'

'Be reasonable, Señor. They're good quality goods.'

'Times have changed,' Garcia told him smugly. 'These days, we can pick up any number of slaves, every bit as good as these, and for half the price we were paying a few years ago.'

There was a lot in what he said and the seamen knew it. The laws dealing with infidels and heretics meant there was a steady supply of criminals sentenced to hard labour. More often than not, the authorities were glad to get the surplus off their hands and sold slaves for next to nothing.

Tempers were beginning to flare. 'I'm hungry,' the seamen's leader said, in an attempt to calm the situation. 'You've seen what's on offer and you know what we want for them. Let's get something to fill our bellies. We can talk while we're eating.' They swung the shutters closed and left with their customer, in search of food.

Ethan and his friends clustered in a feeble patch of light that penetrated the gloom. 'Did you hear what they said on the boat, about Sulieman?' he asked.

Khaled nodded, 'It was that bastard who had us captured.'

When the seamen and their customer returned, they looked well fed and in a better frame of mind. A deal had been struck. Two men were ordered to give the slaves water and bread before chaining them for the night.

The forced march to the mine began at dawn. Shackled to restrict movement, the prisoners were lashed repeatedly for their lack of speed. It was the best part of a day's trek to the mine. They'd eaten nothing but dry bread since their capture and the last water they'd been given was back at the harbour. As the sun burned down, their thirst became ferocious. It was made worse by seeing both guards gulping greedily from their water-skins and spilling a large part of their supply. When Ethan asked for something to drink, one of the overseers answered him with the slash of a whip. 'You'll get water at the mine,' he snarled.

They moved slowly along the rough track while crowds of people gathered to stare and curse angrily. *'Slaves, Infidels!'* the men and women jeered. Others amused themselves by spitting or throwing rotten vegetables and excrement at the stumbling prisoners. Worse by far, were the children. They ran alongside, giggling and mocking the slaves' nakedness. They cut them with sharp stones and poked at their genitals with sticks. Some of the older boys tried to trip the shackled prisoners. Others broke thin, whippy branches from trees and played at being overseers by menacing and lashing their helpless victims.

Worn out, bloody and plastered with filth, the friends dragged themselves through an expanse of barren land. The area had once been fertile but was now nothing but wasted earth, torn at by men, ravenous for what lay beneath. They were halted at a collection of rough, stone buildings surrounding a crater. Filthy and foul smelling, the mine had ravaged its surroundings, as remorselessly as a vulture devours a corpse. The plants and trees that survived lay largely buried by sterile slag tips. They would die later, poisoned by widening stretches of putrid water.

'Welcome to the hell of the infidels,' yelled one of the overseers. 'Take a good look. It's where you'll learn to sweat blood before we send you to Almaden.'

The ropes that had linked the prisoners together were removed but their ankles and wrists remained chained. The guards pushed them towards the mouth of the crater. 'See that ladder?' one of them shouted. 'Get yourselves down it!'

The manacles and leg irons meant climbing was difficult, but the lash made sure they reached the bottom. It was the first gallery of the mine. The stench of human excrement, urine and the hot, dust-laden air burned into their throats. It made them choke and retch, while from all sides, an incessant hammering, the metallic rattle of chains and the harsh curses of the guards drove painfully into their ears.

Nothing in their previous lives could have prepared them for this scene from a nightmare. On all sides, overseers with whips yelled and lashed at sweating gangs of naked prisoners as they pickaxed the rock face. Slaves pounded and crushed the roughly hacked ore before shovelling it into wagons, to be dragged over the uneven ground by pairs of harnessed men.

Originally selected for their strength, the prisoners no longer displayed the confident manner of brawny men. Cowed by whippings, they kept their heads down as they worked and avoided eye contact with their overseers. To come to their attention invited punishment and the lash broke spirits.

Khaled nodded towards a couple of slaves, yoked like mules to a cart loaded with rocks. One of the wheels was buckled, making it almost impossible to drag the truck over the uneven ground. It frequently became wedged, causing the men to trip or fall to their knees. Even so, they were making some sort of progress. It wasn't enough. Their lack of speed infuriated the overseer and he lashed them repeatedly.

One of the guards nodded in the direction of a vat. The friends stumbled towards it, desperate for water. They were allowed to drink but the crack of the whip and a series of barked orders made it clear there would be no respite. An overseer pointed them towards the opening of a small tunnel. Beside it stood an empty wagon, identical to those they'd seen loaded with rocks and dragged by harnessed prisoners. After handing each of them a crude oil lantern, a hammer or a pick, the overseer ordered them into the tunnel.

Crawling on hands and knees, they made their way to the final section that opened into a small, low-ceilinged chamber. The overseer made no attempt to enter but his shouted curses followed them. 'Ten wagon loads before you eat. You've seen the size we want. Start breaking!'

They worked, crouched or lying on their bellies while sweat poured from their bodies and the shock of every blow jarred along their arms. The seaman who'd described the rock face as iron hard hadn't lied. It needed all of their strength to pickaxe loose even small quantities. In the hot, suffocating air, their breathing became laboured, while the dust and smoke from the oil lamps threatened to choke them.

Exhausted, deafened by their own hammering, their limbs cut and grazed, they continued to hack at the rock, pausing only to fill their buckets with the broken-off chunks of ore. They dragged them to the entrance of the tunnel and emptied them into the wagon.

The prisoners lost track of time and worked like mindless beings until the ten wagons were filled and the order was given to crawl back. After so long spent crouching, it was difficult to stand upright. Their breath rasped in their throats as they dragged themselves to the first gallery. Here they were fed and watered like animals.

While gulping desperately from the vat, they saw a stone trough filled with dry bread and hunks of rough, fatty meat. Before they could reach it, another gang elbowed their way towards the food. The guards watched, amused by the sight of starving men fighting over handfuls of scraps. Then, growing bored with the entertainment, they ordered the prisoners back to the surface.

'Enjoy your pig meat, did you?' one of the overseers jeered. 'Something special for our Jews and Muslims.' Danny and Reuben began to vomit the contents of their stomachs over the ground.

The prisoners were herded towards one of the stone buildings and into a dark, filthy cell where they were locked for the night. Ethan made them soak their cut and grazed skin with urine while Reuben cleaned away a coating of filth and took a look at Danny's back. To his relief, he saw that the cuts had started to scab over and showed no sign of infection. When he'd finished, the friends fell into an exhausted sleep on the hard earth floor.

***

16

The rattle of chains and a guard's curses woke the prisoners. Their eyes slowly became accustomed to the harsh light, and the friends were able to make out the silhouette of a second man in the open doorway. It was Garcia and he was keen to know more about the slave who claimed to be a Christian.

He walked around the group of still half-asleep prisoners until he spotted Ethan's straw-coloured hair. 'On your feet!' He prodded him with the toe of his boot and Ethan jumped up as quickly as his chains would allow. 'Get outside. I want the answers to a few questions.' Ethan looked desperately at his friends, as though they could prevent him from being taken away. It was hopeless. Garcia seized him by the shoulder and shoved him through the doorway. He was taken some distance from the building before the interrogation began.

'Let me hear you recite the creed, boy.'

'I believe in God …' Ethan wasn't allowed to finish.

'What about the ten commandments?'

Ethan had got as far as the first 'Thou shall not …' when Garcia ordered him to recite The Lord's Prayer. After a couple of sentences, Garcia seemed satisfied the boy had been telling the truth and started to question him about his previous life. 'Worked as a slave, did you?'

'Yes, Don Garcia.'

'Who did you work for?'

'Sheikh Omar, Señor. I worked in the stable yard.'

'Enjoy working for a Moor, did you?'

Ethan did his best to control his voice. He needed to stay calm and mask the hatred he felt for this appalling man. 'Slaves don't enjoy their lives, Señor. They do what they have to, in order to stay alive and keep out of trouble.'

'The Jews and that Moor?'

'They worked there as well, Señor.'

'Friends of yours, are they?'

It was a dangerous question. Ethan suspected it would be wise to distance himself from his companions. If he could do that convincingly, Garcia might allow him more freedom. 'Slaves don't have friends,' he replied. 'To survive, they have to do a lot of things, maybe even kill each other. They can't afford friendships.'

'I don't like the idea of Christians being enslaved by infidels,' Garcia said silkily. 'It isn't right. Having to obey people you hate and at the same time pretend to respect them. Is that how it was?'

'That's right, Señor.'

The slave owner's teeth were rotten. He moved closer to the young fair-haired prisoner and Ethan had to prevent himself from gagging at the stench of the man's breath. Garcia reached out to touch the boy's hair and then quickly withdrew his hand. The next time he spoke, his manner was brusque, 'Control a gang of slaves, could you?'

Ethan wasn't sure how to reply. 'I think so, Señor,' he said at last.

'That's not good enough. I need someone who can get work out of dead men. How would you feel about driving those friends of yours until they drop?'

'I wouldn't feel anything, Señor.'

Garcia wasn't convinced. 'That's what you say.'

'It's true, Señor. I'd do what was necessary. I'd get all the work you want out of them. Just give me the chance.'

'If you're lying to me …' Garcia's tone was menacing.

'I'm not lying, Señor.'

The man nodded. It was impossible to read his expression. 'We need pit props. You'll make a bit of money for yourself if you get those dogs of yours to cut down and trim-up enough trees. You'll be told how many are needed every day. Make them cut more and you'll earn yourself a bonus. Can you do that or shall I give the job to someone else?'

It was too good an opportunity to miss. If Ethan was allowed to work with his friends, he might be able to get them better food and even look for a chance to escape. 'I can do it Señor. You don't need to find anyone else. You said I could use the men I came with. Will you give me a free hand with them?'

'When you've proved yourself. In the meanwhile, make sure none of them gets any funny ideas. That goes for you as well. We'll be watching. If the work drops off, you'll lose the bonuses you've earned. I'm holding you responsible. If any of them so much as think about escaping, I'll have the lot of you whipped and back underground.'

'Don Garcia,' Ethan began hesitantly, afraid he might be overstepping the mark, 'Last night the guards fed them pig meat. Jews and Muslims can't eat that Señor. It's against their religion. If we want a good day's work out of them, they'll need proper food. Starving men are no use to us.' *'Us'*, the word rang in Ethan's ears like a betrayal.

'The overseers do that sometimes. It's their idea of a joke.' Garcia's manner was surprisingly reasonable. 'But you're right. I'll see to it they get something to eat before they start work.'

'And some water, Señor. So they can wash themselves.'

Garcia gave a sudden laugh. He'd always been amused by the way Muslims and Jews found it necessary to wash themselves. No decent Christian was always swabbing away at his body. 'Very well, they'll get their water. You as well, I suppose?'

'Yes please, Señor.'

'You've lived with them so long, you've caught their habits.' He gave orders that the new prisoners should be fed straight away and then had Ethan's chains removed. A sullen looking guard brought him a couple of buckets of water and Ethan began to wash off the previous day's filth. Garcia stood watching, fascinated by the way the sun highlighted the boy's golden hair while drying his naked body.

Ethan felt Garcia's hand begin to caress his back and shoulders. The movements weren't aggressive and yet they were repulsive. Snake-like, the hand slid slowly across his buttocks, down over his thighs and around to the front, finally taking hold of his genitals. He fought to suppress a shudder of revulsion as the man started to fondle him.

'Do you like that?'

'Please Señor, don't.' Ethan was trying to control his voice, desperate to conceal the loathing he felt.

Garcia let go of him. He handed the boy a rough tunic, identical to those worn by the overseers. 'Put it on,' he said in what could have been mistaken for a pleasant tone of voice. Ethan continued to stare ahead, afraid to look at the man. Terrified of encouraging his touch.

'You'll need this.' Garcia handed him a coiled whip. 'Get your Jews and that Moor ready to move. Fernando will be going with you for a few weeks to keep an eye on things. He'll show you what's needed. Do the job well and it's yours. Try any funny business and the lot of you will be back down the mine. The same goes if you're caught talking to them. Orders and nothing else. Any more than that and we'll know you're cooking something up.'

Ethan knew there was worse to come. Garcia's fondling had been the first move. He needed to speak to Khaled and explain the situation to him and his friends; otherwise it would look as if he was throwing in his lot with the mine owner. He'd have to wait for the right moment; Fernando would be listening to every word, watching every move and reporting back to Garcia. If he was going to be of any use to his friends, Ethan would have to carry out his job exactly as Garcia demanded. Their survival, as well as his own, depended on convincing the man he was trustworthy.

***

There had to be an explanation, some good reason, why Ethan was dressed as an overseer. Khaled took a step towards his friend, opened his mouth to speak but was silenced by the threat of a lashing. Ethan saw the contempt on Danny and Reuben's faces as they turned away, muttering that he'd betrayed them. Harder to bear was the hurt in Khaled's eyes.

Fernando directed them along a path that led through the woods, driving them on until they finally reached a clearing. He pointed out the trees that were to be felled and showed them a pit prop that had already been prepared. They should take careful note of its length, he told them, and the way the branches had been trimmed from its trunk.

It was risky issuing slaves with axes. There wasn't much chance of chained men mutinying, but Fernando didn't relax his vigilance for an instant. Ethan was permitted to direct the felling and trimming of the trees. Apart from that, he had no chance to speak to his former friends.

At night, when they were locked up, he was made to sleep alone in a separate part of the camp. In his solitary cell, Ethan experienced fear-filled nights, followed by traitor-mornings. Waking to sunshine and the song of birds, he'd reach out, only to find nothing of his former life, merely the chain-weight reality of a new existence. It was here, in this terrible place, that Garcia forced himself on the young man.

Ethan's unwillingness to co-operate annoyed him. The mine owner preferred willing partners and he'd tried bribing him with small favours. They'd failed to soften the boy.

'Khaled's a good friend of yours?' he asked unexpectedly.

The conversational tone caught Ethan off-guard. 'I worked with him, Señor. That's all.' His face betrayed him. Garcia noticed a slight movement of the boy's eyes and the beginning of a smile at the mention of Khaled's name. He would put the knowledge to good use.

'How did the Jew earn himself that lashing?' Garcia asked on another occasion. Ethan told him the seaman's story had been more or less accurate. Danny had managed to get his ropes untied.

Garcia sneered, pretending not to believe him. 'Stop trying to cover up for them,' he snarled. 'Muslims and Jews! They're all the same. Give them a chance and they'll be down on you like a pack of wolves. There's only one way to make dangerous animals docile. Castrate them. I'll see to it in the morning.'

'Don't do that Señor,' Ethan pleaded, 'They'll work hard. I'll make sure they don't cause any trouble.'

'You'd do anything to save your friends, wouldn't you?' Garcia knew his threat hadn't been wasted. He had the advantage and he'd play the boy like a fish.

Ethan had tried to ignore his friends' hostility. At first, their faces had shown disbelief. Now, as he was forced more and more into the role of an overseer, they no longer bothered to hide their contempt. He could tolerate their loathing but there was no way he could rid his mind of the pain he'd seen in Khaled's eyes.

He'd worked hard to gain Fernando's trust. The old man was puzzled by Ethan's unwillingness to use the whip. On the other hand, his young apprentice kept the slaves hard at work and they usually exceeded their daily quota. Although he never said so, Fernando must have been satisfied with the bonuses he received because he shared some of them with Ethan. The young man saved the few coins he was given, hoping that one day, they'd amount to something.

Fernando managed to profit from his job in another way. He traded the branches and twigs the slaves trimmed from the pit-props to fishermen on the nearby beach. They needed the loppings for the fires over which they smoked a good part of their catch. In exchange, they gave Fernando fish and other food. Most of this, he kept for himself. Anything he didn't fancy, he gave to his young assistant. The weeks passed and Fernando became more trusting and less vigilant. Ethan began to hope a day would come when he'd be left alone with the slaves while the old man bargained with the fishermen.

By nature, Garcia was a bully. Nevertheless, there were occasions when he showed something that approached kindness. After satisfying himself, he would speak pleasantly to Ethan and even display a degree of remorse. The young man used those times to obtain favours for his friends. He persuaded Garcia to send them extra rations of food and drinking water. They were allowed to eat in the cleaner, better ventilated cell to which they had been moved. This avoided further humiliating fights for food and in addition to goat meat; they now found fresh fish, eggs or fruit with their meal.

More importantly, Ethan had managed to persuade Garcia that the slaves' shackles were hampering their work. Over time, they chafed and threatened to ulcerate the flesh. Instead, they were fitted with light chains, loosely attached to leather belts. These would be easier to break, of course, and they were warned that any tampering would lead to severe punishment.

***

Khaled was struggling with a lopped branch that had snagged in the undergrowth. Fernando was busy with a new batch of fish so he didn't bother to look up when Ethan shouted that there was a problem. Out of the corner of his eye, the old man noticed his apprentice grab a whip before starting in Khaled's direction. The boy was learning, he smiled to himself.

It might have been because he'd seen the lash or perhaps he could no longer bear the sight of his former friend, but as Ethan drew closer, Khaled turned his back and started to move away. Ethan felt a surge of irritation. 'Don't walk away from me!' he snapped.

Khaled ignored him.

'Bastard!' The words began as a curse but ended as a plea. 'Speak to me!'

Fernando was still muttering over the fish. Ethan took a chance and grabbed his friend by the shoulder. It was a move they'd used in the past and had always seemed warmer than words. Khaled shrugged Ethan's hand away.

'I miss you,' Ethan began.

Khaled raised his head, not to look at his friend but to stare blankly through him. 'I wish you were dead,' he muttered tonelessly.

'Things aren't what they seem.'

Khaled's eyes briefly met Ethan's. 'What did I ever do to you?' he asked.

'Try to trust me, Little Brother.'

Khaled let the branch drop. He nodded at the whip in Ethan's hand. 'What are you going to do with that? Lash trust into me?'

'If it was that easy …' He paused, not sure how to continue. 'When did we lie to each other, Khaled?' he asked. 'I've needed to speak to you but they're watching me all the time.' He took hold of the tree branch and tried to help wrench it free. It held fast. 'This is the first chance I've had. If Fernando catches us talking, we're finished. I haven't betrayed you, Khaled. I swear I'm doing what I can to get us out of here but I need your help.'

The words were starting to hit home. Khaled wanted to believe them and looked directly at his friend for the first time in weeks. The change in Ethan's appearance made him gasp. His face was older and the expression in his eyes contained a mixture of pain and self-loathing. But there was something else. It was that same expression of sincerity Khaled had known since the day they first met. 'You're not lying!' he wanted to shout but forced himself to whisper.

Ethan shook his head very slightly, 'I'm not lying.'

'It was you who got us the food and water, wasn't it?' Khaled turned back to the tree with its still trapped branches. For a while, it seemed he was trying to rip it to pieces. 'God forgive me, Ethan, but I've hated you.'

'You didn't understand.'

'Did you mean what you said,' Khaled asked, 'About getting us out of here?'

'There might be a chance,' Ethan said quietly, 'It's no more than that. But if it comes, it'll be soon. That's when I'll need your help.'

'We'll help, you know we will. It's our lives we're talking about!' He was starting to grin and that was dangerous. 'Get that look off your face before the guards see it,' Ethan snapped. 'And for God's sake, make sure Danny and Reuben don't do anything rebellious.'

'I'll warn them.'

'While you're at it, find out which of them speaks Hebrew best.'

***

17

Five Jews had been burned to death in a neighbouring village. They'd converted to Christianity in the hope of protecting their families but behind closed doors, they'd kept to their old ways. Their heresy had come to light when neighbours denounced three of them for not eating pig meat. It turned out that their sons had been circumcised and not one of them had ever worked on the Sabbath. The evidence was overwhelming and the court sentenced them to the stake.

'People I know, saw it,' Fernando gloated. 'They reckon infidels melt when they're burned, and that's a good while before they die.' What with the burnings and the fact he was getting more fish than ever in exchange for the wood, the old man was almost jaunty.

Ethan suppressed a shudder at the thought of the Jews' torture-laden deaths. He urgently needed to make contact with the fishermen and offered to carry the wood down to the beach. Fernando would have none of it. If there was business to be done, he'd be the one to do it. Besides, he knew how to handle the Jews.

But Ethan had sown a seed and a few days later, Fernando decided he'd had enough. 'My back's killing me,' he complained. 'Dragging that wood down to the beach, that's what's done it. It's time you took your turn with the sledge. Make sure you get a good deal. The position they're in, they can't argue.'

Matanza!

The fishermen were waiting on the shore, surprised to see Ethan but keen to do business. They were worried men and their anxiety made them talk. 'It's our houses and boats they're after,' one of them was saying.

'They'll use any excuse to get their hands on our money,' his friend agreed, 'Then spend it running their damned inquisition. How are we supposed to pay the new taxes when they won't let us set up stall in the market?'

Ethan now understood why the wood had become so important. The Jews couldn't sell their fish and had to preserve most of their catch by smoking it. From what they were saying, he could tell things were getting worse by the day. They were now in danger of being hounded out of the village altogether.

'We've been here longer than most of them!' one man shouted angrily. 'Four generations of my family have lived in this village. Now they're saying we've no right to be here.'

'They won't let us sell our fish but they still expect us to find money for the taxes,' another added. 'Taxes for not being Christians, that's what they amount to. They know we'll never be able to pay them and that'll give them the excuse they're looking for to grab everything we own.'

'They've taken my brother's boy for forced labour,' his comrade yelled, 'There's more of it every day. You hear about it in all the villages.' He was eyeing Ethan's blond hair and pale skin as though they were emblems of the oppressor, 'You're happy enough eating our fish as long as it's cheap but you don't want us living next door to you!'

'What's the matter with us?' the first man asked. 'We're no different from you. We used to live and work side by side. We never had these problems. Where are we supposed to go if we can't live here?' He raised his arms skywards as he spoke, as though appealing to heaven for an answer.

'You've got your boats,' Ethan told him. 'You're better off than most of us. You can get away and start again.'

'That's easy enough for you to say,' one of the fishermen spat angrily. 'We're the wrong religion. There's nowhere for us to go.'

'Because you're Jews?'

'You know bloody well it is,' the man spat again. 'That's why you're kicking us out!'

'I'm not kicking anybody out.' Ethan picked up the basket of food and turned to leave. 'Will you be here for a few more days?'

'Until you finally drive us out. God knows where we'll be then.'

***

Fernando eyed the basket of fish greedily. 'You took long enough but we won't go hungry.' He started dividing the food into two piles - a generous one for himself and a meaner one for his young assistant.

Ethan seized the opportunity. Trying to move as casually as he could, he wandered over to where Khaled was working. He glanced back at Fernando and was relieved to see the old man still absorbed by his task. Keeping his eye on the man, Ethan put a hand on Khaled's shoulder, 'Did you talk to Danny and Reuben, about the Hebrew?'

'Neither of them speaks much. Enough to pray. That's as far as it goes.'

'It might be enough.'

'Enough for what?'

'I'm not sure, but it could come in handy.'

Khaled's eyes were alight with hope. 'I've told you before to get that look off your face,' Ethan said. 'There's nothing any of us can do for the time being, so settle down and don't make the guards suspicious.'

The next day, he was allowed to go to the beach again. 'You got a good deal yesterday,' Fernando said, 'Make sure you get a better one today.'

'I'll take the Jews with me. That wood nearly broke my back yesterday.'

'One of them will do,' Fernando told him, 'And don't keep him away from his work too long or there'll be no bonus for either of us.'

Ethan dragged one of the large wooden sledges over to where Danny was hacking the branches off a tree. 'Fill that with firewood,' he barked. 'Be quick about it and then follow me!'

Danny started to wrap a cloth around his waist but Ethan told him to leave it off. 'I want the fishermen to see you've been cut,' he explained, as soon as they were out of earshot. 'They're Jews and they don't trust me because I'm not one of them. They need to get away from here as much as we do. They've got their boats but nowhere to go in them. You've got to convince them to take us to Almeria. If they'll do that, Khaled's father will give them enough land to build homes for themselves and their families.'

Danny wasn't so sure, 'I'm not lying, Ethan. Giving them false hope so we can make use of them.'

'It won't be false hope. Before this happened, Khaled asked if he could marry my sister.'

'He told me.'

'His father said we could have the land from the farm to the coast.'

'He told me that as well.'

'I give you my word, Danny, it won't be false hope you'll be raising. That land I'm talking about, they'll get part of it. So will you and Reuben.'

The fishermen watched Ethan and Danny pull the sledge towards them. '*Shalom*,' Danny called out, combing his memory for more Hebrew words. Most of the men were no more fluent in the language than he was. The few words he remembered, and the fact he was circumcised, persuaded most of them he was a Jew, but there was something wrong about the way he and the fair-haired overseer were standing together. They were too comfortable in each other's company, behaving more like equals than master and slave.

One of the young fishermen circled around them, his suspicious eyes missing nothing. The still-scarred state of Danny's back made him wince. 'He's been lashed!' he shouted angrily. 'That's the way *Straw Hair* treats Jews.'

'It wasn't his doing,' Danny said, stepping between Ethan and his accuser. 'We were taken prisoner together in Almeria. I was whipped while we were on the boat. It was nothing to do with Ethan. He's a slave, the same as I am.'

'So what's he doing, dressed like that and carrying a whip?'

'He's a Christian, so they made him an overseer. We didn't understand what was happening, either. He'd always been a friend of ours so we thought he'd betrayed us. That was until we found out he'd been using his religion and his skin colour to get the mine owner to trust him.'

'You can believe that, if you like!' an old man shouted from where he was smoking the day's catch. 'Feathering his own nest, more likely.'

'That fish he's been getting,' Danny said, striding in the man's direction. 'He's been giving it to us. He got us moved to a better cell and he makes sure we get plenty of clean water to drink and wash with.'

'Keeping you alive,' the old man croaked, 'So you can go on slaving for them. That's all it amounts to. If he's a prisoner, what's he doing with that whip?'

'He's never touched us with it. Not once. They told him to lash us but he wouldn't. He always made some excuse. We were spitting at him, calling him a traitor and even then, he never came anywhere near using it on us.' The fishermen's stares were no longer so hostile and their voices were becoming less strident. They were starting to listen to what Danny had to say. 'We've worked with him for years in Almeria,' he continued. 'He's a good man. His best friend's a Muslim. His name's Khaled. You haven't seen him yet, he's back at the felling site, but his father owns a lot of land in Almeria. Get us there in your boats and you can live and work with us. Free and out of danger.'

For a while, nobody was willing to break the silence that followed Danny's torrent of words. Then, one of the fishermen shouted, 'He's telling the truth, you can hear it in his voice. And the way I see it, we've got nothing to lose.'

'We've got families,' another man shouted. 'There are over fifty of us, counting our children and old people. Can you take us all in?'

'How many boats have you got?' Ethan asked.

'Enough.'

'Get us to Almeria and Khaled's father will give you land to live on. That's a promise. Will you do it?'

'We'll do it,' a group of men shouted enthusiastically.

'Is tomorrow soon enough?' called out another.

'We'll be here by first light. Make sure you're ready by then.'

***

18

As they drew closer to the mine, Ethan and his gang could see a group of overseers struggling with a young prisoner. Man to man, he would have been more than a match for any of them, but there were four guards and they were armed with staves. Garcia stood watching as the youth was stripped and manhandled towards the whipping post. His wrists were secured with chains and his ankles made fast to a couple of rings that had been let into the ground. Meanwhile, the guard chosen to administer punishment, strutted in front of the onlookers.

He paced out his distance, uncoiled his leather whip and carefully shook out the thongs. If they were tangled, the force of the lash might be reduced and his reputation would suffer. Everything was as it should be and, confident he wouldn't disappoint the spectators, the man stood waiting for Garcia's signal.

The mine owner nodded impatiently but the overseer wasn't to be rushed. When ready, he raised his whip, took several brisk paces forward and brought down the lash. It sliced through the air and cracked sharply across his victim's back. The prisoner's body jerked convulsively, ramming itself hard against the post. He fought against the restraints that were holding him, wrenching at his wrists in a frantic attempt to escape the blazing agony. But the chains held fast.

The flogger checked his whip, shaking it again to make sure the thongs were hanging correctly. He was in no hurry, preferring to pause between lashes. Drawing out punishment made it more effective. The prisoner took the second slash across his shoulders and the guards yelled their approval. The whip was shaken out and the overseer positioned himself, ready to deliver the next stroke. Looking around, his victim saw the callous contempt on the faces of the guards. He had taken the first couple of lashes in silence but as the whip cut into him for the third time, a groan escaped through his clenched teeth.

Garcia had been waiting for Ethan and told him to stay behind while Khaled, Reuben and his brother were ordered back to their cell. Ethan saw them pause as they passed the whipping post and mutter angrily to each other. The mine owner took his eyes away from the flogging in order to watch them. What he saw, obviously pleased him. He smiled at their young overseer and beckoned him over. 'You've done a good job,' he said as Ethan moved to stand at his side. 'We've had plenty of work out of them and they're still in good condition.'

Garcia turned his attention once more to the prisoner under punishment. He'd had his eye on the young man ever since the new batch of prisoners arrived. His refusal to be cowed had made a lashing inevitable. Ethan tried not to watch as the whip continued to sear across the slave's torn back. 'What did he do, Señor?' he asked nervously.

'Tried to hit one of the guards.' The mine-owner's eyes had narrowed until they were little more than slits. 'We're teaching him respect. Thirty lashes should do it.' Drooping an arm around Ethan's shoulders he confided, 'You're getting a bigger gang tomorrow. They'll need breaking in. Then, work them like your first lot and you'll make yourself some real money.'

'A bigger gang?'

'To take the place of your friends. You'll be getting fifteen new Jews. He's one of them.' Garcia nodded in the direction of the man at the whipping post. 'Don't worry, he'll know how to behave by the time we've finished with him. They're from families that didn't pay their taxes.'

Ethan remembered what the fishermen had told him at the beach. 'Maybe they couldn't pay, Don Garcia.'

'*Wouldn't* pay is more likely. They know the law as well as everybody else. All non-Christians pay the infidel tax. They broke the rules and examples have to be made. Their eldest sons have been sentenced to hard labour. It's got quite an Old Testament ring to it, don't you think, punishing the first-born? If they won't pay in one way, they'll pay in another.' An attack of self-satisfied laughter made him speechless.

Ethan's loathing for the man reached a new level of intensity; it could as easily be Khaled, Danny or Reuben they were cutting to pieces with the lash. 'How long before they're released?'

'The sons?' Garcia shrugged his shoulders. The man was in a dangerous mood. Ethan was becoming increasingly alarmed for his friends' safety but he knew better than to give any sign of his feelings. 'What's happening to my original gang?' he asked casually.

'They're needed as replacements at Almaden.'

Ethan felt the blood drain from his face. The tales Fernando told about the place were terrifying. It consisted of a labyrinth of underground chambers and tunnels connected to an old prison. Originally a place of punishment for hardened criminals, it was now used for Muslims and Jews who fell foul of the Christian authorities. The life expectancy of workers in the Almaden mines was so short that large numbers of replacements were regularly needed. 'It's the biggest mine we've got,' Garcia continued, with a touch of pride in his voice. 'But it's a good two weeks from here so we're only sending the fittest. The others would never stand up to the march.'

By keeping his friends well fed and fit, Ethan had condemned them to the hell of the cinnabar mines. He remembered Fernando describing the deadly effects of this red crystalline rock from which mercury was extracted. After a few weeks, the miners fell ill with a strange wasting disease. Unable to control their bowels, they became emaciated and their limbs shook uncontrollably. In the final stages of the illness, most of the victims were blind and out of their minds.

Ethan shuddered as he recalled the old man's description of it as *'a sly death'*. It crept up on its victims.

He clenched and unclenched his fists. His first instinct had been to smash them into Garcia's ruthless face, but he knew that would achieve nothing. 'Very well,' he said, his voice flat and devoid of emotion, 'What time shall I have them ready?'

'First light tomorrow morning.' Garcia sounded unconcerned. Sentencing men to a living death was of less importance to him, than deciding what to order for supper. Ethan was fighting to keep his feelings under control. Garcia read the shock in his face but chose not to comment. Instead, he continued to outline the young overseer's new responsibilities. 'We won't increase your quota for a few days. That'll give you a chance to get the replacement slaves broken in. You've proved you can manage on your own, so this time, you won't have to share your commission with Fernando or anyone else. You'll make yourself some real money.'

Ethan's breathing had speeded up. If Garcia had been sending the prisoners to Almaden a day or two later, the escape could have taken place as planned. That was now impossible. He had to talk to his friends and find some way of bringing things forward.

The flogger was pausing between strokes, prolonging his victim's misery. Ethan was made to watch while the full thirty lashes were meticulously laid on. It was only when the guards started to take down the prisoner's unconscious body, that Garcia allowed the young overseer to leave. 'Come to my quarters as soon as you've cleaned yourself up,' the mine-owner called after him, 'I'll need you.'

'Very well, Señor.' The expression on Garcia's face told Ethan why he would be needed. He ran to his friends' cell, but instead of Khaled, Reuben and Danny, he found a group of terrified prisoners who stared at him suspiciously. Ethan's feet felt heavier than wet clay. Unable to move, he looked helplessly at the young men. Their colouring and facial characteristics told him they were the Jews.

At first, none of them had the courage to speak. Then, one of them asked nervously, 'Your name is Ethan, Master?'

'Yes, I'm Ethan.' He turned, surprised the prisoner knew who he was. 'Where are the men who used to be here?'

'We don't know, Master. They were taken away soon after we arrived but one of them, his name was Danny, told us we could trust the young overseer called Ethan. We'd know you because you had hair the same colour as straw. He said to tell you none of this was your fault. By the time they found out they were being moved, it was too late to do anything about it.'

'Garcia lied to me! He said they weren't being taken away until first light tomorrow morning, but he'd already arranged to have them moved. That's why he made me watch the whipping. To keep me away from them.'

'There was a Muslim called Khaled,' the young man continued nervously. 'Do you know him, Master?'

Ethan stared at the youth through tears that threatened to blind him. 'He's my brother.'

'That's what he told us but we couldn't understand it. He had hair and skin the same colour as ours. He didn't look anything like you.' Seizing Ethan by the arm, the young man pulled him towards the wall. 'Look, he's scratched something, up there!' He was pointing to a faintly marked message. 'It's in Arabic, Master. Can you read it?'

'My brother taught me.' Ethan's arms hung uselessly by his sides and before he could explain what he'd read, a couple of surly looking guards pushed their way into the cell. They were half dragging and half carrying the young man who'd been whipped. After letting his semi-conscious body slump to the floor, they left in silence. One of the Jews glanced at the prisoner's savagely punished back before walking over to the vat and soaking a rag in water.

'That's alright for his face,' Ethan told him, 'But piss on it before you swab his cuts. It'll stop them from festering. If it's a long time since you passed water, it'll burn like fire, so do it now, before he's fully conscious.' He watched to make sure his instructions were carried out, wincing as the dark yellow urine flooded the young man's cuts. The prisoner opened his eyes and looked around, trying to focus on his surroundings. Ethan squatted beside him on the ground and asked him his name.

'Aaron,' the young prisoner managed to reply, his voice weak and husky.

'He didn't mean any disrespect,' another man said. 'It was the guard who hit him first. The boy was just trying to defend himself. He stopped before he landed the blow, but that didn't make any difference to them. They said he was threatening the guard, so he'd get a lashing.'

In the short while that had passed since reading Khaled's message, Ethan had experienced a confusing flood of emotions. At first, he'd felt broken, as though his muscles were refusing to obey him. That mood of helplessness had given way to cold hatred. His mind flashed back to when he'd fought Bruno. He'd learned then, that rage added to his vulnerability.

He watched as the prisoners continued to bathe their friend's lacerated back. He saw Aaron grit his teeth as again, the urine burned into his raw flesh. Ethan's instincts urged him to show the boy kindness but he knew how easily that could lead to self-pity. If they were to survive, the Jews mustn't give in to the impotence of despair. The young men standing around Aaron were little more than a leaderless group of frightened boys. They would have to be coerced into action. 'Never mind the whipping!' he barked, 'I want him back on his feet and ready to move out as soon as possible. Get working on him with the cold water and whatever else it takes to get him wide awake and walking.'

'Never mind the whipping?' one of the prisoners shouted angrily. 'He's barely-conscious and all you can think about is getting him on his feet so you can start working him to death. You're the man we're supposed to trust? You're as bad as the rest of them!'

Ethan grabbed his shoulder and thrust him roughly towards the wall. 'You see that?' he was pointing towards Khaled's barely legible message. 'It says my brother knows I'm too late to save him and his friends but he's begging me to save you.'

Moments before, the young prisoner's eyes had sparked with anger. Now, they were focused on the ground. 'I'm sorry, Master. We don't understand what's going on. Danny said we could trust you. Then you told us to get Aaron up and ready to walk. It sounded as if you were on their side. Tell us the truth, Ethan. Are any of us getting out of here alive?'

'I don't know, and that's the truth of it. If we work together, we might have a chance.' He'd spoken sincerely but he knew that was as much humanity as he could afford to show. 'You'd better do as I say!' It was the voice of the overseer who demands instant obedience. 'And you'll keep your mouths shut.' Too frightened to argue, the men murmured their agreement. 'I'll be back before daybreak. Make sure Aaron's on his feet and ready to move out. He's coming with us. If he can't walk, you'll have to carry him.' The men nodded.

Ethan walked quickly out of the cell and called a guard to lock the door. By the time he reached the mine owner's quarters, a plan of sorts was forming in his mind. He'd try playing Garcia along. Let him go so far, and then use the man's frustration to make him change his mind. Similar tricks had worked before.

The mine owner was waiting for him, slumped on a bench at the door of his cabin. 'You're filthy. I thought you'd been washing yourself, like those Moors and Jews you're so fond of.' Garcia's breath stank of stale wine.

'I'm sorry Don Garcia but I didn't have time. I was trying to patch up the man you had whipped.'

'Wasting time with a Jew?'

'We'll need him for work tomorrow.'

The man turned his back; his impassive shoulders told Ethan that a whipped Jew should be of no concern to anyone. Garcia pointed to a red earthenware jug and basin that stood on a low wooden table. 'There's water there. Get yourself clean!'

Afraid of the anger inside him, Ethan stripped and started to rinse off the day's grime. He could feel Garcia's eyes watching him. As much as he loathed any form of physical contact with the man, he would force himself to tolerate it, if by doing so he could help his friends.

Garcia opened the door of a cupboard, took out a clean tunic and threw it onto the bed. He then walked over to Ethan, picked up a sponge and started to wash the boy's back and thighs. Ethan tensed. There was something more repulsive than usual about the man's caresses. Instead of leading Garcia on, as he had in the past, he started to bargain. 'Don Garcia, I want you to bring my friends back.' Ignoring the anger he saw building in the man's face he continued, 'You've sent them to the mine, but they can't have got far. Get them back and you can do what you like with me.'

It was the first time Ethan had found the courage to speak to Garcia in this manner. He was usually afraid of jeopardising his friends' position. Now, there was nothing to lose. 'You can do what you want with me afterwards,' he repeated, 'But you must get them back.'

'*Must!*' Garcia turned the word into a challenge. 'You're telling me what I *must* do?'

Ethan knew he'd gone too far and tried to moderate his tone. 'I *beg* you Señor. I'll do anything you want.'

Garcia snatched up his whip. 'Slaves don't barter with me!' He slashed viciously. Ethan managed to move aside. Instead of coldness, there was a strangely pathetic note in Garcia's voice. 'I've shown you kindness. I've given you every privilege. Still, all you think about are your filthy infidel friends.' His expression reminded Ethan of a pleading child.

'Señor, that isn't true. It's just that I've known my friends for longer than I can remember. I grew up with them. I'm begging you to bring them back. If you do, I swear you can use me in any way you want.'

Again, Garcia's mood changed. 'I'll use you as I like, whenever I like,' he shouted angrily. 'Your friends are going to the mine. You've seen them for the last time.'

'They'll work hard for you here,' Ethan pleaded. 'I'll see to it they do. Why send them to Almaden?'

'It's the way I want it!' Garcia slashed with his whip, catching the boy hard across his back.

Pain released the fury Ethan had been fighting to control. He unleashed a torrent of blows, hammering Garcia about his head and body. The man cowered, attempting to protect himself from the attack. Ethan grabbed the whip from his hand, wrapping the thongs aroundGarcia's throat. He twisted them tighter. 'Bring them back!' he yelled. 'That's all I'm asking. Bring them back!'

Garcia shook his head furiously and began to thrash around. Ethan fought to control him. He dragged the man across the room and smashed his face repeatedly into the stone wall. Twisting the thongs, he begged Garcia to save his friends. The man's breath came in ragged gasps as he shook his head and fought frantically to free himself. Ethan jerked the whip tighter around the mine owner's neck, pleading for his friends' lives. The only reaction from Garcia was a further shake of the head. Again and again, Ethan drove the man's broken face into the wall. The hatred he had controlled for so long surged freely, channelling itself into the obliteration of this monstrous being.

Garcia's eyes rolled upwards. He had long since ceased to struggle when Ethan allowed the limp and bloody body to fall to the floor. He might have expected to experience remorse or even panic. Instead, he no longer felt a part of what was taking place. It was as though he were watching some other, distant figure playing a role.

He went through Garcia's belongings and found a small purse crammed with gold coins. Shrugging his shoulders, he decided he might as well add theft to the sin of murder. Ethan dragged the lifeless body onto the bed, folded a sheet into a thick wad and used it to cover the bleeding head. He pulled a blanket over the entire body then walked to the door. He stood, looking back into the room and nodded. Anyone peering at the bed would think the man was sleeping.

On the floor, Ethan saw an empty leather bag. He rammed into it a couple of Garcia's sheets together with the tunic the dead man had laid ready. After hiding the small purse at the bottom of the bag, he suddenly remembered the windows. Glancing up anxiously, he was relieved to find the shutters already closed. No-one could see inside. Even by day, so little light entered the room that, unless someone walked to the bed and pulled back the sheet, it would be impossible to tell Garcia was dead.

He closed the door of the cabin behind him and a couple of guards peered suspiciously in his direction. Seeing it was Ethan, they relaxed into an idle slouch. 'Been visiting your master?' one of them smirked. The mine owner's liking for fair-haired boys was well known and Ethan had frequently been seen leaving Garcia's quarters in the middle of the night.

He wandered up to them, casually smiling. 'He's drunk so don't expect him to be up early in the morning. Make sure nobody wakes him. He'll be in a hell of a mood.'

'We'll keep well away from him in that case,' one of the guards laughed. 'Thanks for the warning.'

As soon as he was out of their sight, Ethan quickened his pace and was more or less running by the time he reached the young Jews' cell. He told one of the guards to unlock the door and walked briskly inside. His eyes searched the wall for Khaled's scratched message. Placing the palm of his hand over the writing, he stood in silence for a moment before turning to the prisoners. 'On your feet and ready to move out!' he yelled.

They'd done a good job on Aaron. He was badly injured and in severe pain but he could stand. With his friends' help, he'd be able to walk, even if at times, he might need carrying. Ethan handed him one of the tunics he'd stolen from Garcia's room but the man's back was too damaged to bear the weight of it. To cover himself, Aaron tore off a section of cloth and twisted it around his waist. The remainder could be used to swab his back when it next needed attention.

Ethan told the guards to open the door and pointed his men in the direction of the track. They hadn't taken more than a dozen steps when one of the guards yelled after them, 'Where are you going with that sledge and those Jews at this hour?'

'Don Garcia's orders. I've got to get them to the logging site and ready to start work, well before dawn. They're a new gang so they won't be as quick as the old ones. On top of that, he's increased the quota. We'll be needing the sledge for the extra props.' The guards nodded sympathetically. They knew what it was like having extra duties imposed whenever Garcia felt like it.

'I'm not letting a bunch of idle Jews lose me my bonus.' Ethan sounded as though he was trying to make the best of a bad situation. 'I'm going to teach them the meaning of *work*.' Changing his tone, he added cheerfully, 'Don't worry, there's a full moon. We won't get lost.'

The guards muttered their approval as Ethan and his labourers moved quickly out of the camp and along the worn track that led to the logging camp. As soon as it was safe to do so, Ethan took a look at Aaron's back. The cuts were clean. They'd soon start to scab over, provided they were kept clear of infection and the urine should take care of that.

The immediate problem was the boy's lack of speed. Ethan told the prisoners they'd have to give him any help he needed to keep up with them. The sheets he'd brought from Garcia's room could be turned into a makeshift stretcher but Aaron wasn't to be shown too much sympathy. 'Make him walk whenever he can. He's a heavy man to carry but if he can't keep up, that's what you'll have to do. We're not leaving him behind. Once the track widens out, you can put him on the sledge.'

Ethan knew it was only a matter of time before Garcia's body was found and he ordered his men to double their pace. There was another fear nagging at the back of his mind but it wasn't one he could share. If the fishermen's sons were among those who'd been rounded up, their fathers would be unwilling to abandon them and sail south. Ethan and his men would be recaptured and pay a terrible price for killing Garcia.

***

They stumbled onto the beach at daybreak. The sight that greeted them was astonishing. More than thirty boats heaved and settled in the swell, while the fishermen made ready to sail. On shore, about fifty men, women and children were busy loading the last of their livestock and possessions on board.

As soon as they saw the prisoners arrive, the fishermen and their families rushed in their direction. The young man, who had questioned Ethan on the previous day, pushed his way towards the sledge. He'd seen Aaron struggle to his feet and grabbed an arm to steady him. It was then he saw the state of the boy's back. Turning on Ethan he snarled, 'That's two of our men who've been whipped like dogs. This one's my cousin!'

'Don't take it out on him,' Aaron said. 'Without Ethan, I wouldn't be here. Nor would the rest of us.'

'Where's the one you had with you yesterday?'

Ethan opened his mouth to reply, but nobody was listening. The fishermen had recognised relatives and friends among the prisoners. They were crowding around and all talking at once. There were questions to be asked and they needed answers.

Ethan felt a hand on his shoulder. He jumped around; fists raised and ready to defend himself. It was a grey-haired fisherman with two little girls clinging to his ragged tunic. The children looked up at Ethan with large, wide-open eyes, not understanding the danger they were in, but trusting him to be their friend.

Their father spoke quietly so as not to alarm them. 'I'm Aaron's uncle,' he said. 'My nephew has told us what you did for him. I want to thank you and apologise for my son, Isaac. It's been a long time since anybody did anything to help a Jew and we can't help being suspicious. Forgive me Ethan, but this has to be said. If you're playing games, it's the lives of children like these, you're playing with.' He gently tousled his little girls' hair.

'No games!' Ethan replied starkly. 'The stakes are too high. None of us can afford to lose.'

Although he no longer sensed any direct animosity from the crowd, he felt isolated amidst this group of frightened people. For some moments, he stood alone and largely ignored.

'You didn't say where your mates are!' It was Isaac's voice and he was holding out his hand in friendship.

'I was too late,' Ethan replied, 'They've already been sent to Almaden.'

No longer the outsider, he was immediately surrounded by a sympathetic crowd. 'It could be worse,' Isaac told him bluntly. 'Almaden's a long way into the interior but they'll follow the coast track for the first day or so before they strike inland. I've seen them taking gangs of slaves that way plenty of times. Muslims, they looked like for the most part, but there were usually a few Jews among them.'

Crouching down he started to sketch a rough map in the sand with his finger. 'You see this line? That's the coast. And here ...' he was pointing to an indentation, 'It's a small harbour. That's where they bring in the boatloads of prisoners.'

'I know it,' Ethan said. 'That's where we were unloaded and sold to Garcia.'

'Well, that's where they'll pick up the road for the interior. If we get moving, we'll catch them up before they get too far along it.'

'You make it sound easy, Isaac. We both know it's a very long way.'

'By land it is. But we'll be going by sea. Boats travel like birds. They can move in straight lines. The track they'll march your friends along skirts around the hills and they'll have to stick to areas where the trees have been cut down. We've got to catch up with them before they get too far inland. If we do that, we've got a good chance. When did you say they started out?'

'Nightfall. As soon as we got back from work.'

'That's not good. I didn't realise they'd been on the road so long. They'll be three parts of the way to the harbour by now and starting inland before we get to them. We'll be too late.'

'Get on board, the lot of you!' Aaron's uncle spoke with the authority of an older man. 'We're not abandoning them, anymore than Ethan left my brother's boy behind. There's a Levante blowing. We'll make good time to the harbour. If they've started for the interior, we'll catch them on foot. They'll be chained. We're not.'

'We're not armed either,' a man shouted from the middle of the crowd. 'The guards will be.'

'Who's not armed?' Isaac yelled in reply. 'We've got our knives and harpoons.'

The fishermen knew the waters as well as they knew their children's faces. The boats cut through the waves, following the coast and avoiding the rocks.

***

19

Aaron's cousin was right - they travelled like birds. Most of the fishing boats remained half way to the horizon, giving the innocent impression of a medium-sized fishing fleet. The lead vessel tied up in the harbour and Ethan went ashore alone. In spite of his fair hair and skin colouring, he was expecting a suspicious welcome. What he found, was far more disturbing.

The locals were half drunk and stood talking in small excited groups. Full of wine and gossip, they couldn't stop bragging about the gang of infidels they'd baited for much of the morning. The prisoners had been left chained, while the overseers went for a drink. The youngest of the guards had been told to keep an eye on them but he'd soon grown bored and resentful. It was no joke being left outside in that sweltering heat while his mates swilled beer in the cool of the tavern.

To relieve his frustration, he'd begun cursing and lashing the chained men. The row attracted a jeering mob, eager to poke and prod at the captives. There was no point in trying to stop it. The young overseer would only have made himself unpopular. Besides, it was just a bit of harmless fun.

Not so long ago, Ethan and his fellow prisoners had been marched through this same village to the jeers of onlookers. He felt his fists clench as he heard these red-faced, drink-bloated creatures boast about their treatment of his friends. He needed to lash out. But not yet. For the time being, he'd laugh with the men as they boasted, he'd tolerate their reeking breath and put up with their sweaty arms around his shoulders. His anger would keep.

The more he aped their gestures and shared their prejudices, the happier the locals were to open up and answer his apparently casual questions. He told them he was a messenger and in big trouble. He'd been sent by the authorities with orders for the chief overseer. His instructions were to meet up with the gang before they set off inland. One way or another, he'd managed to miss them. The villagers sympathised. He was an underdog, the same as they were, at the beck and call of anyone with money. Now, he'd be punished for something that wasn't his fault.

Suddenly, they were all talking at once, keen to show off their knowledge and outdo each other with advice for this friendly, fresh-faced young stranger. He needn't worry, they assured him, he'd soon catch up with the slaves. They were on foot and could only move slowly, on account of their chains.

He asked if the gang was a large one and they told him it wasn't. There were no more than half a dozen guards - enough to control a band of twenty chained prisoners. The overseers were on horseback and not heavily armed, but they weren't expecting trouble. It had been years since rebels had tried to free a gang of infidel prisoners. They'd been hunted down and tortured to death in the village square. Since then, it had been quiet in these parts. Ethan nodded approvingly.

More banter, more back-slapping and he shook himself free of the drunks. 'You'll be back?' one of them shouted as he walked towards the wharf. Ethan turned and waved. 'If I am,' he muttered to himself, 'It'll be to burn your village and every trace of you to the ground.' By the time he was on board, he'd come up with a plan. He'd be the overseer again only this time, he'd be driving a different gang of slaves.

'They're not a very welcoming lot as far as your people are concerned,' Ethan warned the young Jews, 'So we're going to skirt around the village instead of going through it. We shouldn't have much trouble picking up the track to the interior. I got a good look while I was there. I know the way it runs.'

Ethan told Aaron and two other men to stay on board and guard the boat. He led the rest of his gang past the village. Several of them had sections of chain draped over their shoulders; others had knives and harpoons hidden under their clothing. They could hear drunken voices in the distance but for the time being, Ethan decided against telling them the reason for the villagers' high-spirits. There'd be time for that later.

They followed a series of narrow paths that threaded between densely planted fields until they reached a broad, well-beaten track. From what the villagers had told him, Ethan knew it led to the interior of the country. In spite of the heavy chains and concealed weapons, the men moved urgently along the dust layered road until they came to an area that had once belonged to Muslim farmers.

Groups of men, women and children now wandered aimlessly through charred crops while others, numbed by hopelessness, sat beside the few items they had managed to salvage. Formerly fertile fields had been burned or laid to waste while wells, water-wheels, reservoirs and irrigation canals had been mindlessly wrecked. The resulting drought was an impartial scourge. It destroyed the livelihoods of Jews, Muslims and Christians alike. Food and water were all that mattered. On either side of the track, impoverished farm workers stood gaunt and dull eyed, desperate to sell or barter everything they possessed.

A group of old men who had worked as carters were hoping to sell their mules. 'How much for all four of them?' Ethan was astonished by the pitifully small sum they were asking. 'What about the carts?'

'They're no use to us without the mules to pull them. Give us what you can afford and they're yours.' With the few coins he'd saved while working for Fernando, Ethan had more than enough. He told a couple of his men to drive the mules. The others loaded their chains and weapons into the carts and climbed in behind them. The animals were used to hard work and kept up a steady speed. Even so, it was late afternoon before Ethan spotted a distant shadow moving slowly along the track. The shimmering heat robbed the figures of their detail but he managed to make out the six mounted guards and what he estimated to be about twenty prisoners. For a moment, the haze lifted and he saw Khaled, Reuben and Danny. He opened his mouth to yell with relief but managed to control himself. For a while longer, his joy, as well as his hatred, needed to be curbed.

'Let's have the gold!' he shouted to one of his gang. The others watched in amazement as a young man handed over his heavy neck chain.

'That's all your family's got left,' one of his friends muttered, unable to believe what he'd just seen.

'It's alright,' the youngster smiled. 'I've a good idea what he wants it for.'

Ethan halted his men. 'You remember what we practised on the boat?' Their faces answered for them. The plan was as simple as it was dangerous.

'You see those guards,' he began quietly. 'They've brutalised prisoners! They've worked them to death! They've lashed them and starved them! They've raped Jewish women! They've castrated Jewish men and slaughtered Jewish children!'

His voice had risen in volume. He saw anger burning in the men's faces and knew his words were cutting deep. 'That row you heard, while we were passing the village. Do you know why they were celebrating? I'll tell you. They'd been torturing Jews and Muslims!'

His companions' fury threatened to become uncontrollable. Ethan needed to rein it in, and then channel it in the direction of their enemies. 'You're angry! I'm angry!' He paused, to make sure he had their full attention, 'But anger can be dangerous. It makes men careless. Act without thinking and they'll beat us. Do it the right way and we'll destroy them.'

The Jews' growl of agreement told Ethan they knew what to do.

'We'll have to get the guards down from their horses,' one of the young men shouted. 'Mounted, they've got the advantage.'

'Leave that to me,' Ethan told him. 'Wait until I've got them distracted, then move slowly and quietly into position. Don't let them suspect anything and above all, make sure nobody makes a move until I give the order. Is that clear?' They nodded.

'Right! Get those chains up where the guards can see them. Make sure you're in control of them. At the same time, you've got to look like prisoners. Everybody know what to do?' The men growled again. They were as ready as they'd ever be.

Ethan jumped to his feet and started to yell. The guard at the rear of the slave column turned in his saddle. He saw the approaching carts and what looked like a cargo of male prisoners. He shouted ahead to his superior and the column was halted. The lead guard wheeled his horse around and sat watching the wagons as he waited for them to draw closer.

Ethan bellowed at them again, 'Hold up! I've got another load for you.' He jumped out of the cart and ran towards the guard. 'Señor Garcia changed his mind. He wants us to take this new gang of slaves to Almaden along with the others.' The guards recognised Ethan and jumped down from their horses to talk. He was well known as one of Garcia's favourites and disliked because of it. Nevertheless, they'd treated him with grudging respect, never knowing what he might report to his master.

As the wagons drew up to the column, one or two of the guards began to show interest in the new prisoners. Ethan recognised the danger. From a distance, their chains looked convincing enough. Close up, they wouldn't deceive a child.

'They're Jews,' he scoffed. 'Fishermen. They smell of rotting fish. Don't get too close or you'll end up stinking like they do!' The guards sneered their distaste but weren't surprised. All slaves stank. Especially infidels.

One of the overseers was dressed differently and standing apart from the others. It was difficult to see his face but there was something familiar about him and the way he held his whip. As the man turned, Ethan's stomach lurched. 'Sulieman, you bastard!'

'Watch your tongue or you'll be hacking rock instead of driving a gang of slaves.' Gesturing towards Khaled, Reuben and Danny, he sneered, 'I've got your friends where I want them. One word from me and you'll be underground, alongside them.'

The sunlight picked out the chain around Ethan's neck and its glint caught Sulieman's eye. 'Where did you get that, Pretty Boy? A present from a grateful customer?'

'Señor Garcia gave it to me.' Ethan's tone was defensive.

'Like I thought,' Sulieman sniggered, 'For services rendered. They said you were his whore. Now he's dressing you like one!'

The guards looked with hungry eyes at the chain and mumbled to each other as they moved closer. It would be easy enough, in this isolated spot, to dispose of the yellow-haired catamite and strip his corpse of the gold. They eyes continued to follow his fear-filled movements and, as Ethan scrambled desperately in the direction of the carts, the guards closed in.

'Hand it over!' Sulieman reached out menacingly and attempted to snatch the chain from the young man's neck.

Ethan backed towards the carts. 'Why should I?' he stammered. 'It was a present. Señor Garcia wouldn't like it, if I gave it away.'

'Señor Garcia wouldn't like it,' the man mocked as he and the other guards drew closer to the cowering boy. 'Señor Garcia isn't here to protect you now!'

'You're right,' Ethan shouted, 'Señor Garcia isn't here. He's dead!'

Sulieman stepped towards him, a puzzled smile forming on his lips. He was still smiling when the young man drove the long fisherman's blade deep into his heart.

'Do it, men!' Ethan yelled. His gang swarmed out of the carts and leaped at the remaining guards. Four of them fell, no longer recognisable as human, their heads pulped by the flailing chains. The last of them died more slowly, their chests opened by the fishermen's blades.

Ethan searched among the stunned prisoners until he found Khaled chained between Reuben and Danny. For a while, the three of them were unable to move or speak. Eventually Khaled managed to whisper, 'We knew you'd come.'

'That was the easy part,' his friend told him. 'There's a long way to go before we're safe.'

Ethan watched while the guards' bodies were stripped and dragged behind a couple of boulders. 'Leave it at that, men!' he shouted. 'The vultures can finish the job for us.' The guards' horses were a bonus. By using them as well as the carts, the men could be transported more quickly. They had to get back to their boats before the attack was discovered.

A short distance from the port, Ethan told those prisoners in chains to get down and walk. Six fishermen, in the guards' blood-stained clothing, would ride the horses. In the dark, with their overseers' whips, he hoped they'd convince any suspicious onlookers they were on official business. They were half way to the boat when their luck had run out.

A group of rowdy drunks emerged from one of the run-down buildings and stood, blocking the way. 'What's going on?' their leader slurred aggressively.

'That message I was carrying. It was for the guards,' Ethan told them. 'Plans have been changed. We're taking them to a different mine.'

The villagers were muddle-headed with wine, but a few of them recognised their old drinking partner. Ethan found himself surrounded by slobberers and it took what little patience he had left to shake free of them. He was under orders to make good time, he explained. Much as he wanted to stay and drink with them, he had to get on. There was one thing they could do for him, though. He needed another boat. Would they let him have one of theirs in exchange for the six horses, the mules and the wagons? Drink hadn't softened the villagers' cunning. The answer was *'No'*. Which only became *'Yes'*, when Ethan offered them the remainder of Garcia's gold.

The vessel was old, half rotten and barely sea-worthy but with the one Aaron and his mates were guarding, it got them as far as the flotilla. Once the men were on board, the boats got underway and the fishermen set about hacking off the prisoners' chains. Ethan and Khaled sat, watching the waves scud past the bow of the boat. Neither of them spoke for a while and Khaled went to put a hand on his friend's shoulder.

'I need some rest,' Ethan said and climbed slowly to his feet. Khaled watched his friend clamber unsteadily across the deck and disappear below.

***

20

Morning began with a warm sun and light ripples. The boats skimmed past scorched rocks and coasts speckled with stunted pines. Dolphins, arching in groups, kept pace with the flotilla. Until, growing bored with their game, they melted below the surface as unexpectedly as they'd arrived.

But weather is a creature of moods. By mid-day, the wind had stiffened and its bee-hum became a roar in Khaled's ears. He no longer heard the creak and groan of pulleys as the crew hefted ropes and trimmed sails. Instead, he saw knots of men point anxiously at clouds that ganged up to menace them. Experienced crew members stayed confident. The following day, they told their mates, they'd round Cabo de Gata and enter the bay of Almeria.

Few of the fishermen had been this far south and several were still suspicious. Were they and their boats being used by Ethan and his friends as a means of escape? If so, the Jews might be betrayed as soon as they'd delivered their passengers to Sheikh Omar.

Khaled walked towards the prow of the boat and stood looking at the sea. *Wine-dark*, Homer had called it but it was nothing of the sort. At times, the water was the deepest of blues and at others an emerald green. Wine-coloured it was not. So much for his tutor and those endless Greek translations. And yet, he couldn't wait to see the man again. He was a part of home and family life.

Khaled moved erratically across the deck, making use of grab ropes to steady himself. He felt the bitterness of a wind that penetrated his clothing and heard the thud of white-capped waves. The crew took them as a warning. Before long, they would taste the full power of the Levante.

His attention was caught by a weirdly strange, almost unearthly sound. At the same time, he saw Reuben scrambling towards him across the pitching deck. On land, there was no one more firm-footed. At sea, his friend floundered as clumsily as the rest of them.

'You've got to come,' Reuben gasped urgently. 'It's Ethan. He's gone mad. Danny and I can't do anything with him.'

'It's Ethan making that noise? He sounds like somebody in hell.'

Reuben pulled him towards the stern of the boat and down into the cramped cargo area where their friend had fallen asleep the night before. Danny was standing, limp armed and helpless, while Ethan writhed and clenched his fists over his head. He'd pulled his body into a tight ball and was struggling to force himself into a corner of the storage space.

Khaled crouched down and put an urgent hand on his friend's shoulder. 'What's the matter, Brother?' Ethan was incapable of hearing and his eyes remained shut as he flung himself against the bulkhead. He reminded Khaled of a trapped gazelle he'd once seen. Hunted to exhaustion by a pack of dogs, the beautiful, doomed creature had fought frantically against the net and then lay panting until its heart gave out.

Ethan's friends tried to hold him but he struggled and roared in an attempt to kick free. Khaled hit him hard across the face. The blow shocked him into temporary silence. Before he could start to thrash and scream again, Khaled gripped Ethan's head between his hands. 'It's me,' he shouted. 'Talk to me for God's sake!'

Instead of answering, his friend began to pant and moan. Khaled struck him again. Briefly under control, Ethan stared around with unfocussed eyes. 'Don't hit me. Please don't hit me,' he pleaded like a terrified child. Then, grabbing hold of Khaled, he began to scream.

Danny and Reuben looked at each other, astonished to see their friend behaving like this. He was gripping Khaled's arm so tightly it took all of their strength to loosen his hold and control his convulsive jerking. They held him for a very long time, until, slowly, his movements became less violent and his breathing moderated.

'Where's Reuben?' he asked, looking around in panic.

'I'm here. Danny and I are both here.'

Ethan looked at them with a confused expression, 'Did they hurt you?'

'Not much,' Danny told him. 'We're safe now.'

'Did they do anything bad to you?'

'Nothing that won't mend. My back's healed and the marks are fading.'

'Khaled?'

'I'm here and I'm alright. Don't keep asking the same questions.' His words displayed an increasing irritation. 'You've had a bad dream, that's all!'

'It wasn't a dream.' Ethan was struggling with reality, 'I was awake and I could see what they were doing to you. It was my fault but I couldn't take it any more.'

'What are you trying to say?' Khaled snapped. 'You're talking in riddles!'

Once again, Ethan's eyes were tightly closed, as though blocking out images that returned to torture him. 'It's nothing I can tell you about.' Danny motioned his brother in the direction of the door and Reuben caught his meaning. They'd leave Ethan and Khaled together for the time being.

'You're behaving like a frightened child,' Khaled told him, as soon as they were alone. 'You're supposed to be the strong man. The fighter.'

Ethan's face was marred with pain. It reminded Khaled of a similar expression he'd seen at the logging site, on that day when he and Ethan had finally broken their silence. 'Something happened, didn't it?'

His friend looked away, unable to meet his eyes.

'Garcia?'

'I don't want to talk about it.'

And then Khaled knew he was right. He remembered the look he'd seen on Garcia's face, when the mine owner first set eyes on Ethan. 'You've got to tell me about it,' he told his friend. 'If you don't, it'll become a silent area between us'. He saw fear in his friend's eyes and it made him soften his words. 'The only times we've had trouble, you and me. They've been when we haven't talked things out. Like when I didn't tell you about Inga. We swore this would never happen again. Now you're doing the same thing. You're cutting me out.'

Ethan's head hung down and when he finally spoke, it was in a guilty monotone. 'If I tell you, you'll never want me for a friend again. Nor will Danny and Reuben.'

'What do you think we are?' Khaled's voice displayed a mixture of exasperation and sympathy. 'We owe you our lives. There's nothing can change that. What happened, Ethan? Did Garcia fuck you or something?'

Ethan looked away, his face burning.

'And there's something else. Something about Reuben and Danny. That's why you kept asking if they'd been hurt. I'm right aren't I?'

'Garcia said he'd have them castrated.'

'And me? Did he threaten to do that to me?'

Ethan sat without moving, his face turned away. Then, through lips that hardly moved, he finally said, 'I told him to fuck you.'

'You're lying!' Khaled yelled, unable to believe what he was hearing. 'You'd never have said that.'

'I said it.' Ethan's voice was little more than a whisper.

'There must have been a reason. You'd never have said it otherwise.'

'There was a reason. A very good one. I hated you.'

Khaled stared at his friend, 'You're making this up. I don't believe a word of it.'

'I'm not making it up, Khaled. I wanted him to hurt you, the same way he was hurting me. I begged him to stop but he kept laughing and saying I liked it as much as he did. I hated you Khaled. I hated you because you weren't there. One day, the pain got so bad, I begged him to do it to you, instead of me. I didn't care what he did to you, just so long as he left me alone. I hated you Khaled. You were with Danny and Reuben and I was alone with Garcia.'

'I don't believe you, Ethan. You'd never have told him to do that.'

His friend didn't reply.

'Even if you did, it was the pain talking, not you. Any of us would have done the same in your place.'

'Don't start saying you forgive me,' Ethan told his friend angrily, 'I don't want to hear that. Some things are too big to forgive.'

'That's not too big to forgive. You gave us back our lives. You'd never have come for us if you'd hated us. What you did, that's the important thing. Not something you said when you were frightened and in pain!'

'Forget it, you mean? The past is the past. Better to leave it there. What if I can't leave it there? What if it keeps coming back?'

***

21

The gale had blown itself out and the sun was shining from a cloudless sky. Khaled and Ethan stood in the bow of the lead vessel catching excited glimpses of home. The friends were clean-shaven for the first time in months. Their hair had been washed, brushed and tied back by some of the girls and they were dressed in the crisp, white cotton tunics a couple of women had worked hard to finish in time for their arrival.

Glancing at his friend, Khaled recognised the same young man who had walked out of Floria's room with him on the night they were captured. The tense expression on Ethan's face reflected the cruelty of the past months but he was acting more like his old self. 'The sleep's done you good,' Khaled told him.

'It wasn't the sleep,' Ethan gave him a sheepish look. 'It was the talking to you gave me. I don't know what happens at times, something takes me over from inside. I know what I'm doing. It's no good pretending I don't, but I can't stop myself.' He shook his head in frustration, knowing he'd made a poor job of explaining.

'You remind me of Alexander the Great.'

'And you talk a lot of rubbish.'

'It's true! Remember what our tutor told us?'

'He was always going on about him. It was as good a way as any to keep our attention.'

'Apparently, Alexander was possessed. At times he could be *murderous and melancholy mad*. Anyway, that's what Plutarch said.'

'His *daemon*, he called it.'

'That's it, his *daemon!*' Khaled smiled, grateful for having the word handed to him. 'When Alexander was in control of it, he could conquer the world. But when his daemon took over, things weren't so rosy. He killed a couple of his best friends when he was like that.'

'It was usually when he'd been hitting the bottle!' Ethan's face cracked into a half-smile, which was more or less what Khaled had been hoping for. The danger now was that his friend might take the words too much to heart.

'I might do something like that when my daemon takes over,' Ethan said uneasily, 'After all, I killed Garcia.'

'That was no worse than putting down a mad dog.'

'If I started on Danny and Reuben, you wouldn't be so forgiving.'

'Then you'd better learn to master your daemon.' Khaled noticed his friend shudder. He suspected Ethan was terrified of being in the grip of something he couldn't control. 'Think of it like riding a horse,' he told him. 'The ones with spirit are the best. You've got to master them, that's all. Do that and they'll take you to the ends of the earth.'

'What happens if you can't master them?'

'They get you on the ground and trample you to death.'

'I don't know about you,' Ethan spluttered, 'But I'll be walking from now on. Anyway, how come you know so much about it?'

'Arabs and Berbers have got their daemons as well, you know, only we call them *Djinns* or *Genies*. Sometimes they're on your side. Then you've got *genius*. Other times, they work against you. A lot depends on how you tackle them.'

'You sound like a teacher.'

'That's because I haven't got genius. The ones who've got it, use it. People like me, tell others what to do.'

Ethan started to scoff, so Khaled tried another tack. 'Remember when I used to write poetry? I'd get an idea, work hard and try putting it into words. I'd write, rewrite, correct and polish it until it was the best thing I'd ever done. And do you know something? Given enough time, plenty of effort and a lot of luck, I'd turn out something that was almost second-rate.'

This was more to Ethan's taste. He was always happy to help Khaled laugh at himself. It took the sting out of his own shortcomings. 'Your poetry wasn't up to much, then?'

'You told me it was shit.'

'Sometimes, a good shit makes you feel better!'

'Good or bad, it was the best I could do. A few people manage to write or compose things and they're perfect from the first to the last stroke. Some say it's God working for them. Others say it's their genius.'

Ethan was obviously intrigued by the idea, so Khaled went for the kill. 'You should try and get to know your *daemon* a bit better. You're good at everything you do. Riding horses, fighting, there's nobody can touch you. Getting us away from the mine, that's the best example of all. You made it happen. The rest of us couldn't have done it on our own. Your *daemon* was working for you. For all of us.'

'Garcia liked the colour of my eyes.'

'You made them work for us, those blue eyes of yours. It was your *daemon* that showed you how to do that.'

'I was Garcia's whore.'

'You were our friend.'

'And the killing?'

'Necessary.'

'Leave it in the past?'

'Until we think of a better place for it.'

***

22

The bay of Almeria looked even lovelier than the friends remembered it. The Jews were astonished by the size of the port and its boats of varying types. 'It's the biggest harbour in this part of the Mediterranean.' Ethan's grin was that of a proud proprietor. 'It's why the Romans called it Porto Magno.'

Most of the fishermen were finding it difficult to take their eyes away from the massively walled Alcazaba. It promised security to anyone lucky enough to be inside. Other members of the crew, however, were pointing to a group of fast-moving boats. Earlier, they'd been pottering aimlessly. Now, they were heading straight towards them. The flotilla was surrounded in no time and the Almerians set about closing the net.

Sun glinted on weapons and a shot was fired. Ethan's head was wrenched backwards and a knife jabbed at his throat. 'This is the welcome you promised us?' It was Isaac's voice. 'You won't live long enough to enjoy it, you treacherous bastard.' The blade was pressed close to Ethan's jugular vein.

And then there was a second voice, louder and coarser than the first. It carried a warning a man would ignore only if he was tired of life. 'You're my cousin, Isaac, and I love you. But, as God is my witness, cut Ethan and I'll rip your heart out!' Isaac felt the prick of a fisherman's knife and loosened his grip on Ethan's neck.

'Get that blade away from him,' Aaron continued in the same deadly tone. 'Ethan hasn't betrayed us, nor has Khaled. Drop the knife or, believe me, I *will* kill you!'

Isaac let the knife fall from his grip and Aaron slammed his foot on top of it, pinning it harmlessly to the deck. Isaac stood in front of the younger man, his head bowed in shame and his arms across his chest in the position of surrender. Aaron embraced his cousin before kissing him on both cheeks.

'Talk to your family,' Ethan said. 'Tell them they're nearly home.'

***

'Who are you?' a voice cut across the water. 'State your business here!' The cry was taken up and repeated by the crews of the Almerian boats.

Khaled pushed his way to the bow of the vessel and waved both arms vigorously in the air. 'I am Khaled, son of Omar,' he shouted at the top of his voice. 'Inform my father that I have returned with my brother Ethan. Ask him to receive us and extend sanctuary to our comrades.'

The captain of the lead vessel called to several of his senior crew members and, together, they scrutinised the young man who was continuing to shout and gesticulate from the bow of his boat. As soon as Ethan, with his mane of fair hair, appeared at Khaled's side, there was no longer any doubt about their identity.

'Thank God for your safe return, Khaled, son of Omar,' the captain yelled across the distance between them. 'I will send word that you are requesting sanctuary for your comrades. Follow us into the harbour, but do not allow your men to disembark until we receive your father's reply.'

The boats were moored but the men, women and children remained on board. Khaled jumped ashore and ran from vessel to vessel. He saw husbands place comforting arms around terrified wives, while weeping children clung to their mothers' clothing.

'They're waiting to hear from my father,' he cried out. 'That's all it is.'

Ethan joined his friend on the quayside and the people surged to the sides of their vessels. He was the man they knew. The one they were learning to trust. 'Everything will be alright,' he assured them, 'I give you my word.'

Even so, Ethan couldn't be certain of Sheikh Omar's reaction to such a mass of people looking for a new life on his land. He might not be willing to grant what they had been promised. It was a fear Ethan kept to himself.

***

In spite of the dust, Khaled recognised the figure of his father among the approaching riders. He grabbed Ethan by the arm and the friends ran to meet him. Meanwhile, the fishermen and their families waited anxiously. They'd taken note of the man's fine clothes and the armed guards that protected him. From what the Jews knew of the world, people like him had little sympathy for the poor.

Sheikh Omar jumped from his horse and embraced his son and Ethan before thanking God for their safe return. 'And thank God for these Jews,' Khaled told him, pointing to the boats loaded with desperate families. 'It's because of them that we're here.' He detailed the role played by the fishermen and their need for a place of safety, then watched his father walk briskly to the water's edge.

'You are welcome,' Sheikh Omar shouted to the families still waiting aboard the small boats. He repeated his words then beckoned them vigorously to come ashore. Among the confused and nervous groups at the harbour-side, Khaled spotted Aaron and his uncle. He turned to his father and asked whether Hamdi still lived in Almeria.

'Of course he does. He's been studying with several of our best doctors since the end of Ramadan. They tell me he's got the makings of a first rate surgeon.' Sheikh Omar's expression clouded. 'Why do you ask?' he said anxiously. 'Are you in need of treatment?'

'For one of our friends,' Khaled explained. 'He was whipped a few days ago. We've done what we can with his cuts, but it's time a proper doctor had a look at him.'

'And you think Hamdi would be the man? You wouldn't prefer someone with more experience?'

'He's about the same age as the man we're talking about. They should get on well together.'

Khaled worked his way through the crowd until he reached Aaron's uncle. Then, putting his arm around the man's shoulders, he led him gently forward. As soon as he found himself in front of the sheikh, however, the old man fell to his knees and raised his arms in the manner of a supplicant.

Omar stooped and helped lift the man to his feet. 'It is I who should kneel to you for bringing my son and his brother home to us,' he said. 'They've told me what you did for them and we'd consider ourselves honoured if you and your people would agree to make your homes with us.'

'We're fishermen, for the most part,' Aaron's uncle managed to say, 'But among us there are shepherds, farmers and men who work with wood or metal. Our women are clever with needles and can earn a living making and embroidering clothes. Sheikh Omar, we have not come to burden you or your people. If you allow us to stay, we'll prove ourselves useful.'

'Perhaps my son has told you that both he and Ethan are to be married?'

Khaled looked up in amazement. For the past months, marriage and a normal home life had seemed less than a distant dream. Ignoring his son's confusion, Sheikh Omar continued to explain, 'He and Ethan will then have more than enough land for themselves and their new wives. Close to the sea, there is a large area that is unsuitable for farming. It would, however, be ideal for a fishing community. Further inland, they will be able to accommodate farmers and shepherds. We'll have to work out the details carefully. We can't have those people who are already living there disadvantaged by your presence; that would only cause bitterness and make for future problems. But with good will on all sides, and the help of God, I am certain everything can be achieved to our general advantage.' Turning to Khaled, his father said, 'Their most urgent need will be for a roof over their heads. I'll send for our architects.'

'Architects won't be necessary,' Khaled smiled. 'They're looking for homes, not palaces. If we can provide them with the basic materials, they'll build the houses for themselves. In the meanwhile, they'll be happy enough sleeping on their boats.' His father shrugged in agreement and Khaled continued, 'I would like Ethan, Danny and Reuben to stay with me in my quarters tonight, if that is acceptable to you. It would also be a good idea if the young man I told you about stayed as well. In that way, Hamdi can start the treatment as soon as he arrives.'

Sheikh Omar nodded. 'Of course, that would be the most logical thing for all of you to do. Early tomorrow morning, we'll start out for the farm.'

Once again, Khaled's puzzlement showed on his face, 'We've just got back and you're talking about going to the farm. We want to see Inga and her family, of course we do, but why the rush to get us married in a few days?'

Floria had been living with Inga and her family since Khaled and Ethan's disappearance. It wasn't much of an explanation but, for the time being, it was as far as his father would go. On their way to the farm, they could show the Jews the land that would be theirs.

***

Hamdi was conducted to Khaled's quarters by a respectful house servant. He displayed even more self-assurance than he'd previously possessed. He greeted Khaled and Ethan briefly, and then turned his attention to Aaron. The well-being of his patient was of greater importance than gossiping with old friends.

He told the young man to take off his tunic, and then set about peeling away the makeshift bandages.

Matanza!

'How many lashes did you get, my friend?'

'Thirty, Master.'

'I thought it was more. The brute who gave them to you knew what he was doing. I'm not your master, by the way. My name's Hamdi.' He examined the cuts carefully and finally smiled with relief. 'I don't know which of you has been treating him but you've done a good job. There's no sign of infection, that's the important thing.'

After checking Aaron's general physical condition, he announced, 'You're a tough young devil to take that lot and still be standing. The main problem is that you stink of stale piss. Informed medical opinion tells us that urine is of no use whatsoever in the treatment of wounds. Country people, on the other hand, find it works well. Maybe it's a case of doctors not knowing everything!'

A servant arrived carrying hot water in a large ceramic judge. Ethan and Khaled sluiced the young Jew clean and then helped him to dry himself. Hamdi smoothed on some of his famous healing ointment but told Aaron to leave his cuts uncovered so the air could get to them. 'You'll have to sleep on your belly for a few days,' he told him, 'And only use bandages if you put on a tunic. They'll stop it from rubbing. Apart from the cuts, you're probably the fittest man in Almeria.'

Aaron managed to raise his arms and flex his muscles. 'My friends tell me I'm strong. There aren't many men who'll take me on in a fight.' His cockiness was returning and Ethan recognised something of himself in the young Jew. 'I'll take you on as soon as you're fit.'

'You, Master? I'm not fighting you. You saved my life.'

'You didn't do too badly for me on the boat. I hope Isaac isn't the man to bear a grudge. It's a bad thing when there's resentment in a family.'

'He'll get over it. We're more like brothers than cousins. Do you know why he dropped the knife?'

'You were going to kill him, weren't you?'

'Nah! Me kill Isaac? I'd never do that.'

'You convinced me.'

'You, maybe. Not Isaac. He got rid of the blade because he heard what I said about you and Khaled. He'd made a bad mistake.'

'Whichever way it was, I felt a lot better without that dagger at my throat.'

'I'll tell you what, Master. If you're ever in trouble and need someone at your back, I'm your man.'

'Thanks Aaron. I'll remember that.'

Khaled smiled to himself. Aaron was what Ethan needed. Someone he could lick into shape. He'd done it for him. Now he could do it for this promising young Jew. When Khaled had been his master, Ethan had been the man in charge. Now they were equals, Khaled had started telling him how to live his life. His friend was missing someone to boss.

'You'd better stay here until your cuts heal,' Hamdi told his patient. 'I'll come in every day to see how you're getting on.'

'Here? I'm not staying stay here! I'm going to have a look at the land.'

'You won't be going anywhere for a few days. You want to be fit for the weddings, don't you? They lay on a good spread here. It'd be a pity to miss it.'

'I won't miss it. I only want to see where we'll be living. That won't take long.'

'No, but dying might spoil your appetite and that's what'll happen if that back of yours gets infected.'

Aaron's face showed his alarm. Dying wasn't what he'd had in mind at all. 'Maybe I'll do as you say. My uncle and cousin can look at the land.'

'A wise choice,' Hamdi told him. 'The food's good here but the cemetery's nothing to write home about.'

**

23

They set out while the air was cool. Ethan, Khaled and his father were on horseback, the fishermen in their boats. The journey to Aguadulce was short and the groups met up again after sunrise. It was a magnificent morning. The blood red sky over Cabo de Gata lent traces of colour to the mountains and the countryside smelled fresh with dew. To the settlers, it signalled a new beginning. Sheikh Omar had warned them that the impoverished earth by the coast was of little use for agriculture and that apart from a handful of fishermen, few people wasted their time there. The Jews saw it as a promised land.

The men who worked the inshore waters eyed the newcomers with alarm, afraid this small army of cuckoos would force them from their nest. Sheikh Omar promised them nothing could be further from the truth. He pointed to the Jews' boats. They were bigger and better designed than those the local fishermen were accustomed to sailing. In exchange for letting them settle along that stretch of coast, the incomers promised to teach the Almerians their boat-building skills. They would then be able to share in the more productive offshore fishing, previously beyond their reach.

While Sheikh Omar was busy reassuring the fishermen, Danny and Reuben led a group of farm workers inland, pointing out areas where they could set up home. The men would spend the next few days on foot, examining the soil, the availability of water and the direction of the prevailing winds. They would then be able to calculate which parts were best suited to the raising of livestock or the growing of grapes, citrus fruits, and the mulberry trees that were essential fodder for silk worms.

Ethan, Khaled and his father shook hands with the local men before starting up into the mountains and towards the farm. Climbing higher, they saw the odd rabbit venture into daylight, while a pair of bee-eaters circled them, their blue-green plumage flashing like steel in the sunlight. Ethan looked at the lush, fertile landscape and shook his head, 'It must have been like this around the mine before men made it ugly.'

'They've hacked down and burned more or less everything that was growing there,' Khaled said. 'They've turned farms into wasteland and left the people without the means of making a living or feeding themselves.'

His father nodded. He knew more about the disaster that was overtaking Al Andalous than either Khaled or Ethan had realised. 'People bring me different information every day,' he said. 'Most of the tales are so harrowing I can hardly believe my ears. The reports vary but they agree on one thing; wherever the Christians gain control, they celebrate their victory by burning the crops and slaughtering the animals. Not content with that, they throw the carcases into the wells to poison the water supply or leave them to rot while the people starve.'

'We saw that with our own eyes,' Khaled told his father. 'And it wasn't only the Muslims who went hungry. In some areas, they'd left whole families of Christians to starve as well.'

'We managed to buy mules and wagons for next to nothing,' Ethan added. 'Some old men were so desperate for food they sold them to us for a few coins. I admit it suited us at the time, but it doesn't alter the fact that people are dying because of what those fools are doing to the land. They won't be happy until they've wiped out all trace of anything associated with your people. If they carry on like that, they'll turn Al Andalous into a desert.'

Khaled shook his head in despair, 'By wrecking the irrigation systems, uprooting the trees and reducing the countryside to a wasteland, they think they're hurting us. They don't realise the harm they're doing to themselves. God only knows what we've done to make them hate us so much.'

'It's not what we've *done*,' his father replied. 'We're here. That's enough for them.'

***

The dog had heard the pounding of hooves on hard packed earth. It growled suspiciously then ran to sniff out the intruders. Khaled and Ethan watched Rabo bound towards them. He'd grown into a powerful young hunter that barked excitedly before whisking them a welcome with its tail.

Ethan's young sisters thrust inquisitive heads out of the doorway and, in no time, the yard was full of excited women who cried with relief and laughed with joy. Conversations were impossible and words unimportant. They needed to see, to touch and to hold; to know that this was happiness and not merely a dream.

Sheikh Omar was standing beside Ethan's mother. They saw Floria take Ethan by the arm and lead him away from the others. Catching hold of his hands, she placed them on her belly and whispered quietly into his ear. He stiffened, pulled briefly away, then lifted her in his arms and carried her to where his sister and Khaled were standing. Their conversation was short and ended with the four of them hugging.

Khaled looked for his father and found him by the door of the cottage. He was chatting to Inga's mother and the pair of them were smiling happily. 'The weddings are next week, did you say, Father?'

***

24

Inga had always known that the haremlek was an area apart from the men's section of the house. When she and her friend first stepped inside, they had expected to find it a place of gloomy silence in which bored, unfortunate women passed their monotonous lives. Instead, she and Floria were welcomed by a group of light-hearted ladies who flitted like butterflies in exquisite gowns or giggled as they gossiped on softly piled cushions.

The girls were invited to join them and choose from a selection of honeyed pastries, glasses of mint tea and freshly crushed fruit juice. While sipping her drink, Inga watched her friend gaze nervously around the high vaulted, interlocking rooms. The intricately honeycombed ceilings and latticed domes appeared to float above stuccoed walls with their incised patterns of interlaced leaves.

At first, they spoke little, taking refuge behind shy, uncertain smiles but Inga's confidence grew and she tugged at Floria's arm. Together, they wandered to an elegantly arched window from where they caught glimpses of an inner courtyard. Two of the harem ladies beckoned them and they stepped eagerly through a doorway into the loveliest garden the girls had ever seen.

It was a secret place in which they first heard and then saw, tree-shaded fountains splash into broad alabaster basins. The water sparkled and coloured fish drifted between the extravagant flowers and plate-like leaves of water lilies. In this cool oasis, bees busied themselves with myrtle blossom and small birds darted among citrus trees, ornate with glossy leaves and waxy fruit.

Khaled had told Inga about these inner courtyards. He'd said one was a small intimate patio, close to his own quarters. The other, was this light, airy garden in the haremlek. He'd done his best to describe them but in spite of his enthusiasm, he'd failed to picture the enchantment that Inga now sensed.

She remembered that special evening in late spring, when she'd been sitting with him under the vine-covered pergola at the farm. 'The Persian word for a garden is *paradise*, he'd told her. 'I used to love playing in them when I was a little boy. That's when I realized why it was that, in your religion and mine, *paradise* has come to mean the place where God and his angels live.'

He'd leaned closer and placed a small, heavily-scented sprig of jasmine onto the seat beside her. She remembered his rich, deep voice and the way her body tingled. He'd spoken in Arabic so she hadn't understood. Then, seeing her puzzled expression, he'd moved closer. 'On our wedding night,' he whispered mischievously in their local dialect, 'We'll taste the joys of paradise together.'

She'd pushed him away, pretending to be angry and telling him he should be a poet. Then, before he could move too far, Inga had caught hold of his hand. She'd needed to hear that voice again.

***

The girls were beautiful; Khaled's mother told them so. But soon they would be brides and there were things to do before the wedding. To a woman's eyes, Floria's pregnancy was clearly visible and she'd been terrified about how it would be viewed. To her astonishment, nobody raised an eyebrow. She was marrying Ethan and that was good enough. He'd always been popular. Now he was a hero. The part he'd played in Khaled's escape meant he could do no wrong, and neither could his bride.

After his conversation with Floria, Sheikh Omar had realised the baby she was carrying might well be his grandchild. He'd spoken to his wife and they'd decided to remain silent. The young couples weren't uncomfortable with the idea. If anything, it strengthened the ties between them. When the child was conceived, Ethan, Khaled and Floria had been lovers. The baby would be brought up by Ethan and Floria but belong to the four of them. Nothing could be simpler.

Two serving girls laid out sample rolls of cloth for Floria and Inga's inspection. They were encouraged to take time over their decision making. Selecting the material for their wedding gowns was a serious matter. There were shoes to be made as well, and the excited harem ladies showed them an almost limitless number of styles.

Once their decisions had been taken, the makers could begin work and there was no time to lose. The weddings were only a week away. The preparations were directed by Khaled's mother with a little help and a lot of hindrance from well-meaning sisters, aunts, cousins and friends. The girls played no part in the planning. They would spend the seven remaining days in the hands of the haremlek ladies who would make certain they were ready for the wedding night.

Ethan and Khaled got off lightly. The day before the wedding, their hair was cut by Mohammed, the young man who usually performed this quick and simple task for them in his shop by the souq. Their weddings called for special measures, or so he told them. He arrived at the house with a bag full of painful-looking instruments and an eager cast to his eyes. They could have their body hair removed with a razor or hot wax, he explained, and was astonished when they chose neither option.

Apart from the curls at the base of his belly, Ethan didn't have much in the way of body hair. The little there was, he intended to keep. Khaled, on the other hand, was proud of the dark growth that embellished his legs, arms and chest and said he didn't want to end up looking like a hairless eunuch. He managed to dodge most of Ethan's clouts.

Floria knew them as they were. She'd never complained about their appearance and Inga had glimpsed enough of her brother's body over the years to guess what to expect from her husband on their wedding night. In any case, she knew she could rely on Floria to plug any gaps in her knowledge.

Mohammed was disappointed. He'd hoped to do more for his customers than cut the hair on their heads. The occasion was a special one, however, and they gave him a free hand. The young barber sculpted their hair, making sure it showed their profiles to best effect. When he'd finished, the friends looked at each other and nodded.

'Why don't you do it like this when we come to you in the souq?' Ethan wanted to know. Mohammed rubbed the thumb and middle finger of his left hand together. They took his meaning. The fee for today's work would be higher than usual. Never mind. They were satisfied with their haircuts so they let him loose on their feet and hands.

He worked with pumice stone and oils to soften and then remove the hard, dry skin that walking barefoot had produced over the years. 'There's not much I can do with them,' he grumbled repeatedly and the friends agreed. He was grappling with the impossible. They let him cut, file and buff their nails then thanked him and asked for the bill. They'd put up with enough *chewing around*, as Ethan called it.

Mohammed wouldn't be required to shave them on the morning of the wedding. 'We'll do that for each other,' Khaled joked. 'We wouldn't feel safe with the razor in anyone else's hands.'

The young barber looked crestfallen and Ethan knew why. His visit to Khaled's palatial home was going to be less profitable than he'd hoped. The tip they gave him made sure he'd speak well of his young clients, even though he was secretly troubled by their lack of hygiene. 'It's your wives I'm concerned about,' he told them in a slightly condescending tone. 'Most well-brought up young gentlemen, such as yourselves, prefer to consummate their marriages with shaved bodies.'

He'd done his best to advise them but at the end of the day, the man who paid was the man who ruled. Mohammed pocketed his tip and turned to leave. As he reached the door, Khaled called after him, 'See you at the wedding.'

'You said you wouldn't be needing me.'

'Not to shave us. We want you here as our guest.'

'That was a nice touch,' Ethan told his friend as soon as they were alone. 'Mohammed's as happy as a seaman in a whore house. He's been well-paid, over-tipped, and now he can look forward to a square meal as well.'

Inga and Floria objected to nothing the harem ladies had in mind for them. Their wedding gowns were gorgeous concoctions of silk and their shoes had been skilfully made of matching materials. Their bodies were soaked, bathed and softened with perfumed oils before the gently heated wax was applied and all bodily hair was removed. Their eyes were outlined with kohl and their hair dressed and decorated with pearls. One of the last people to attend them was an elderly lady whose job it was to paint intricate and swirling geometrical patterns onto their hands and feet. She worked meticulously with a minute brush and henna until the ladies of the haremlek were satisfied that no girl's hands had ever been more beautifully decorated.

On the wedding morning, Khaled and Ethan were woken by a couple of servants carrying jugs of hot water into their room. For once, the friends were quickly out of bed, it was going to be a big day for both of them. Nevertheless, they'd slept well. They washed, pouring the water for each other, and lathered their bodies with sandalwood-scented soap. Taking it in turns, they shaved with Khaled's razor. He'd given a similar one to Ethan but they kept it at the farm, so it was ready for them at the week-ends. Preparing for their weddings was a nervy business but they followed their usual routine and wore out the same jokes. That helped.

The women who'd made their clothes on the boat, had tailored a new pair of white tunics. Ethan and Khaled had asked for them to be simply designed and, apart from the gold edgings, they were. Khaled's mother had supplied the silk. Imported from Damascus, it was of a superb quality, both light and comfortable to wear.

As soon as they arrived in the majlis, Khaled's father presented each of them with a Khunja. These curved daggers, with their gold filigree sheaths and woven belts, had been brought from Yemen and each of them was an indisputable symbol of its owner's manhood. He then tied a length of silk around Khaled's head and, using a solid gold pin, attached a peacock feather to the front.

Ethan stared admiringly at the elegant wine-red of the turban with its multi-coloured feather that dipped and caught the light with every movement of his friend's head. 'Now you really are a Sheikh,' he told him.

Khaled motioned to one of the attendants and the man handed him the strip of blue silk he was holding. He tied it carefully around Ethan's head and finished by attaching a peacock feather, identical to his own. 'So are you, my brother,' he winked.

For much of the day, male friends and members of the household gathered in the majlis, keen to congratulate the young men and give them the benefit of their experience in conjugal affairs. Several of them hadn't heard about Khaled and Ethan's visits to *The Three Barrels* and described in detail what was expected of men on their wedding nights. The friends listened politely, not bothering to tell them their apprenticeships had already been served.

Two days before the wedding, servants had been sent to the high mountains. Snow could be found there throughout the year and they'd brought back blocks of ice packed in straw. These were stored in the thick-walled chambers of the ice-house until the day of the wedding when chunks were hacked off, crushed and blended with fruit juice, egg whites and cream. It would be served with fresh and preserved fruits, walnuts and almonds bathed in honey. But first, the guests would enjoy a banquet of meats, fish and rice that legions of cooks had worked throughout the night to prepare.

Ethan had been surprised to hear that there would be no exchange of vows, as in the Christian tradition. The legal transaction between the families of the bride and groom had already taken place. Today's celebrations, Khaled explained, were for the enjoyment of family and friends. In the evening, the girls would be taken to their bridal chambers, undressed by excited, chattering women and made ready for bed.

The two rooms were close to each other in Khaled's section of the house. He and Ethan had chosen them, partly because they were far enough from the rest of the house to guarantee privacy, but mainly because of the large arched windows that led to the inner courtyard. It was a happy place where Ethan and Khaled had spent long evenings talking and joking with their friends. Here, for the duration of the next month, their *honeyed moon,* they would be alone with their wives.

Word was brought to the young men that their brides were waiting for them and, smiling self-consciously, Ethan and Khaled left the gathering. The festivities would continue for several days but without the newly-weds.

Outwardly, the men looked confident enough. Inside, Khaled was quavering. There'd been lots of girls before. Well, a few. Then, Floria had taught him to make love. With Inga, things would be different and he couldn't help wondering if he'd be up to the job. He turned anxiously to his friend, but Ethan had his worries, too. He'd slept with Floria plenty of times but there'd been more flops than he liked to think about. Still, they were in the past - at least, he hoped they were.

***

Half asleep and drowsy from making love, Ethan and Floria were relaxing in each other's arms when they heard a sharp cry of pain. It was his sister's voice and it startled Ethan into full consciousness. He was about to jump out of bed when Floria caught him by the arm. 'Don't be silly,' she whispered and he lay back, amused by his own naivety.

The next morning, Floria watched as he took a knife, made a cut across the palm of his left hand and allowed the blood to drip freely onto the sheets of the marriage bed. A display of stained linen would normally be expected - to prove a bride had been a virgin on her wedding night. Floria's pregnancy was an open secret but Ethan wasn't the man to disappoint his guests. Besides, it would give them something to think about.

***

25

Inga handed her son a small bundle of leaves and watched as he fed them, one by one, to the rabbits. 'That's it, Nuri. They've had enough. Now go and play.'

She'd noticed the rider some time before but it wasn't until he was close to the farm gate that she realised who it was. 'Khaled!' she shouted, 'Leave whatever you're doing, we've got a visitor.'

Sheikh Omar eased himself from the saddle and embraced his daughter-in-law. 'I look and smell like a wadi,' he laughed, slapping brown dust and sand from his clothing, 'But I had to come looking for you. You're both too much in love to visit us.'

Inga's smile reflected the affection she felt for Khaled's father, 'Come into the house and I'll get you something to eat and drink.'

The idea of taking it easy was appealing, he told her, but after so long on horseback, what an old man needed was a walk - to loosen up his joints.

'In that case, Khaled can show you the changes to the farm while I get the food ready.' Inga walked back to the farmhouse and her father-in-law noticed that she was pregnant again. He said nothing. His son would break the news when he was ready to do so. Until then, it wasn't appropriate to comment.

Khaled took his father's arm and directed him proudly towards the newly planted fruit trees. 'This part's protected from the winds,' he explained, 'So the orange and lemon trees grow really well.' The saplings certainly looked healthy. Their leaves were a shiny rich green. A sure sign they'd taken to their new soil and were beginning to thrive. 'They need plenty of water and luckily, there's no shortage of that,' Khaled continued. 'The diviners have found several new spots where we can sink wells. Then there's the spring, near the cave, and some others higher up in the mountains.'

'Plenty of fresh water, for the houses and land around them. That's good.' Omar spoke as enthusiastically as his son.

'Can you see what Ethan and Floria have been doing over there?' Khaled was keen to show off his friends' achievements. His father looked in the direction of the new house and saw a broad belt of young trees. 'I recognise the flat leaves,' he said. 'They're similar to those on the ones you've planted lower down the valley, but for the life of me, I can't remember what they're called.'

'Mulberries. They're for the silk worms. The leaves are about the only things they'll eat.' Khaled described how Ethan and Floria bred them while the Jewish women wove the thread. 'They're already producing enough good quality silk to start selling. It's a lot cheaper than importing it from Damascus.'

He was being modest. Silk manufacturing was one of their most profitable ventures. The skill the Jewish women displayed in spinning, weaving and embroidery, meant their finished products were selling better than they could have hoped. The silk was prepared during the winter, woven into cloth and sold from June until September throughout Almeria, Granada and Malaga. And it wasn't only in Al Andalous that it found a market. The fishermen's boats were kept busy transporting the finished products to various Mediterranean ports. 'Some of them take our silk over to Africa,' he said. 'I'm planning to go with them one of these days, to see where our family came from.' The old man fell strangely quiet.

'What's the matter, Father? Don't you like the idea?'

'It's just that you've got me thinking about our future, here in Al Andalous.' He wouldn't say any more. Instead, he asked for news about the fishermen and their families.

Khaled told him they'd not only finished the houses in which they lived, but they'd also built a small school and a synagogue. 'They're fine people,' he continued. 'They keep their boats in good repair and they've helped design and build better vessels for their neighbours.'

Sheikh Omar's attention was suddenly caught by a mixed flock of sheep and goats. They were grazing the terraced hillside but a kid had begun to stray. Both men watched as the young shepherd used his sling to hurl a pebble in its direction. The stone cracked sharply against a nearby rock and the minute animal sprang into the air. It landed splay-legged, hesitated for an instant, and then scampered back nervously to the protection of the herd.

'That young shepherd isn't called David, by any chance?'

'Like the one who killed Goliath? You're half right. He's a Jew but his name isn't David, it's Nathan. He's Reuben and Danny's nephew. He's the one who bred most of the goats you're looking at.'

Khaled was proud of the young shepherd's achievements but he was starting to have his doubts about the animals. 'We're getting worried in case they multiply to such an extent they overgraze the land. I'd better have a word with Nathan and Ethan. They know more about goats than I do. Ethan's been teaching us to skin them. It's not as easy as it looks but he can do it in no time. He's a real expert with the knife. The Jews call him *Skinner.*'

'To his face?'

'Not if they've got any sense. A few of them might get away with it. Young Aaron, for one. He calls him *Skinner* all the time. Ethan caught him at it, the other morning. It was *Skinner* this and *Skinner* that, until Ethan grabbed hold of his ear and clouted him. He thought he was for it, especially when Ethan told him to get three horses saddled up. He told him we were going hunting and he'd better make sure we caught something. If we did, he'd teach him how to skin it. If we didn't, he'd skin him instead.'

'And did you catch anything?'

'A couple of rabbits. Enough to save Aaron's hide!'

Khaled led the way to a group of wooden hutches where the rabbits were still nibbling the leaves Inga and Nuri had given them earlier. Father and son stood for a few minutes, fascinated by a litter emerging, still partially blind, from the nest.

'They'll have their eyes completely open by tomorrow,' Khaled told his father. 'Nuri loves feeding them. He does it whenever we'll let him.'

Sheikh Omar's face brightened at the mention of his grandson's name, 'How is the boy?' he asked.

'Growing quicker than a mushroom. You know he's over three years old now? Inga says he looks a lot like you.'

Khaled's father roared with laughter, 'You mean he's got a beard already?'

'Not a beard, but she says he's got your nose.'

'That's alright, there's nothing wrong with my nose. I've always rather liked it. I hope he hasn't got my hair, though. His was golden, like his mother's, when he was a baby.'

'It still is.'

'What about his eyes, are they as blue as Inga's?'

'Exactly the same. And his skin's closer to her colour than mine. But everybody says he's got my chin. He runs all over the place. It's impossible to control him at times. He talks more every day and he's always chattering about Grandpa and Grandma. Khaled's face had started to burn. Then, realising his father would be delighted with the news, he blurted, 'Inga's pregnant again.'

'I couldn't help noticing! When's the baby expected?'

'In about four months, God willing. We're hoping for another boy. But come on inside and you can see Nuri.'

His father nodded. The thin mountain air was making him feel breathless. 'Before we do, I'm afraid I've got some bad news. I don't know whether we should talk about it in front of your wife, especially in her present condition.'

'We don't have any secrets,' Khaled said, shaking his head. 'Inga and I tell each other everything. The good as well as the bad.'

'It's your brother Ali,' his father began. 'It seems he's been busy building up an army of supporters. He claims it's to defend the area around Abdera against the Christians but King Abu Abdullah, in Granada, has treaties with them. I see no reason why they should threaten us.'

Khaled wasn't so sure. In the past, Christian monarchs had sought alliances with Muslims, whenever they'd found themselves in conflict with other Christians. Now, King Ferdinand and Queen Isabella so dominated their co-religionaries, they no longer needed Muslim support. 'As long as the threat is no closer to home than Abdera,' he began.

'It's Abdera for now.'

Khaled nodded slowly. He had no reason to show sympathy for his brother, yet he'd often wondered how Ali must have felt when a younger brother was born. To find he had a rival after spending several years as the only son couldn't have been easy. 'Sometimes I feel sorry for him. Inga and I have so much and he has nothing.'

'You've got what you deserve and so has he.'

'But do you ever wonder if we judged him too harshly?' Khaled tried again. 'I was lucky to find Ethan when I was young. Ali was never blessed with friends. Maybe his loneliness made it easier for Sulieman to drag him down.'

'You may be right,' Sheikh Omar sighed. The estrangement had hurt him more than he was willing to admit and in his heart, he still hoped for reconciliation. 'Anyway, let's go in and see my grandson.'

With his bright blue eyes and mass of blond hair, Nuri was a delightful child. As soon as he saw his grandfather, he started to giggle and climbed onto the old man's knee, eager to pull his beard. 'You did that when you were his age,' Sheikh Omar told his son.

Inga was busy laying out bowls of fresh fruit and jugs of juice for them to enjoy while she prepared the meal. 'Has Khaled told you?' She looked conspiratorial and placed her hands on her pregnant belly. Sheikh Omar crossed the room and embraced his daughter-in-law. 'He had to tell me. He was too excited to keep such wonderful news to himself. He says the baby is expected in about four months.'

Inga nodded, 'And it's not only us who have good news. Ethan and Floria have another little girl, did you know that?'

'No, I didn't,' Omar replied. 'That goes to show how long it is since we last visited each other. Khaled pointed out Danny and Reuben's cottage to me, earlier. What do they do for a living these days?'

'They fish of course, but mainly, they breed and sell horses. We'll go and have a look at their herd later, if you like. You might find a few things about them you recognise.'

'You mean they've stolen them from us?'

'No, not stolen. I gave them a few mares, to get them started. I stable a couple of our stallions with them from time to time. They're reliable studs.'

'No wonder they don't need to work for me any more. They must be making a fortune, those two brothers! So, one way or another, you've kept your old gang together.' Sheikh Omar sat back and for a long while, he said nothing. Khaled knew these silences. His father was weighing up a situation and considering the best way to proceed. He'd speak when he was ready.

'Now that I've seen you again, and everything you've worked to build up,' he began slowly, 'I realise I have no right to disturb your lives by asking for help.'

'Ali is getting ready to cause trouble for us.' Khaled started to outline the situation for his wife's benefit. He didn't dwell on the Christian threat; it might amount to nothing, in which case, he'd have alarmed a pregnant woman unnecessarily. On the other hand, if the danger was as grave as he was beginning to suspect, he'd have to think long and hard about how to tell her. 'I'm going to fetch Ethan,' he said, 'He needs to be a part of this conversation.'

The hens stopped their scratching and cackled their irritation while Khaled crossed the yard and knocked at the door of Ethan's farmhouse. Without waiting, he walked straight into the kitchen and found Floria feeding her new baby. Startled, she looked up. Then, seeing it was Khaled, she smiled her welcome.

'I'm sorry, I should have waited. I didn't think …' he began.

'Don't pretend to be embarrassed, you've seen more than this!'

'That was before we were respectable.'

At that moment, Ethan burst into the kitchen. He'd seen Khaled arrive and sprinted to the cottage, eager to see his friend. 'What's this, a Moor raping my wife?'

'Give the man a chance,' Floria giggled, 'He's just walked through the door!'

'Beer?' Ethan offered.

Khaled shook his head. 'I can't. Father's here.' Turning to Floria he asked, 'Can I borrow your husband for a while?'

She put on her furious face. 'You had him all day yesterday!'

'That was for hunting, this is different.'

'Fishing?'

She was keeping up her angry act rather well and Khaled decided she'd earned an explanation. 'This is important, Floria. Father has a problem and I need Ethan.'

'Go on then, take him!' Her attempts to be stern never lasted more than a few moments. 'If Inga's cooking something special for your father, tell her I'll lend a hand. That's if she needs me.'

The two men crossed the yard, terrorising the hens as they went, and swung straight into Inga's kitchen. 'I need a few herbs from the garden,' she told them. 'It'll give you a chance to talk.'

As soon as she'd closed the door behind her, Sheikh Omar began to describe the situation for Ethan's benefit. He'd always believed that reason and common sense should be applied to situations where conflict threatened. Nobody could be right all of the time and truth usually lay somewhere in the middle. Ali, on the other hand, thought that compromise amounted to fighting with one hand behind your back and would lead to ruin.

'A lot of people agree with him,' Khaled said. 'What we see as making fair and reasonable concessions, the Christians mistake for weakness.'

'That's Ali's point, exactly,' his father said. 'I hope he's wrong, but he says we've allowed them the freedom to undermine our liberty for too long. Furthermore, he thinks men of my age are too old to mount an effective challenge. He's probably right. By nature, I am not a man of war. Ethan, forgive me for saying this, but we are now facing a very real threat from the Christians. One that people like me have been too slow to recognise.'

Ethan was usually content to let others work out political matters on his behalf. This time, however, the situation was too serious to ignore. Looking across at Sheikh Omar, he said, 'We'd better find out the truth. And the sooner the better. But whatever happens, there'll be one Christian and a lot of Jews ready to stand with you.'

***

26

They had been spotted. Ethan drew Khaled's attention to a burst of reflected light, high in the mountains. Moments later, they saw an answering flash from a point lower down. By straining their eyes against the glare of the sun, they were able to make out the movements of several small figures peering at them from the distant rocks. There were two further flashes of light and a couple of lookouts could be seen scuttling away.

It was more or less what Khaled and Ethan had been expecting but that didn't make them feel any the less uneasy. 'We're approaching openly,' Khaled said. 'They can see we're no threat to them.' He was trying to sound reassuring but Ethan wasn't taken in. 'We never were a threat to your brother, except in his mind. He's a born schemer and he thinks we're made from the same clay.'

Khaled was no longer listening. A group of horsemen, partly concealed by their own dust cloud, had emerged from the mouth of a dried up river bed and were heading towards them. He and Ethan would soon know whether they'd been fools to take Ali at his word.

***

Three days earlier, they'd been astonished by the arrival of a messenger. It was the first time they'd heard from Ali since his row with their father and now he was seeking to make contact. His words seemed conciliatory enough but the friends remained dubious about his motives. Ali claimed he was eager to heal the breach with Khaled and was asking for a meeting. Surprisingly, he wanted Ethan to be present when they met.

Sheikh Omar agreed that contact with his elder son was desirable. Nevertheless, he was suspicious and had been inclined to reject Ali's request. Khaled had taken a more generous line. If Ali were sincere, the rift could be healed and future conflict avoided. 'We won't be in any danger while we're there at his invitation. He knows the traditional law as well as we do. Guests are entitled to his protection for three days. If he violated the code of hospitality, the whole of Al Andalous would be outraged. He'd never stand the loss of face.'

**

The riders drew closer. Their leader raised his right arm and his men pulled up in a shower of sand and grit. Alone, he urged his horse forward until he was within easy hailing range of the two friends.

'Peace be upon you Sheikh Khaled,' he called.

'Peace be upon you,' Khaled shouted in reply, surprised to be addressed so formally. 'We come at the invitation of my brother.'

'Sheikh Ali will be pleased see you,' the man replied. 'Follow me but I must ask you not to close the space between you and my men. They are nervous and easily startled.'

They were also heavily armed and in spite of the man's politeness, the severity of his expression made sure his instructions would be obeyed. From their clothing, Khaled could tell the men belonged to one of the hill tribes with which Ali had allied himself. Good fighters, they were loyal to their leaders but disinclined to compromise. 'We'll do as you say,' Khaled shouted, 'But, as I told you, we are here at my brother's invitation.'

Five of the horsemen led the way back to the wadi from which they'd emerged. The friends followed, maintaining their distance. The other riders fell in behind them. No-one spoke as they moved steadily upwards, following the dried up river bed and skirting the massive boulders that generations of flash floods had ground smooth. Apart from the odd scuttling lizard, the only sounds were those made by the horses. Their hooves crunched the gravel, causing occasional falls of sand and stones, as they moved through a narrow defile and rounded bends overhung with rocks.

Khaled and Ethan found themselves approaching an encampment guarded by groups of armed men. The leader of their column dismounted and walked towards a small hide-covered tent. He called out, and then waited respectfully until he was told to enter. Moments later, he emerged accompanied by a figure dressed in white.

Ali's skin had been darkened by the sun and he looked leaner and fitter than when the friends had last seen him. His face, however, was expressionless and gave no clue to his feelings. He glanced first at his brother and then at Ethan. 'You are welcome,' he said at last. Khaled's eyes narrowed suspiciously, surprised by this apparent warmth. Looking in Ethan's direction, Ali offered his hand in friendship and the three men walked together into the simple tent.

Apart from cushions and a few worn, goat-hair rugs, there were no comforts. After the parching heat of their journey, however, the interior struck Khaled and Ethan as refreshingly cool. Ali invited them to sit with him on the cushioned floor and, after seeking their approval, had the tent flaps opened to improve the flow of air.

Satisfied that his guests were comfortable, Ali clapped his hands and a youth, naked apart from a linen loin-cloth, entered and stood waiting for instructions. Ali told him to bring refreshments and the boy fetched jugs of water, drinking cups and a large pot of coffee which he placed carefully on the rugs in front of his master's guests. Moments later, he returned carrying trays of dates, oranges and peeled pomegranates. He handed each of the seated men a small conical cup into which he poured cardamom scented coffee. The boy allowed it to stream from a great height, ensuring the surface was generously covered with a frothy *face*. He had learned better than to insult his master's guests by serving them faceless coffee.

The friends noticed a flicker of embarrassment distort Ali's features as the youth moved without thought to sit at his side. The expectant expression on the young servant's face reminded Ethan of a puppy accustomed to its master's fondling. Ali glanced uneasily at his guests before waving the boy impatiently away. The youngster started to back respectfully towards the opening of the tent but Ali, once more in control of himself, told the boy to remain within earshot.

For long frustrating moments, hypocritical politenesses were exchanged during which, all of them were careful to avoid making reference to previous disagreements. Ali asked after the health of his father and mother. Only then, did conversation turn to the matter in hand.

'In the past, you and I have quarrelled,' Ali began, waving his hand dismissively. 'It is also true that at times, your friend was treated unjustly.' Turning to Ethan he made an upturned gesture with his hands, indicating that the matter had been something over which he'd had no control. 'But you must believe me when I tell you, I never felt anything but deep affection for you both.'

Ethan was losing patience, 'You and Sulieman arranged for us to be taken prisoner. We were treated worse than dogs!' Khaled sucked in his breath causing Ethan to glance briefly in his direction. The glare on his friend's face temporarily silenced him.

'That terrible business was none of my doing.' Ali's voice was becoming high-pitched. Khaled remembered this tendency of his brother's from childhood and fought to prevent himself from smiling. When under pressure, or afraid he wouldn't be believed, Ali had always protested by squealing like a pig.

'It was Sulieman who arranged for your capture,' Ali continued. 'I heard about it, of course, and immediately did everything I could. Unfortunately, by then it was too late. Sulieman acted alone. You cannot believe that I, your brother, would be capable of such a wicked plan.'

Khaled did indeed believe his brother capable of such wickedness but whether the story was true or not, he would accept the face-saving excuse that had been offered.

'Believe me,' Ali continued, 'There are more serious matters that should concern us than unimportant family rivalries.'

Ethan clenched his teeth. Their enslavement had been no petty affair. Furthermore, bitter experience had taught him never to trust this man. However, he remembered Sheikh Omar saying it was better to negotiate than to fight. 'Words cost nothing,' he'd told them, 'But their consequences last forever.'

If there was a chance that tragedy could be averted, they should conceal their distrust with gestures of civility and accept as true the diplomatic lies that Ali offered. He was smiling which was not a good sign. Khaled and Ethan remembered that in the past, it had often been the prelude to acts of cruelty. Warily, they allowed him to continue.

'We have recently found ourselves in possession of infidel prisoners.' Ali paused in order to judge the effect his words were having. Satisfied he had Ethan and Khaled's attention, he continued. 'They were persuaded to give us certain information concerning their activities and the intentions of their armies. From what they have told us, we must urgently recognise the perilous nature of our position. We can no longer count on being left in peace in this part of our territory. In fact, it is only a matter of time before the infidel forces move to extinguish our civilisation.'

It was Ali's use of the word *infidel* that jarred most with Khaled and Ethan. Their captors had used the term repeatedly when sneering about Muslims and Jews. *Infidels* were regarded as less than human and therefore fit for any cruel and degrading treatment their masters chose to inflict.

Ali continued to describe the atrocities regularly committed by the Christian forces and the friends found it easy to believe a good part of his story. Their bodies and minds carried the scars inflicted by their captors and there were times when memories of their enslavement were all too real. The word *infidel,* however, evoked not the blind hatred that Ali intended, but a fear of the intolerance that it implied.

He ended by showing them a map and the information it contained was certainly shocking. Small areas around the cities of

Granada and Almeria, including their own section of the Alpujarras, were still in friendly hands. However, enemy forces now controlled most of the land that had previously been Muslim. Isolated within their paradise, they had ignored the outside world and closed their ears to rumours about the advances made by Christian armies.

'You can see what I meant when I told you we had more important things to concern us than family disagreements.' Ali believed he had said enough. The evidence argued for itself.

Even so, Khaled tried to take a more optimistic view, 'Father is convinced that in the end, reason will prevail.'

'Father is a dreamer,' Ali interrupted brusquely. 'He believes the world and his fellow men are as he would wish them to be.'

'Father is a man of great learning!' Khaled replied angrily.

'He lives in a world of words and not of realities. While he and other so-called learned men are busy with their books and their fine ideals, our enemies circle like wolves, waiting for the moment to attack.'

'Father would say that if we cannot persuade them with justice and reason, we have no right to prevail.'

'Justice. Reason. Tolerance!' Ali sneered, 'That's all Father and men like him think about. They think too much! They can see good in everyone. Believe me, a lot of men have died from too much tolerance on the part of their leaders. The problem with people like Father is that their education was dominated by the teachings of Greek philosophers. Their idealism has prepared them to live in a world that no longer exists.

We have tolerated the presence of Christians in our midst. Most of them, like your friend Ethan and his family, have been good and loyal citizens. There are, however, other fanatical members of their faith who, instead of respecting us for the freedoms we have allowed them, seek to impose their beliefs and laws upon us. Believe me, this war will not be won by the preachers of reason. It will be won by the strong and it will be their version of the truth that future generations will read.'

*

'How long do you think we've got?' Khaled asked his friend as they rode home. His question didn't come as a surprise. Ethan had been thinking along similar lines from the moment Ali had shown them the map. 'A few weeks. A year at the most.'

***

Three months later, Ali brought the news to his family in person. To avoid further bloodshed, Abu Abdullah had surrendered to the forces of King Ferdinand and Queen Isabella. In exchange for assurances that the Muslims would be permitted to found a new kingdom in the Alpujarras Mountains, he had handed the keys of Granada to the Catholic Monarchs.

Although the last Muslim king of Granada and his entourage had been permitted to make a dignified departure from the city, the shock of the surrender had reduced most of his followers to silence. It was left to the aged Queen Mother to speak for them. Hearing her son's sigh as he turned for one last glimpse of his beloved Granada, she cruelly told him, 'You do well to weep like a woman over that which you could not defend as a man.'

Fearing the worst and hoping to find a place of refuge for his family, Sheikh Omar made urgent contact with blood relations who'd continued to live in North Africa. Khaled allowed himself a brief period of optimism, arguing that since their farm was in the Alpujarras, they'd be left in peace. Ethan spoke of living on borrowed time.

***

27

For the second time that week, Inga woke up screaming. The bad dreams had begun shortly after Ethan and Khaled's visit to Ali. Now, they were happening more often. Khaled reached out to his wife and cradled her patiently in his arms, waiting until she'd cried herself free of the nightmare. When she seemed calmer, he asked, 'It was your dream again, wasn't it? The one about the mountain?'

'Yes, the Cerro. The dream's never quite the same but it's always about us.' She was sounding less anxious, but her voice was still coloured by fear. 'This time we were higher up, but we couldn't escape from whatever it was that was chasing us. We kept trying but we weren't able reach the top. Something was holding us back.'

Khaled hated seeing her in this terrified state and blamed himself for letting her know about the latest Christian advances. She'd sensed the situation was serious and he'd ended up telling her everything he knew. Maybe he'd over-estimated her inner strength.

It was increasingly doubtful that their family and friends had a future in Al Andalous. Some of them were looking to brother Muslim states for military support. Others would settle for a place of refuge. His own mother and father had left for North Africa, hoping to reach an agreement with blood relations who'd continued to live there.

Khaled stroked his wife's hair and was relieved to feel her tensed body relax against his, 'You said we were trying to escape?'

'Yes, but the worst thing was the blood.'

'*Blood?*' he repeated, horrified by the picture his wife was starting to paint.

'Yes, the dream's different every time but there's always blood. It's on the ground and all over the people lying there.'

Khaled wasn't surprised she was frightened; her description would be enough to alarm anyone. 'Who else was there, apart from you and me?'

'Nuri, of course. He was with us. Ethan, Floria and the children were somewhere close. I couldn't see them but I know they were there. They were trying to reach us but something was stopping them.'

'Inga, it was only a dream.' He kissed his wife gently, hoping to soothe her fears.

She shook her head, desperate for him to take her seriously. 'Khaled, I've dreamed all my life and sometimes those dreams have turned into nightmares. None of them were like this. It was as real to me as you are now. I can still remember everything about it. You know what dreams are like; they start to disappear as soon as you wake up. Then, after a while you can't remember them at all. This one's different; none of it goes away. What frightens me most is that it's happening more and more often. Sometimes I'm afraid to go to sleep in case the nightmare, or whatever you want to call it, comes back.'

Khaled pulled her tense, frightened body closer. 'You're safe with Nuri and me. Nothing bad is going to happen to any of us.' Guilt nagged at his words. He'd intended to comfort his wife; instead he was giving false hope.

Inga welcomed his arms around her and the security his strength provided. As long as this man was protecting her, she knew there was nothing to be afraid of. His body smelled good. It was a sweet, male muskiness that spoke to her of his potency. She kissed his cheek, her lips brushing the dark stubble she would enjoy removing for him in the morning.

Before their marriages, Ethan and Khaled had shaved themselves or, more often than not, each other. Inga remembered that first morning when she'd brought the soap and water for him. 'You don't have to do that,' Khaled had told her, reckoning without his wife's determination.

'Sit down my husband.' She remembered the words, '*My husband*' and how good they'd felt on her lips. 'Let me serve you, as a faithful slave should serve her master.'

'You're no slave …' he'd begun angrily, only to look foolish when he realised she'd been joking. They'd known each other for years and there was still so much to learn.

'Ethan lets Floria do it for him,' she'd said, 'And she baths him at night. Didn't he tell you?'

'I think he said something about it.' Khaled had done his best to sound casual but she knew he was thinking about the bathing sessions he and Ethan had enjoyed with Floria before they were married. He was probably wondering whether Inga knew about them. Her laughter made it plain, it didn't matter either way. The touch of her fingers, the coolness of the blade and the caring way in which she removed all traces of facial hair, left her husband smooth-skinned and alert. His morning shave was a luxury he'd never willingly give up. Just as in both homes, the evenings had become a time for leisurely baths and massage with scented oils.

Inga snuggled up to her drowsing partner. 'Heaven must be a beautiful place,' Floria had told her, shortly before their weddings. 'Your brother takes me half way there and Khaled will do the same for you.'

Ethan had spoken endlessly about Khaled for as long as she could remember. She'd watched them talking quietly together, their arms around each other's shoulders. Boys of their age shared close, intimate relationships. Inga knew that, but their faces told her there was more than friendship between them. 'Do you think they can really love us when they care so much for each other?' she'd once asked her friend.

'There are more ways than one of loving,' Floria told her. 'Khaled will love you more than any woman has the right to be loved but never make him choose between you and Ethan. Do that and you'll lose him.'

Inga knew she was right. 'The next time you're talking to Khaled,' she said, 'Take a good look at his face. There's a small scar above his right eyebrow. It happened the day we first talked about getting married. Ethan caught us together and nearly killed him. He thought he was going to lose the most important person in his life. That isn't me, Floria, and it isn't you.'

***

Khaled told Ethan about his wife's nightmare. It was strange having the same dream more than once but the darkness had gone and in its place, the mid-morning light streamed down. It was hard to take terror seriously. Talk of the Cerro reminded them it had been too long since they'd climbed it. The view from the peak excited them, which was why, as youngsters, they'd so often scrambled to the top. It was good hunting country, too. There were plenty of quail, hare and rabbits to be flushed out and they always returned with something for the pot. Giving that as their excuse, they set out with Rabo for company. He'd turned into a fine hunter, old Rabo. It took a good dog to run down a hare and he did that more often than not.

They pushed through cool, shoulder-high grasses that closed behind them, leaving no sign of their passage. Higher up, scrub and gorse edged out the lushness. It was replaced by bushy herbs that caught at their clothes and scented the air with rosemary. The tang reminded Ethan of roasting chicken, of kid and of juicy lamb. Higher still, and their feet rasped against crust-dry ground and panicked partridges into breaking cover.

The Cerro was balanced by a similar mountain to the east. There had always been something reassuring about their symmetry. Highlighted in turn by the sun, the peaks protected the valley between them. 'We used to call it *our mountain*,' Khaled panted.

They'd reached the half-way point. Oregano and sage sprouted from between the rocks, while vivid red poppies livened the rust coloured earth.

Ethan pointed to an eagle. It was circling the crag that reached skywards above them. 'Come on,' he yelled, 'Let's get as close to him as we can.'

The view didn't disappoint and for a time, its wildness reduced them to silence. They sat near the summit, unconcerned by the jagged gorge that lay below.

'How many more times do you think we'll do this?' Ethan asked.

Khaled didn't answer. Being so high up, they could gaze further out to sea than was possible from the farm. 'Can you see it on the horizon?' he was pointing excitedly. 'It must be the Jebel. That's where my family came from.'

Ethan strained to look and at last made out a greyish-yellow streak in the far distance. 'If you say so. More likely it's a cloud or a trick of the light. Not your range of mountains in Africa.'

'If we were able to fly like birds, we could go over and take a look.'

Khaled's words provoked Ethan's memory. 'Somebody else once talked about flying like birds,' he said quietly. 'It was Aaron's cousin. He told me their boats could move in straight lines, as easily as birds fly. Before that, I'd all but given up. You'd got such a start on us, I thought we'd never reach you in time. When he talked about the birds and their boats, I knew we had a chance.' Ethan's voice carried a warning. He might have brought up the subject, but he'd said all he wanted to say.

They approached their memories differently. Khaled needed to talk, hoping that in that way, the terrors would turn stale and powerless to hurt. Ethan chose what seemed the easier course of action. He pushed his memories aside.

'If you hadn't come ...' Khaled's eyes were smarting and his voice was choked.

'Don't think about it!' Ethan was suddenly angry, more with himself for opening the conversation than with Khaled for baring wounds. 'We'll go insane if we remember. We've got to forget. Those things belong in the past. We've got to leave them there.'

Khaled wasn't ready to let go. He needed to thank Ethan for the life he'd given him back. He supposed it would be like that for as long as they lived. But he'd misread his friend's mood. 'If you hadn't come for us ...' he began again.

'You won't let me forget, will you?' Ethan grabbed the front of his friend's tunic, bunching it in his clenched fist. 'It was bad for me as well!' He saw the pupils of Khaled's eyes dilate with fear. 'I'm sorry,' he said quietly, 'I was thinking of myself.' Admitting to selfishness helped make him feel less guilty. He looked away, trying to lose himself in the beauty of their surroundings.

'Sometimes I forget you took more than the rest of us put together,' Khaled told him. 'No, it's not that I forget. It just seems important to say how much we owe you.' He put his arm around Ethan's shoulders and for the first time in their lives, his friend shrugged it off.

'You don't owe me a thing!' There was a bitterness in Ethan's voice that Khaled hadn't heard for a long time. 'If you knew the sort of man you're talking to, you wouldn't think so much of me. Killing Garcia and the guards taught me what I am.'

Khaled's attention had been caught by the sheerness of the drop beneath them. 'How many greens can you see?' he asked.

It was a game they'd played as youngsters and Ethan was glad of the distraction. 'I don't know. I've tried to count them but they always defeat me. There are so many shades. When you think you've got it right, the light changes and the greens become browns or the yellows become greens and you have to start again. You taught me to see those colours, you know. When we were boys you showed me that yellow corn fields weren't yellow at all. There were a hundred different tones that together, we call yellow. You helped me to see things differently, to write Arabic and to listen to your poetry. You encouraged me to think like a man and not like a boy. You taught me all of those things, and in return, I taught you to kill.'

'You sell yourself short, Brother.'

When he spoke again, Ethan's voice had become a monotone, sounding more like prayer than conversation. 'I try to be a good husband and father. I want to be a good brother to Inga.'

'You're all of those things. You make Floria happy and, as for me, you're the best friend a man could have. Why do you hate yourself when we love you so much?'

'Because I can't forget what I am and what I did.'

'I've told you about that. We all have. We've told you the truth a thousand times, but it's not what you want to hear. You enjoy whipping yourself with guilt.'

'I'm a murderer. I've killed people.'

'And if you hadn't killed them, they'd have killed us.'

'Khaled, what would you say if I told you that I enjoyed killing those men? As I smashed their heads or hacked them with my knife, I was happy and excited. I felt more alive than I'd ever felt before. Well, what do you think of your beloved friend now that he's told you that?'

Khaled picked up a stone and hurled it into the ravine. He watched as it cracked into one rock after another before continuing downwards and finally disappearing from sight. 'You forget I was there when you killed the guards,' he said at last. 'It's hard to say how I felt because there was so much happening at once. At first I was too terrified to feel anything but fear. Then, I remember being excited because you were giving us a chance to live. I felt angry because I was chained and couldn't do anything to help. Then, I was frightened again; in case you weren't able kill them all. Everything happened so quickly and there were so many feelings. There's one thing I am sure of, though. I was happy when you killed the guards. They were dying and we were going to live. None of us would be here today, if you hadn't done what you did.'

Ethan smiled his gratitude, 'It's not forever, though, is it?'

'Nothing is.'

'Our future here. We don't have one, do we?'

'Not here, maybe. But we have a future. You gave us that.'

Khaled noticed his friend shudder. Rocks that normally held the sun's warmth had grown strangely cold while a dark sky began to menace them. Rabo leapt to his feet and bolted after a rabbit. There was the usual short, frantic chase with an inevitable end, before the dog returned with its broken-necked victim.

'Good boy, Rabo! Good Boy!' They were habitual words spoken without thought. Ethan took the torn body and handed it to his friend. It was something he'd done a hundred times before. Now, as they watched a trickle of blood start from the dead creature's mouth, they sensed a difference.

The liquid flowed faster. It splashed fresh and red onto the ground then merged with the flood of poppies. The friends felt a flicker of revulsion which, in the stormy half-light, turned swiftly to fear. The flowers layering the ground had lost their innocence and the entire Cerro looked as if it were drenched with blood. The peaks, once magnificent in their sharp angularity, loomed and threatened. Dark, low-hanging clouds shrouded the valley and closed down the day.

They'd lost sight of the house and Ethan felt a surge of panic. 'Let's get down!' he said urgently, as though by retracing their steps all would be well.

Back at the farm, Khaled tried laughing at their fears. 'It was getting dark, that's all it was!'

'No, it was more than that. You felt it as well, didn't you? We were walking through Inga's dream.'

***

28

'Can I come with you Daddy?' It was a question Nuri was burning to ask and yet, he wasn't sure he should. The damp winter air was ripe with the smell of horses. In the past that would have meant a ride on his pony or better still, a trip out with his father and Uncle Ethan. That had been before. They never took him anywhere these days. He didn't think he'd been bad but he must have done something wrong if they didn't want him with them.

He was jumping around, watching the riders make ready and hoping to be noticed when a shining bush caught his attention. Moving closer for a better look, he saw it was hung with spiders' webs. Woven during the night, they were now spangled with dew. Nuri twitched the twiggy branches and found he could make the droplets jump and shimmer as they caught the watery light. He poked the largest of the webs and watched the spider stir.

Disappointingly, it didn't run and seize his finger. Instead, it hunkered down, on guard and hoping for better things. The boy tried scrunching up a leaf and flicking it at the web. This time, the spider came rushing to investigate. It was a good game and Nuri could have played it forever. But the spider grew wise. No longer tricked by lifeless fragments, it returned to the centre of its web and lay in wait.

The mountain fog, thick and impenetrable for the best part of a week, was starting to clear. He'd heard his father say something about the sun burning it off before midday but it was still early morning and difficult to see beyond the farm house.

Nuri had been giving the matter some thought these last few days and he'd come up with the idea that it was steam from the horses' nostrils that caused the fog. He wasn't sure about it, but his Daddy would know, if only he could talk to him.

There was an urgency about his father's behaviour this morning that warned the boy not to butt in. Something new was happening and Nuri longed to be a part of it but that wouldn't be allowed. He couldn't understand why things had changed.

'Stay at home and look after Mummy for me.' His father said that a lot these days. None of the other men had time for him either. Before, they'd stay to chat about his pony or play games. Now, they went off together in large, noisy groups. Some of them he didn't see again. Others came back, sad and serious, like his father was looking now. He was like that when Nuri had been naughty but he hadn't done anything wrong today. He knew that for a fact because it was still early, and he hadn't had time to get up to those things his parents called *mischief*.

Why was his father taking so long to say goodbye to Mummy? The horses stamped impatiently and Nuri lost interest. He went off to feed the rabbits. With luck, he'd catch sight of the new babies. He decided to give them some more leaves. Mothers needed extra when they had little ones, so they could make plenty of milk. His father had told him that, just as he'd said to move quietly and not frighten them. Mother rabbits sometimes killed their babies if they sensed danger. That was another thing he couldn't understand. It seemed all wrong to him, a mother killing her babies. It must be true, though, because his daddy had told him so.

Nuri watched his father ride off with Uncle Ethan and their friends. Then, suddenly, he couldn't see them anymore. They'd vanished into the mist. He heard his mother calling and, as he ran up to her, he saw the tears shining on her face. He knew she wouldn't tell him why she'd been crying, so he didn't ask. She cried a lot these days.

'We're going to see Auntie Floria,' she said at last. Nuri could see she was struggling with a smile. 'You'd like that wouldn't you?'

Yes, he would like that. He could play with Cousin Bella and Auntie Floria was always kind.

But even she was different today. When they arrived, they found her in a hurry and too busy to talk. She kept darting about, collecting food and blankets. 'We're going to the cave,' was all she'd tell him. It was exciting going to Daddy's cave. It smelled of the old wood fires where they cooked food and warmed themselves while listening to Uncle Ethan's stories. They'd been there lots of times, so why were Mummy, Auntie Floria, his Grandma and Aunties so serious? They didn't seem to be looking forward to it at all.

***

By attacking from the sea, the Christians had intended to take them by surprise but Reuben spotted the flotilla long before it made the shore. It was the way raiders had come in the past and they'd been made to pay a heavy price. He immediately ordered Aaron and his men to repulse this new band of invaders. The young Jews had protected their families before and would do so again, but the raids were becoming more frequent and the rumours of Christian advances more serious by the day.

The small garrison in the Zugaiba fortress had watched, not overly concerned, when Khaled and Ethan rode in support of their comrades. As far as the visibility would allow, they'd followed their friends with their eyes but although the mist was starting to clear, much of the landscape remained hidden.

The guards felt themselves fortunate up here, protected by the almost impassable mountains. The chance of an enemy incursion was scarcely worth considering. It was from the coast that an attack would come. They doubted if this morning's raid would amount to much – they never had in the past. Things could safely be left to the Jews.

Why do they keep doing it, Khaled thought to himself as he and his men drew closer to the sea. It didn't seem to be much more than a small Christian raiding party - not enough to cause real trouble but a nuisance that had to be dealt with. In all probability, they weren't an organised band at all. Just adventurers looking to snatch a few slaves and disappear as quickly as they'd come. Aaron and his men would be more than a match for them. But it was strange the raiding parties hadn't learned their lesson by now. Khaled smiled confidently to himself, not realising the Christians had learned, and like Nuri's spider, grown wise.

***

'Goats need to eat,' Nathan told his uncle. 'No amount of weather changes that.'

Danny watched his nephew shrug on a second sheep-skin before trudging into the mist. The dawn light, pale and feeble, scarcely cut the gloom. 'I'll be there as soon as I've had a look at the horses,' he yelled after the boy. 'I'll bring you your food.'

Danny's wife shook her head. 'He'll get frozen, up on that mountain,' she told her husband. 'You'd better take the boy a blanket.' She was right, but she'd never hear Nathan complain. Danny knew what they'd got in his nephew. He was a tough one. A man, more than a boy. He'd stand any amount of harsh weather as long as he could do a good job. Sheep and goats? Nathan knew more about them than men three times his age. But it was a cold morning.

Danny checked the horses, making sure they had food and water. He and Reuben could see to the mucking-out later. He went back into the farmhouse, picked out a good thick blanket and grabbed Nathan's bundle of food.

He found his nephew sheltering between a few rocks. He dropped down beside him and threw the extra blanket over the young man's shoulders. 'Knew you wouldn't forget,' Nathan smiled. He took the bundle of food and held up a piece of wood he'd been working.

'It's shaping up well,' Danny told him. 'You're good with your hands.' By the time he'd finished whittling, the stick would be a doll.

Nathan's mother could dress it and give it to his little sister.

While the goats grazed around them, Nathan and Danny sat on the ridge above the village, tearing off chunks of bread and sharing the cheese. 'There's a funny noise,' Nathan told his uncle. 'It started before you got here. It sounds like horses on the move. I can't make out what it is. The mist's too thick.'

Danny could hear it too. It was getting closer and now they could feel the ground tremble. The dogs barked an alarm into the damp fog. They were trying to warn them, but of what? There was nothing to see except for the goats. They were darting backwards and forwards in small fragmented groups, not herding together like they usually did. Echoes played tricks with sound while the mist, in some parts wispy but for the most part dense, hugged the mountains. Danny and his nephew couldn't make sense of things at all.

***

The villagers had trusted in their position, high in the Alpujarras, believing it gave them security. The time taken by an enemy climbing the steep goat tracks would give the Al Zugaiba garrison plenty of time to prepare. The possibility of a serious attack from the interior of the country wasn't worth considering. The mountains provided an almost impenetrable bulwark and an enemy's approach would be noticed well in advance. But they'd reckoned without the fanaticism of the Christian forces. By trekking through the mountains, they'd achieved what had been thought impossible. They took the thick concealing mist as a gift from God and as a clear sign of his approval.

***

The shock of their numbers immobilised Danny and Nathan. As the Christian army emerged from the murk, the two men found it hard to take in what they were seeing. There must have been hundreds of foot soldiers, all carrying shields on which were painted large red crosses. More terrifying were the mounted troops, bearing guns of a type Nathan and his uncle had never seen before. They were called harquebuses but they would never know that, just as they wouldn't see these weapons, crueller in their accuracy than any guns before them, take the lives of their friends and family.

One of the riders moved in their direction. Danny pushed his nephew behind him and walked towards the advancing soldier. He had started to raise his hand in greeting when the blast from a harquebus ripped through his chest.

Nathan knew he had to warn the village. Still clutching the doll he'd made for his little sister, he turned to run. A rider cut him down more easily than a farmer scythes hay.

✷✷✷

The early morning had begun normally enough. There was a braying of donkeys and a few dog-bark echoes that bounced around the mountain-side. But when the people of Felix woke up, they found Christian troops surrounding the village.

Old men and boys attempted to organise some sort of defence but they weren't soldiers. Farmers and shepherds for the most part, they had no plan, no deeply thought-out strategy, only the desperate need to protect their homes, their women and the children. They fought with what lay to hand until the Christian forces over-ran them.

 The terrified women tried to hide the children and themselves in their homes but were steadily driven out by smoke from fires lit by their attackers. Most were cut down or raped as they tried to flee. Others took refuge in the mosque. Solidly built, it should have withstood a siege but this too, became a place of death. Suffocating smoke poured from burning hay that soldiers piled high to block the doorways.

The Cerro was the only place left to them. Women and old men fit enough to climb, helped children and the sick reach a temporary sanctuary. From it, they watched their young men slaughtered.

***

Nuri was bored. There was no fun in the cave this afternoon and Bella was being silly; she didn't want to play with him. Outside, he could hear the screams of horses. Why were they making that noise? His mother and Auntie Floria wouldn't tell him. They were behaving as though they hadn't noticed, and kept on talking quietly to each other. He couldn't make out a word they were saying.

There was a savage clash of metal. Auntie Floria told him not to worry; it was only the goats. Nuri knew better. Goat bells didn't sound that loud or so harsh. The noise from outside was growing stronger. He could hear the deep-throated roar of angry men and the rumble of horses getting closer. That meant his father was coming home. He started to jump with excitement. There were questions only Daddy could answer.

Nuri looked around the cave, to make sure nobody was watching. The grown-ups had told him a hundred times to stay where he was. If they caught him, he'd be stopped for sure. Bella was crying and Auntie Floria was desperate to keep her quiet. His mother and aunties were helping to soothe the little girl. Nuri took his chance and edged slowly towards the entrance. He wrenched open the door and darted outside.

The sunlight was blinding. He slapped both hands across his eyes then opened his fingers ever so slightly until he could peer between the gaps. There wasn't much of anything that made sense and it sounded as if the horsemen were moving off. If he didn't hurry, they'd be gone. Still dazzled by the light, he pushed his way through the bushes and ran to find his father.

But these were different men. Some of them were wearing clothes like those of his father and Uncle Ethan. Most were dressed strangely and carrying swords. Nuri didn't like them at all. They were angry and kept hurting each other. There was a lot of noise and it frightened him. He wanted to go home but he'd started to wet himself. He hadn't done that since he was a little boy. He couldn't help it and he hoped his Mummy would understand. It was only because he was frightened.

Nuri moved his hands away from his eyes and used them to cover his ears. If he could block out the noise, everything would be alright and then he could look for his father. He needed to pee again, but properly this time. He tugged at his loin cloth. It was wet and starting to smell. He yanked himself free of its clammy shame and threw it into a bush. He pulled back his foreskin, just like his daddy had taught him and started to pee. One day, when he was grown up, he wouldn't have that little piece of skin, and that would be good because then, he'd be strong and brave like his daddy.

He realised a soldier had been watching and must have seen everything. Nuri's face began to burn. But it was alright, the man was smiling so he couldn't be angry. The boy smiled back and the soldier walked towards him. There was a big red cross on the front of the man's clothes and he was carrying a very large sword.

***

Ethan was shouting and pointing wildly in the direction from which they'd come. Khaled strained his eyes against the glare of the sun and realized they'd been tricked. The mist had cleared from much of the mountain but now, columns of smoke obscured their homes.

At that moment, a detachment of Christian cavalry appeared from the east. The landing from the sea had been a feint. It had lured Aaron and his men forward and they were in danger of being encircled. His skirmishers had enjoyed some initial success but they'd found themselves outnumbered by a disciplined enemy. The Christian infantry savaged Aaron's left flank. It started to crumble and the cavalry pressed home their attack.

Khaled and Ethan's first reaction had been to divide their forces. Half of them would return to the village and lend support to the garrison. The other half would ride in support of Aaron. They immediately realised that would be a mistake. Two weakened units, each of them vulnerable to attack, would be incapable of initiating their own offensive.

Burning the village was almost certainly the attacking army's final act. Their principal objectives had been attained and any help that Khaled and Ethan's men could give would arrive too late. The bulk of their force would continue in support of Aaron. Khaled, Ethan and a handful of men would return to Felix and try to link up with troops from the Zugaiba garrison.

The return journey was a slow one. There were few places in which Khaled and Ethan could give the horses their head and as they picked their way higher, the narrow mountain tracks grew steeper. Khaled and Ethan rode in a deepening silence. At first, they'd expected an attack or ambush at every turn but the absence of opposition confirmed their worst fears. The Christians' work was finished.

Closer to the village, the friends noticed particles of black and white powder settling like snowflakes. Ash had risen high into the air as flames swept furiously from house to house and along the narrow streets. It now returned, dusting the ground, their shoulders and their hair.

***

Light from the open doorway poured into the cave. It took moments for Inga and Floria to notice that Nuri was missing. His mother dashed desperately to look for him but he was nowhere to be seen. The fighting had moved closer to the Cerro, leaving behind it the reek of blood and the excrement of dead men. To the moans of the dying, were added the screams of wounded horses. One of them writhed on its back while Nuri's pony, blood-soaked and with one leg dangling brokenly, looked in Inga's direction and staggered helplessly towards her. The vomit rose in her throat as she watched two more of their horses struggle to stand, their entrails dragging yellow and steaming from ripped bellies.

She saw the blood, the abandoned weapons, the dead and dying men trampled and made unrecognisable by horses' hooves. Then, as she took in the wide area of slaughter with desperate eyes, she heard her son's voice. A Christian soldier had hold of him.

Nuri screamed and the man turned to look at her. The anger on his face changed to fury as he strode in Inga's direction. She saw the danger in his stare as he took in her pale skin and fair hair. They were the same colour as the boy's and both of them had eyes that were bluer than the sky. The woman was as lovely as she was careless and her child was not an infidel. The soldier had known that as soon as he'd seen the boy was uncircumcised.

'You bloody fool of a woman!' he spat out his anger as he spoke. 'Get him away from here. This is no place for a Christian child.'

Nuri ran to his mother and she clasped him to her. Her eyes filled with tears of relief as she buried her face in her son's golden hair. Later, when she looked up, the soldier was gone.

***

The women fought like hell-cats. They beat the horses and their riders with sticks, and then attempted to blind them with handfuls of grit they'd scraped from the ground. They attacked the foot soldiers with bare hands, gouging at the men's eyes and faces with their nails. The troops wanted the good-looking women alive. They'd sell for a high price in the slave market. Young girls and boys were worth even more.

The Christians promised honourable treatment for men who surrendered. But as soon as they'd laid down their weapons, the old men were shot or cut to pieces. The young ones, fit and strong enough for labour, were taken prisoner.

The women saw the brothers they had loved and the husbands who had fathered their children, loaded with chains and destined to end their days in the mines. They watched as their sons were herded like livestock, divided as booty then led away to be castrated and sold as slaves.

Sterile, tamed and docile, these boys who could never be men would live and work for their Christian masters. A few of them would labour in those same terraced fields their ancestors had won from the barren mountainside. Like the generations before them, they would plant, water and make the earth fertile, but it would not be their seed that peopled this land.

The women on the Cerro lived long enough to hear the screams of daughters beaten by Christian men. Their fate was to be raped until pregnant with Christian off-spring. The fruit of their wombs would be raised in Christian charity by the church. Educated to despise their ancestry, they would regard their mothers, as animals of a lesser species.

When the soldiers returned, the old women, the disfigured and the heavily pregnant were hacked to death and their bodies thrown into the ravine. Others were beaten, raped and mutilated before they were hurled alive onto the sharp rocks below. The soldiers laughed at their screams, mocked as their bodies tore and broke, then laughed again at the silence.

Some of the young women broke twigs from bushes and twisted them into small crosses. They held them in front of their terrified faces as they begged for their lives. 'We're Christians,' they screamed, 'For the love of Christ, spare us! We're Christians!'

What if they were, the soldiers jeered. They'd only be converts, so they weren't proper Christians, anyway.

Other women made the only choice available. Before the soldiers reached them, they flung themselves into the ravine.

***

Inga had expected Nuri to resist when she took hold of his hand. Instead, he walked with her in silence to the cave. Once inside, he sat motionless on her knee. She tried speaking to him, hugging him and holding him close but her little boy didn't react. Bella was playing close by on the ground. She tried to involve him in her game, but when she tugged at his clothes and tried to kiss his face, Nuri looked blankly into the distance.

***

Ethan and Khaled were too late by more than half a day. The village and the small Zugaiba fortress had become a place of carnage. The members of the garrison had been killed, their genitals hacked off and their bodies mutilated. All that remained were the distorted, fly-blackened corpses of men who, hours before, had joked while sharing their bread, their cheese and their olives or swapped tales of girls they had loved and others they would marry.

Khaled retched at the slaughter-house stench of blood and putrefying flesh. He looked helplessly at Ethan. His friend returned the stare then ran cursing to drive off the crows that pecked cruelly at men's ruined faces.

***

It wouldn't be long before the women's hiding place was discovered. Bella sensed their unspoken fear and sat silently on her mother's knee while Nuri stared emptily in front of him. There was a rasp of wood and a stream of light as the door burst open.

'Daddy! I'm sorry Daddy!' Nuri rushed towards his father and Khaled scooped him into his arms. Inga reached out and the three of them clung tightly together. Ethan and Floria were on their knees with Bella close between them. There were tears but not for long. Tiredness had leached the strength from their bodies and they took refuge in sleep.

***

29

Khaled and Ethan's families had two horses between them; enough for the children, the others would walk. 'What about our things?' Inga asked, then bit her knuckles as she realised the truth.

A handful of neighbours had survived. Their farms were ruined but a few stone outbuildings had escaped the worst of the flames. They provided temporary shelter and a place to share out what little food was left. So far, the Christian forces had seen no need to occupy the area and the demoralised survivors prayed that they'd be left in peace. Ethan and Khaled owed them the truth. From what they'd seen in the north, they knew this was nothing more than a pause in hostilities. The soldiers would return, ready to slaughter or enslave anyone who had lived through the initial attack.

A few of the younger men had hidden themselves in the hills, planning to fight for their homeland. Those with families to protect needed to escape and, if the fishermen's boats were intact, a limited evacuation might be possible.

Reuben's wife found two more horses and offered them to Inga and Floria. 'They're yours anyway,' she told them. 'Without the start you gave us, we'd never have had anything.'

For the Jews, the slow journey to the coast was uncannily similar to the one they'd made a few years earlier. Then, they'd been buoyed by the hope of a fresh start in a new land. Now, the whole of Al Andalous was in Christian hands.

An evacuation would take time and there was no telling how soon their enemies would return. Khaled and Ethan led their friends towards Roquetas, a small village where they'd fished as youngsters. It had its own natural harbour and was a good distance from the Christian's new base in the Alcazaba of Almeria. If an evacuation was to succeed, it made sense to attempt it from there.

The cluster of fishermen's huts and cottages was frantic with men, women and children collecting possessions and loading them onto boats. To survive, they had to leave, but like the farmers, had no idea where they'd find sanctuary.

'Can you get us across to Africa?' Khaled shouted urgently to one of the fishermen.

'What's there for us?' the man asked doubtfully.

'Life,' Khaled replied.

***

A rumble of horses warned them they were under attack. The sounds were coming from more than one direction and, moments later, they saw a detachment of riders approaching at speed. The red crosses on the soldiers' shields glared menacingly through the dust and they were armed with harquebuses.

Gaunt faced women and children clutched each other as they saw two further groups of horsemen heading in their direction. But they were not carrying harquebuses, nor were they wearing red crosses. These were Aaron's men and, at the head of the second column, Khaled recognised the figure of his brother.

Aaron launched a feint attack. Thinking this was the main assault, the Christians committed themselves. They surged forward and locked with his riders. The weight of the Jews' resistance was overwhelming. Having no time to ready their weapons, the Christians gave ground and fell back in great disorder.

Ali led his horsemen into an oblique assault, driving the enemy forces into the sea. Following a period of chaotic indecision, the Christians found themselves outnumbered and out-manoeuvred.

They retreated in the direction of Almeria.

The euphoria was short lived. 'Get into the boats,' Ali shouted. The Christians had withdrawn only to reform. When they returned, they would have their deadly firearms at the ready. 'Leave your possessions,' he ordered. 'Get yourselves on board!'

Hearing the urgency in Ali's voice, the families struggled to obey his instructions and as soon as each boat was full, it pushed off. By the time the troops returned, most of the fishing boats with their human cargo were far enough off-shore to be beyond the range of the fire-arms. Two remained, however. They were crewed by older men, skilled sailors but slower than their younger mates. As the seamen fought to get the last of the women and children on board, Christian marksmen prepared their harquebuses.

'Allah Akbar!' Ali screamed, launching himself towards the enemy. The Christians were shocked into brief impotence as he hacked his way through their lines. Eventually, several of the more experienced marksmen gathered themselves and fired.

Ali and his horse took the full force of the fusillade. Incredibly, they still moved forward. Ali continued to slash with his sword until, weakened by loss of blood, his horse collapsed beneath him, throwing its dying rider to the ground.

The Christians were slow to reform. None of them had witnessed anything to match the dead man's courage and by the time they had reloaded their weapons, the last boat was moving out of harm's way.

'Where's Khaled?' It was Inga's panic stricken voice that screamed the question repeatedly. Floria tried to explain but her friend was beyond hearing. 'They've gone to link up with the other young men,' she attempted to tell her. 'They said I had to look after you and the children until they can join us.'

Incapable of understanding how quickly the world she'd known had been reduced to nothing, Inga asked again, 'Where's Khaled?'

Floria put her arms around her and spoke quietly, 'He's safe. He's with Ethan.'

***

30

The figures groping around the burned out huts, strained their eyes and searched for anything that had been overlooked. The sea was calm and they moved quietly, so as not to attract the attention of soldiers camped at the far end of the beach. Their scavenging had turned out to be more rewarding than expected. They'd managed to gather together half a dozen fishermen's knives and some lengths of rope which they stuffed into a sack.

***

Three soldiers were more than enough to keep an eye on an empty beach. They were in for a quiet night with no Muslims or Jews to worry about. The dead were no threat and the live ones had fled. Two of the guards were content with wine, a warm fire and tall stories but their mate was tired of worn out jokes. The rustle of a rabbit gave him his excuse. He left the security of the camp and wandered into the darkness. He'd just picked out the glint of the creature's eyes when a knife opened his throat. His mates had time to hear a startled gasp before they joined him in death.

Ethan, Khaled and Aaron wiped their blades on the dead men's clothing before rifling their belongings. There was a little money. The harquebuses were of greater value. Khaled took charge of them and loaded them onto the soldier's horses. Skilled Arab gunsmiths would copy their design and help arm the resistance fighters.

Hamdi had taken no part in the killings. He didn't condemn his friends but his duty was to preserve life, not take it. Aaron opened his mouth to mock but the warning in Ethan's eyes made him shut it twice as quickly. It was a medical man's quibble, Khaled explained. Time would temper it.

They headed along the coast, two of them on horseback, the others driving a heavily loaded cart. When they came to a cluster of rocks, they jumped to the ground and made sure the wagon was well hidden. Hamdi and Aaron would stand guard while Khaled and Ethan continued on foot to the small fishing hamlet. Its few inhabitants were known to be Christian and, so far, it had remained untouched by the army. Even so, it was possible a few soldiers had been billeted there, to keep an eye on the fishermen and watch out for resistance fighters. The friends moved cautiously, grateful for the thick dust that deadened their footsteps.

As they passed the first of the cottages, a door was flung open and light spilled into the alleyway. An elderly woman yelped with fear as she saw the strangers. She was immediately joined in the doorway by a group of men. One of them pushed his way past her and grabbed hold of Ethan and Khaled. 'Get inside,' he hissed. 'Be quick, before anybody sees you.' He manhandled them into the cottage and slammed the door shut. 'If the army finds out …' he began.

The woman was listening. Turning to her, the man snapped, 'Get them something to eat and be quick about it.' She hesitated and, for a moment, it seemed she might refuse. 'They're with the Jews who helped build our boats,' he told her by way of an explanation.

Ethan opened the sack and emptied the contents onto the table in front of him. The men nodded their thanks. Knives were useful to fishermen. 'I was wondering how long it would be before you turned up,' one of them said.

The anxiety in the man's voice told Ethan he was worried about his family. 'We need a ride in your boat,' he told him bluntly, 'Across to Africa. You'll be paid in gold. Later, we'll need you again.'

'We owe you,' the fisherman said reluctantly. 'But not enough to risk our lives. The ride you need now, that's agreed. As for the rest, we'll think about it.'

Ethan knew they wouldn't think for long. They had no love for him or for his men but they knew better than to get on the wrong side of them. Besides, he paid well and always in gold.

The woman returned with generous servings of fish stew bubbling in earthenware pots. The tang of herbs reminded Ethan of that other lifetime when he'd had a home and his family around him. 'There are two more of us,' he said. 'We need food for them as well. Something dry so we can carry it.'

The woman bundled up some bread, cheese and olives. Khaled nodded his thanks and carried the food to where Hamdi and Aaron were waiting. 'Get the cart down to the water's edge ready for unloading,' he told them. A few of the fishermen helped get the chests on board. The quicker it was done, the sooner they'd be rid of their unwelcome guests.

The crossing was long enough for Hamdi to earn a little gratitude and some grudging respect by treating two of the crew members for sea-water boils. It was a messy business, all yellow pus and blood, but it held the men's attention and gave Khaled and Ethan the chance to check the chests. Their gold and weapons were safe.

The fishermen helped unload their belongings and watched the men jump ashore. 'We're grateful to you,' Khaled said.

'We helped you out,' one of the fishermen yelled in reply, 'Don't forget it!'

Ethan walked back to the boat, reached up and shook the man's hand. 'Your village, your families and your boats. They won't be touched. I give you my word.' Turning to Aaron, he said in a voice that wouldn't be argued with, 'Did you hear me?'

'I heard you, Skinner!'

'They're not to be harmed.'

'I heard what you said, Skinner. What about the rest of them?'
'They'll get what they deserve.'

***

BIBLIOGRAPHY

Luis Lopez Navarro: *Felix - En Torno de su Vieja Historia*

Antonio Domínguez Ortiz: *Historia de los Moriscos; Vida y Tragedia de una Minoria*

Manuel Barrios Aguilera: *Granada Morisca - La Convivencia Negada.*

Nicolas Cabrillana: *Almeria Morisca*

Jose Enriquez Lopez de Castañar: La *Conquista de Granada - El Testimonio de los Vencidos*

Andrew Wheatcroft: *Infidels*

Jason Webster: *Andalus*

Godfrey Goodwin: *Islamic Spain*

About the Author

Michael Horrex was born in southern England but has lived abroad for most of his life. He has travelled extensively throughout North Africa and The Middle East, working for many years in Egypt, Libya, Oman and Qatar.

For more than twenty years, he lived in southern Spain where he owned a Cortijo in the beautiful Alpujarras mountains of Andalucia. The view from the farmhouse swept south to include the Mediterranean and, on very clear days, the coast of Morocco. In the grounds, there was a cave and to the west, a beautiful small mountain called El Cerro de la Matanza.